Praise for *The World Without Us*

'A triumph on every level' The Judges of the *Victorian Premier's Literary Award for Fiction* 2016

'Juchau's prose is a thing of wonder. It's the perfect mix of poetry and restraint … Juchau treats us to the shadows of many souls. She reminds us that life itself has a force that is difficult to suppress' *Saturday Paper*

'A bright, bracing marvel of a book … Juchau's prose, too, is a marvel of balance: witty and sensual, self-aware but not jaded, and capable of making poetry from anything' *The Australian*

'We are in the hands of a poetic writer in control of language and ready to invest every sentence with resonant detail' *Australian Book Review*

'I was enormously impressed by Mireille Juchau's haunting exploration of an ecologically fraying world' James Bradley, *The Australian Book of the Year*

'*The World Without Us* is one of those novels that does everything right, all at once: gorgeous writing about people, place, grief, loss and our changing environment. Juchau balances all these elements perfectly, raising questions rather than proposing answers to the big themes she explores' Jo Case, *The Australian Book of the Year*

'Juchau's style is ... Almost any page of this ... great poetic power ...

'Powerful and poetic ... The slow unfolding of the truth, layer after layer, is superbly done; though this novel is too classy to pigeonhole as a thriller, it has all the pace and invention of the classic thriller. What makes it unforgettable is Juchau's sensitive portrayal of a family poleaxed by grief' Kate Saunders, *The Times*

'She creates constant suspense ... Juchau artfully counterpoints personal loss with the destruction of the environment ... The achievement of *The World Without Us* lies in its suggestion that our relationship to a changed environment is today's rather than tomorrow's story' *Financial Times*

'Reading the novel is akin to being inside a hive, a constant whirr of activity as plots are picked up ... The honey comes in Juchau's wonderfully vivid writing and powers of description ... Juchau has a lyrical style and a great appreciation of the natural world ... The world emerges as a vast and bracing place, one that goes on – with or without us' *Irish Times*

'Juchau creates a subtle but elaborate population, all with their own fully formed pasts. The novel, like Evangeline, is understated and calm, and yet thoroughly captivating ... Juchau confirms an eternal concept: when the past holds such pain, and the future such dread, sometimes all one can do is muddle through the present' *Independent on Sunday*

'A haunting tale of climate change and the effect of industry on the environment. Beautiful and sad' *Emerald Street*

THE WORLD WITHOUT US

MIREILLE JUCHAU

BLOOMSBURY

LONDON · OXFORD · NEW YORK · NEW DELHI · SYDNEY

Bloomsbury Paperbacks
An imprint of Bloomsbury Publishing Plc

50 Bedford Square   1385 Broadway
London   New York
WC1B 3DP   NY 10018
UK   USA

www.bloomsbury.com

BLOOMSBURY and the Diana logo are trademarks of Bloomsbury Publishing Plc

First published in Australia 2015
First published in Great Britain 2016
This paperback edition first published in 2017

British Library Cataloguing-in-Publication Data
A catalogue record for this book is available from the British Library.

ISBN: HB: 978-1-4088-6650-4
        TPB: 978-1-4088-6651-1
        PB: 978-1-4088-6652-8
        ePub: 978-1-4088-6649-8

2 4 6 8 10 9 7 5 3 1

Typeset by Integra Software Services Pvt. Ltd.
Printed and bound in Great Britain by CPI Group (UK) Ltd, Croydon CR0 4YY

To find out more about our authors and books visit www.bloomsbury.com.
Here you will find extracts, author interviews, details of forthcoming
events and the option to sign up for our newsletters.

For Roger and Guy

The murmuring of Bees, has ceased
But murmuring of some
Posterior, prophetic,
Has simultaneous come.
Emily Dickinson

If you would fain not meet with
Torment – neighbour, sleep!
Marina Tsvetaeva

THE WORLD WITHOUT US

One

For indeed the ascetic workers, her daughters, regard the
queen above all as the organ of love, indispensable, certainly,
and sacred, but in herself somewhat unconscious ...
Maurice Maeterlinck

I

He'd been climbing for three hours when he saw the odd colour through the tawny trees. In a clearing by the Repentance River, a pale column. As he drew closer he realised it was a woman. She was barefoot and partly clothed, her head skewed back, eyes on the sky. Evangeline Müller, his neighbour from that large wooden house on Fox's Lane.

As he entered the glade, his heavy boots shattered sticks and dry leaves and he thought he ought to exaggerate these noises or call out – she was still undressing. He'd have quite liked to linger, just watching. But that would be creepy, he chided himself, don't be a creep. And then she turned, her chest completely bare, and, without flinching, caught his eye.

It's you, she said.

Her tone was dull, as if she'd been expecting him, or maybe someone else. Or perhaps it was simply relief in her voice. She shifted a hip to one side, folded one arm across her body. It was then he noticed the waxy scars, roping her chest and back.

Jim Parker, he said, offering a stupidly distant hand. I walk up here most Sundays. And you're …?

… Going in, she said as she tossed her shirt to the ground.

Jim, not trusting his eyes to stay on her face, glanced instead at the river. He'd spent his adulthood trying to be decent; it was in his raising, it was in his mother's quiet asides, which after her death had gained the solemnity of commandments. James, don't ever be that kind of guy, she'd say after some encounter with some male, and he'd wonder what had offended her, which leery word, which gesture. Lately, though, he'd been letting this credo slide – it might not have sprung from himself after all, though he could not say what other substance he was made of.

There was no towel near the woman, he noticed, just the small mound of clothes to which she was adding her skirt. A strange place to swim. The river was broad here, then narrowed sharply as it flowed towards the cliff. You could hear the cascades, a two-hundred-metre drop said his map; you could feel the earth's tremor from the force of that falling current. Upstream there were more tranquil, sunnier swimming holes. And she surely knew those – she'd spent her childhood at the nearby commune. Jim had wandered through its gutted remains: the burned husk of a hexagonal hall, the charred footings of the former cabins.

After just three months in Bidgalong Valley he'd come to know the Ghost Mountains well, following trails on a map bought at the town market. As he walked he realised the fey place names – Rainbow Hill, Naiad Gorge, Moonbeam Falls – had replaced all the indigenous names, and were absurd. This morning he'd set out early, following the river to a tapered ridge, pausing at a creek to scoop and gulp water, glorying in the wild-man spectacle of his thirst. He could pretend, in the surround sound of wind, water, leaf and bird, that the forest was pristine, that he was born to it and belonged.

Evangeline was still undressing, unperturbed. Jim, ignorant of what to do with hands, eyes, unruly thoughts, crossed to the embankment, then stuck a hand in.

Wow, that is cold, he said, as if he hadn't already felt that water, minutes back, down his throat.

He scanned the river, guessing the distance from here to the falls, the depth and speed of the flow, assuming the guise of another, less febrile man, the sort to coolly gauge and secure things – risks, locks, errant nails, threats, trip hazards – the dependable, sexless dad of the hardware store and the back shed of widgets, to tamp down his desire.

Now the water was strung with reflected clouds, and the canopy, backlit, was dark as the earth. This world, two hundred and fifty above sea-level, inverted. The river, beyond his reckoning. It seemed as cryptic as the woman readying herself to swim in it.

He shook out his hand. Then wrung his shirtsleeve and watched the drips hover in the green air. In the valley you'd hardly know it was winter; in the valley, the unceasing treacly sun.

When he turned back she was just about naked – a habit maybe from her commune days and her unself-consciousness persuaded him: he was surely guilty of something. After all they were practically strangers – he'd only seen her a few times before – at the market where the family ran their honey stall, and late one afternoon at the River School when she'd come to collect her youngest's things. Jim watched from the office as she crossed the playground. She was arresting – stately maybe was what you'd call her, with blue-hued skin and large grey eyes. She had the long-skirted sandalled look of other hippies around town, but had made this uniform hers, the tuck of her shirt, the way her sleeves were rolled, the hair somehow both secured and falling down. She wore no make-up and he fancied he could see grief's traces in the dull rings beneath her eyes. In one hand, an umbrella, despite the dry weather. She folded it slowly before coming in. She's taken her time, said the office secretary. It had been nearly two years since the funeral and the girl's belongings were gaffered up in the storeroom. The eldest – Tess – was in Jim's class and yet to speak a word. From the glassed-in office, Jim watched the woman lean, shuck off a shoe and edge a foot up the wall behind her. She remained there, stork-like, for some minutes. Poor soul, said Jane Bond, stapling worksheets. But Jim had felt no pity watching Mrs Müller; her left leg bared to the knee, he'd had other feelings entirely.

She was bending over her clothes now, wearing nothing but plain cotton knickers. Sylvie wore this kind of thing on weekends. But Jim didn't want to think of her and weekly texts. Or the postcards featuring the Sydney hotels they'd stolen into last summer, where they'd fucked by the rooftop pools. Sylvie had tried guessing – which hotel had they conceived at? The Radisson or Hilton? The Park Suites or The Quays? But Jim, newly ordained a father, had not been able to think of anything but her cells dividing, her augmenting blood. And now felt guilty – he'd deleted her texts, he hadn't phoned her since moving away – and as he looked fully at the body of this woman stepping into the Repentance River, his mind turned soupy, then entirely blank.

Evangeline stood naked, arms out and teetering. Even sunk to the ankles in river mud she was imperial. He knew the rumours, which Ms Bond had glossed between each staple crunch. How she was seen very rarely in town, and always below that umbrella, in cloudy or clear weather. How she'd been spied walking back roads with an empty pram, intent on something, but never, he got the sense from the staffroom chorus, doing what she ought.

And here she is, breaking his morning's *samādhi*, his wilderness *vipassana*, the goals he'd set since arriving. Here she is fucking with his silent walking attempt *to come out of suffering*, out of mental impurity, his quest for non-delusion. He'd been on his way, hadn't he, ticking off the precepts – no killing, stealing, sex, false speaking, intoxicants. He was advancing, with some exceptions, and after fasting and celibacy had even reached step 8: *to abstain from using high or luxurious beds*. He ticked that off grandiosely, without protest, or even laughter.

But what's he thinking now, unlacing his boots and saying, Perhaps I should – ah?

She hesitates in the knee-high, hectic water. Then a new sound makes him straighten. Not far off, a labouring grunt, a threshing, as if something's being dragged through the scrub.

They wait and listen, tuning in together.

He checks her face, then tugs off his right boot, unpeels a sock. Her body, waist deep, is mirrored, and her long twin, conjoined at the hip, undulates on the water. Then she slides completely under and for minutes, she is gone. Fifty metres upstream, her arms slicing very precisely through the current.

Jim piles his things beside hers then – right away – regret. His lifeless clothes, her underwear, adjacent, incriminate him, and his empty boots, just ahead, seem a kind of manifestation. Their toes are angled away from the water, as if to say, *abandon*.

He stands, shivering in an old pair of boxers. Tall, broad-chested, hunched over his own flesh. He'd prefer to just forget his body, and its limited power over others. Swimming's the last thing he feels like, but he can't just leave her alone in there. That wouldn't be chivalrous, considering the falls. And again, that sound, drawing closer, though nothing can be seen through the leaning bloodwoods – no animal with prey, no human.

She seems to be treading water, paused – or waiting. Her face with the hair slicked off, more vulnerable. Then, as he nears the riverbank, Jim notices, a short distance from where she's left her things, a hammer and some rope.

2

Tess sees the bare feet first, whizzing through the air. Then the chopstick shins and saggy knickers, the vulnerable dip where the spine meets elastic. It's her sister Meg, practising handstands and cartwheels outside their mother's studio.

Tess strides through the brassy winter light. Tall and loose-limbed with dark snaggy hair and a wide red mouth. She's thirteen, in a frayed skirt and singlet with Band-Aids on both knees. She's nearly always hungry but can't say what for; a feeling no amount of bread or milk can dampen, a gnawing that swells or fades in the presence of her mother.

She scans the undulating paddocks, the busted fences of the family's farm. It's eleven o'clock. Where is she? Her mother gone since early light. Far off, her father passing the white huts, smoke uncoiling above his head. Behind him there are new bald stripes on the Ghost Mountains and matchstick piles of freshly felled trees. Squint and you can pretend he's an astronaut – in his boots and white zip-up suit, his folding veil and helmet. Tess watches him high-stepping over a field as pitted and dusty as the moon.

Meg springs back to earth, her hands in the air, her bum jutted like those gym-obsessed girls at Fernery Sports and Rec. Her face, right way up, is flushed pink. She pulls out her inhaler and sucks on it, eyes briefly flashing.

Despite that breathlessness Meg is all grace. At least that's how their mother described her, years back, in the studio. Tess was sprawled in the wingback chair, watching her mother brush alizarin onto canvas. Propped around the room were the newest paintings with their heavy oils and their single, repeated subject. Always horses. Always hills, and two distant, watchful figures. Her mother had paused with her brush held out as Meg passed. Look at that, she'd said quietly, as if to herself, *all grace*. And Tess, turning to watch her sister, thought, OK, but what am I? Before she could ask, her mother was back to painting, her arm arcing so swiftly through the air that Tess decided what she'd really meant was, Meg is just like me.

Both Meg and her mother are fair-skinned with smoky blonde hair. Tess's hair is dull and unruly, the colour of pitch, and her limbs tan fast in early summer, her face dusted year round with freckles. Tess is straight as a ruler from chest to hip so her jeans always need hitching. Her small breasts have nipples that seem, wrongly, to point in opposite directions, breasts that throb with such raw pain she wonders if to develop is to be permanently injured. She binds them in crop-tops nicked from Big W.

The sisters' arms, side by side at the table, catch Tess's eye but no one else seems to notice how much like piano keys they are, the dark and the pale, one more plaintive, one calmer, fuller. Pip, the youngest of the sisters, had been – well – Pip had just been Pip, her green eyes growing as the rest of her faded. Her illness had left her less recognisably theirs, but also made her belong more fiercely.

Where are you going? Meg asks, slapping dust from her palms and twisting her clothes into place. The skater skirt that used to be Tess's, the unicorn T-shirt that Pip once coveted.

Dad said stay by the house till Mum comes back, says Meg. Then flexes a leg in the air, does the pinch-test on a fatless midriff.

Tess throws up her hands, questioning, jabs her watch theatrically. A purple slap-band Lorus, recently stolen.

How would I know? says Meg, narrowing her eyes. She wasn't even here when I got up!

She was not in the laundry, not out back, nor in the studio, which hadn't been used for years. Only the shadows on the walls from where their mother's canvases had hung. In one corner, a stack of old paintings, covered in sheets. But now, as Tess reconnoitres the studio, she notices a gleam in a corner, wet paint on a new palette. She sees what's gone missing – the pram.

Both Meg and Pip had had their time in that Peg Perego. But Tess was mostly carried in slings, their mother said. The pram came into its own after Meg's high-forceps birth, when schlepping a baby got hard. Even picking you up would make me wee, she told Meg, when I wasn't planning. Something about a pelvic floor. The girls had loved hearing about it – uncomprehending, irresistibly horrified. What happened to mothers, after all, might happen to them as well. Blood, babies, some parts of you giving way, like a house with bad foundations.

After Pip the pram became a trolley, wheeled by their mother through fields at dawn. It was packed with paint, solvent and palettes, with sketchbooks and canvases and a waterproof cover so it could stay out in all weather, night and day. Whenever Tess saw it, parked alone in the cow paddock, her heart raced till she remembered – no baby in there, just tubes of oils leaking on to the patterned lining. It was fascinating, said the parent community, to be the child of a painter, but then came the difficult questions about when the work would be exhibited.

The girls ought to be used to their mother going off. But the missing pram's important. And if she's painting again? Could mean anything. Tess doesn't know if she preferred it when, for a year after Pip's death, her mother barely left the house.

So – how about town? asks Meg as Tess returns from the studio.

On the back porch, their mother's black umbrella hangs like a sleeping bat. She wouldn't go without it.

And what would she do in town for that long? She wasn't the sort of mum who *went for coffee* and she did not attend the many *studios*, the preferred term for local businesses. She didn't practise any of the ten types of yoga, t'ai chi or Pilates. She wasn't a mother who had things done to her like nails or hair, Bowen or tarot. She hated shopping, and when she visited the library she raced home to tuck herself in with the hardbacks. She liked mysteries in blizzard lands, books with snow and ice on their covers, and would turn first to their final pages. In these stories, she told the girls, each of the disappeared had their faithful, dogged searcher. In these the lost were usually found, even if they had but one breath left in their body. Beside her bed, the dictionary, for what she called the stumble words. The way she read, with one finger dragging the page, caused the girls to look away.

Tess considers the missing pram. What it could mean. Then she plucks something from the dirt. Another single butterfly wing. Brown and orange ovals with a sham black eye. What's happening to these insects? Can a one-winged butterfly still fly? Perhaps a sign, like those Tom Tucker lists in his weekly *Survival Report*. Once, Tess might have collected these wings for Pip. On the nature table in their bedroom are egg cartons full of botanical treasures: seed pods, dragonfly wings, lizard tails, bunya nuts and old olive pits gnawed on for hours by Meg.

How long are you going to keep this up? asks Meg. You can't be silent for ever! You'll burst.

Tess shrugs, drunk with power, gives herself an imaginary star; then, seeing her sister's puckered face, grants herself another. Six months now without a word. The longer she lasts, the more she understands about silence. It isn't like withholding other things – breath or food. Who can it injure? Though lately she's realised how dependent she is on others to keep it a living, working thing. She hadn't planned that. On your own you're just yourself, unspeaking.

She launches into a handstand, feet pedalling, legs scissoring, skirt slipping over her head. Then blinks at a newly pixilated world. Upright, she bats at her face – *glasses*? – grubs blindly along the ground till she finds them.

When her sight's restored she sees Meg staring, open-mouthed, one finger wagging at Tess's thigh.

Blood, she's saying. Down there.

Later, in the musty privacy of the honey shed, Tess holds her breath, crosses her legs, then bows to take a look.

Jesus, she says under her breath, thinking hard about what she'd been told, in some class, by some teacher, in that clip sponsored by Johnson & Johnson where a girl marked a wall calendar in emergency-coloured calligraphy. An awful worry had tolled whenever Tess thought of it, even though some girls said the trick about your period was being *confident* and others said they were *like so totally* ready for the *challenge*. Prime numbers were also a challenge – and comprehension – but these could eventually be mastered.

Through the shed door, her father crossing the bee yard, the sky around him pocked with insects, his slow ambling making him seem incapable of anything Tess might need him for. Today he'll kill the old queens. After squashing them with his boot he'll leave their crushed corpses beneath each hive so the bees can smell she's dead. *Queens produce pheromones which exert a great power over the surrounding bees. If they begin to perform poorly they should be replaced.*

In The Hive commune, where their mother once lived, they'd kept twenty hives. But they never killed the old queens up there, she said. They'd let nature take its course.

That's no way to run an apiary, their father said. I couldn't believe how Jackson Hodgins kept those hives when I saw them, he laughed. Homes for old-lady bees!

The commune was modelled on the bee community and everyone worked for the good of the group, said their mother. *Una apis, nulla apis.* One bee is no bee. Up there Jackson was hive leader. *King Bee*, their father sometimes called him, though everyone knew there was no such creature. At other times he called Jack *Schwärmer* – fanatic – and also something to do with the swarming of bees.

Were you a worker bee up there, Mum? Or a queen? Meg asked once.

It wasn't like that, their mother replied, blinking fast, a tic that appeared when they spoke of The Hive.

But Lina was my queen, said their father, doing a totally awk dance across the kitchen flagstones, a sideways thing with a shifty hip and snapping fingers, a move Meg called groinal.

Listen, girls, he'd say. When I am first seeing your mother she is in the distance, with such beautiful long hair and skirts. She floats across the bee field like a *Phantasie*. The vibes I was getting, you chust could not believe!

They'd seen one photo. Mum and Dad in faded Kodak. Posing by the Nursery Cell. Most other pictures from the commune had burned. There'd been no time, in that fire, to save their possessions, only to rescue themselves. In this photo the background looks pale and smouldery, as if The Hive was already ablaze and disappearing.

Vibes, Tess had repeated, back then when she was speaking. Dad, how completely yuck!

And weren't you the Arcadian Poster Boy? said their mother. Picture your father, girls. Long hair. Tight purple trousers. Busting his moves by the nightly fire pit. In his mind crossing time zones means Australia will still be in the seventies.

She'd never seen such a man at The Hive, she said. His Euro-mullet and slow surfer's gait, his sun-starved skin and awkward German formality. A man who brought to the mountain the rimy scent of the sea.

But this kind of talk hasn't happened for ages. Not since their mother started carrying her umbrella, or leaving early for the forest then coming home with stringy hair and muddy clothes. She'd become a person seen from a distance talking to trees, applying an ear to the flank of a horse, lying alone in a paddock with one leg lifted skyward.

Before Pip died the family had the Mood Chart with rainbow colours to map the spirit of your day. They'd had the Wonder Jar filled with paste gems by those who'd witnessed Miracles, Kindnesses, Unsought Praise. When the jar was full the sisters were promised a family excursion, a new game, book or toy. But it's totally a relief, Tess tells herself, to be done with all that. Explaining these Müller rituals, which had evolved from routines at The Hive, had made visitors smirk and peer as if the sisters were dim, or some quizzical type of human. And in the colourless months of the family's grief, in days stripped back to survival, hunting out benevolence had become impossible, even offensive to them all. Before Pip died they'd had their mother, mostly present. They had promised visits to the town pool; her strong hands beneath their spines, her face dappled with reflected water, her steady, unbroken gaze. When they were very small, she'd held a mirror over their floating selves, wordlessly showing how on earth they could be as weightless as in the womb.

Tess jumps down from the hayloft. With pelvic muscles clamped, she walks gingerly through the meadow, shoving back her unruly hair, her mind frantically searching the house for what she can use to hide or stop the blood.

Six kangaroos bound from the forest right up to the barbed wire, then bow and billow under. In the high bronze grasses they shake their dark, strokeable ears. Tess hobbles past, stiff-legged. And sees where the roos have caught on the fences; at each barbed interval, the torn-out clumps of their coarse brown fur.

Some sufferings must go unheeded, her father says. The day he put their Kelpie down, the night the old mare died with its head in their mother's hands. The time he shot the poisoned wombat. But Tess, very alert, very loyal to any living thing, has sworn she'll never grow impervious. She's stayed awake to hear her sister breathe; her parents far down the hall, the morning even further off as Pip exhaled and sometimes in sleep made animal noises, pawed the bed and sang in new languages. It was the antibiotics, it was the low blood count, it was the painkillers or the constant fevers. Who would witness it all if Tess did not?

By the time she reaches the house there's a red line down her inside thigh, a blood blotch on her sock. She turns back and runs an eager eye over the mountain for the mother who cannot say any more what a person ought to do.

3

Stefan tugs off the lid of a hive, peers in, then straightens, *scheisse, scheisse*, his cinching bones. He looks at the blank, unanswering sky, at the Ghost Mountains and the sheen of river through the forest. He gives each element his deliberate attention, trying not to let yesterday's facts hew everything up, trying not to picture what he'd found by the western boundary in a swathe of bramble and gorse. He's told no one about his discovery – there's always a cost to unburdening. Well, no one but Nora Roberts. And how will that sound to his wife?

Evangeline had already vanished when he woke to the *verdammte* birds. Kookaburras, hysterical on the wires. Their chortling drilled into his ears and jabbed the headache, which lay in wait every morning. He turned in bed and flung out an arm, then a leg, calling, Lina? No one there. No ministrations as there once might have been – the frosted glass of water, the cool palm on his brow. Her bending over was medicine itself. There'd been a time when he opened his eyes in this new country, stood up, did fifty *vinyasas* and had no thought before amaranth and almond milk but: holy holy holy, I've arrived in *Paradies*.

Fifteen years since he'd left Germany and floated into Bidgalong with a backpack and a copy of Maurice Maeterlinck's *The Life of the Bee*. This had become his personal bible and so, after a dope-hazed, partying spring in Thailand, he headed for the lands to find what that Belgian writer had so loved in the bees: *passion for work, perseverance, devotion to the future*. After a week of surfing, he'd trekked up to the commune because he'd heard it was modelled on bee communities. Instead he found an eco-Puritanism diluted with Buddhist mantras, a commune leader whose ideals had been whittled into zealotry. Jackson Hodgins was lazy by then, and had run to fat. Never mind, Stefan had played along. Your youthful convictions can fade in the blaze of other inducements – the lush, paradisiacal forest, the unworldly young women. He'd been full of ridiculous, half-formed dreams, even – watching Hodgins at the podium – the brief dream of succession, and yet he's still a bit fond of the young man he was then, each morning swollen with hope.

As he kicked back the rucked sheets, bare-chested, arms bisected by tan-lines, he'd tried invoking peace, recalling child-hood bodies of water. Schlachtensee, Krumme Lanke, the Hundekehlesee. Thought of his grandfather tending bees. Henrik Müller had built his first Berlin hive after the war. It sat on his Pariser Strasse balcony with tubs of *Tomaten*. High above the bombed courtyard, he'd watch his workers hurtle in from recon-naissance, alighting on the hive landing strip loaded with pollen. So heartening, that flowers could be found in a city of ruin! Later, he'd grown all his food on a Neukölln allotment. Now you can buy *Stadtbienenhonig* from bees foraging in Berlin yards; now the countryside with its aerial spraying and GM crops can no longer spruik its purity.

The cold needling shower. The breakfast bespoke for migraine. And Stefan picturing everyone gone, draining the short black to the grit before his thoughts hovered on Pip, his youngest, his little house bee. Pip, who'd looked most like his mother, Gretchen. He'd not been able to bury one, because the other was so ill. Both had died in the same month, in different hemispheres. Acute lympho-blastic leukaemia. Stroke. He was not a believer, but would some-times dream of them in some alternate atmosphere, helping each other blow balloons. When they loosened their grip those balloons drifted off, carrying their mingled breath. In these dreams his mother and daughter exhaled, but kept quiet, which turned his thoughts to his eldest, Tess, silent for how long?

Now he stands by his fifty hives, bathed in the cold shadows of the Ghost Mountains. He watches his cows in the adjacent paddock circle the round of hay. He's in overdraft because of it, but won't let his animals suffer through winter. Steve Johnson had his back-field mounds of killed beasts, Paul Betts the pet-food company visit in the plainclothes car. Both very po-faced when you tried asking them about it at the pub, both keen to buy another, drown-ing round. Strange, how they're all capable of sectioning off the different kinds of death on their land. Time to check the price for Charolais. Some year-old steers are ready for sale. But for now, the bees.

Stefan eases the hive tool into the chambers, prises the combs apart. He ought to stop tampering – bees don't like it – but after losing fifty colonies in the past season, he's determined to work out if it's pests or disease. He holds the combs up to the sun – scattered cappings over the honey; checks the hive floor – the cleaner bees still hard at work. No silk-filled wax-moth tunnels. No disquieting slime of hive beetle. Nothing. He's almost disappointed.

Just last week Duke Hany's bees had swarmed, and then were found, flightless as worms, three fields away. José Torres was a hundred colonies down. The beeks were talking like doomers now, calling it the Bee Rapture, discussing Colony Collapse Disorder, electromagnetic fields, radiation, fracking. In Germany, *die Bienenzüchters* had registered their perishing colonies, blaming Bayer's clothianidin. Some locals accuse the Birkenstockers, inept hobbyists whose designer hives are merely a badge of righteous living.

In the fifth hive, confettied pollen in purple, orange, gold, pink.

In the town, someone's pasted WANTED posters for bee rustlers. Which is pointless, Stefan thinks; after all, bees are just cows without fences. Bees are cows with wings. The most you could hope, say the pub soothsayers – the thief gets multiply stung mid-heist and ends up sooking at A&E. You'd rarely recover your insects.

Stefan locates the ailing queen, isolates her, then scans the mountain. Where is his wife? And what will his news do to her – the wreck of that particular vehicle, the bones he's found?

As he hammers the resinous propolis off a frame, he makes a jaunty song of his loves: the green arcades of macadamias at dusk, the machinic stuttering frog. The other day, a filigreed snakeskin wound through the wisteria arbour like a snagged bridal veil. The whickering of the mare in the back paddock, a horse that for a time stood in for the horses in his wife's paintings. She'd sketched old Lucie for months, trying to master the proportions. Coaxing that creature with sugared palms and a conspiring tone. The results were confounding. Abstract, his wife said, which was code for a horse doesn't look like a horse in this variety of art. A horse might seem to say freedom, or if it were tethered, restraint. If he peered long enough he could make them out, horse parts, rearranged.

He loves the place, even though it's failing. The new bees taking a long time to settle, the older colonies unproductive. Some cattle grazing only in balding sections, getting bogged in a quagmire searching for salt. This too was abstract – creatures where they oughtn't be, things obeying no natural order. Yet, Evangeline has always said he's a man not easily put off. Perseverance, devotion to the fucking future – he's tried sticking to Maeterlinck's tenets. A man who'd had enough vim mid-breakdown to rollerskate around his rented French abbey. But the Belgian's optimism had waned – his *Life of the Bee* was the work of a hopeful youth, not a neurasthenic.

Stefan can't imagine leaving the farm, even if it's making a loss. The land, more valuable to industry groups now than any private buyer.

In the distance, by the house, the hazy tableau of his daughters doing gymnastics, still interacting, though Tess has locked something up inside. His throat feels barbed thinking of Pip – two years tomorrow since her death – and of his wife, who he's crazy in love with in spite of her being mostly gone, and him not knowing exactly where or when to expect her. Had he won her on false pretences? Maybe taken advantage after the fire, of her amnesia, her trauma, though they hadn't had such terms back then. They'd simply named what was evident on the body – third-degree burns, head injury, missing tooth. He'd sat with her while she lodged the complaint but later, fearing repercussions, she withdrew it. He'd taught himself patience, as he waited for her to piece it together; he was steadfast, dog-loyal, abiding.

Only once, during the last rainy months of Pip's illness, had he gladly stepped out of his life. He'd been heading home up the access road when he found the creek flooded. He'd forded it so often he'd outgrown all caution, but this time the ute lost traction halfway. He drifted from the farmhouse – lamps burning, curtains drawn – and had a curious sense of peace as Chopin soared from the radio. A lizard paddled by, its head propped above the water like a matron saving her do at the town pool. He rocked gently in the cabin. He could float for miles, a journeying away, accidental, for which he might be forgiven. But as darkness fell, he'd reluctantly bailed out, tethering the ute to a stump. Walking back up the road to the house, he noticed for the first time the many toads flattened against the gravel as if they'd been trying to paddle upstream. There are ways and ways of being gone. Apart from that one, unmoored moment he'd never been more present than in the final months of Pip's life.

He ranks his problems. His wife, her suffering. The farm, how to make it prosper. The letter from the gas-mining company, with all its inducements, its dodgy corporate vibe among the bee books on his desk. Tess's silence, which he's almost used to. When the cows have Bovine Ephemeral Fever their ears droop, their eyes water, their snouts are strung with viscid mucous. They're almost comically morose. But three days in the fever breaks, the lameness passes. It's not the same, Evangeline once pointed out, with humans. He thanked her politely, then drained the Côtes-du-Rhône.

He tends his animals, ploughs the fields, resists disease with natural embrocations. He makes his Preparation 500, stuffing cow horns with shit, burying them, then striding counterclockwise to spray the stuff under a waning moon. More warlock in this midnight rite, than farmer. Is it his failures that make him feel phoney, or maybe he wasn't invented for life on the land? He's followed the instructions to the letter. And yet. He loses a child; his wife stops painting and turns in bed; the bees, disappearing.

Then yesterday, after tractoring up to the property's furthest reaches, a creek giving on to a steep embankment bounded by the Lower Mountain Road, he found the first bone, and then another. Tibia, femur, scapula, clavicle.

Seconds later, Nora Roberts, her slim legs scissoring the broken fence, then leaping the green water, her purple hair aglow, a new thigh tattoo drawing the eye to where it didn't actually want to go.

Nora, with her sleepy hazel eyes and the scent, his daughters tell him, of bananas ready for cake.

Because of their past, when she appears the air around him starts shimmering intensely. He'll fix his eye elsewhere, on a leaning angophora, or a rocky outcrop, while she strolls around. She'd visited more after Pip's death, with the meals by the door, and the regular bag of dope. She'd come inside, protesting feebly, for cups of tea and after midday was a welcome joiner for something harder. She liked her whisky straight, no ice. She liked to chase it with a glass of red, or two, depending. One afternoon, the cold Fino, hay-coloured, very sweet.

There was always some agenda in Nora's eyes. She admired Stefan's land and cursed him – she wished she'd bought it first! Like Evangeline she'd been raised at The Hive, and had left with nothing after the fire. Her acres by Lunar Lake were deeply shadowed for most of the day – depressing, she said, not to mention the eerie human sounds that whorled from the water on dry afternoons.

So what was she doing on the Lower Mountain Road, late on a Thursday? Someone had mentioned a wild swarm. She'd come to take a gander. But as she headed up the Mountain Road she'd spied his tractor. An odd place for Stefan Müller, she'd thought – the cow pasture way off, nothing round here but blackberry, wombat and rabbit. And so she'd pulled over.

She glanced down at the bone in his hands. He was some distance from where he'd found them and she could not see the wreck of the vehicle, metres back, its white paint flaking into the scrub.

What you got there, Stefan? she asked. Foxes been at the roos again?

And then, she'd looked a bit closer. A skull.

He'd seen plenty of bones in his life. The bones of cows, the bones of cats poached from the pansy yards of old ladies. He'd seen bird bones; the chewed-out hulls of cow and sheep; the delicate rungwork of snake and lizard, ant-clean, weather-scoured. And of course, back home, the documentaries.

Stefan raked his hands through his hair, coursing with shame and guilt. Holding such a relic put him in need of an answering gratitude. Life, teeming all about him. He felt the skull's weight; heavier, it seemed, than when clothed with sinew, muscle, flesh.

Those bones were unmistakable, and who knew how old? Clavicle, femur, tibia. A whole *verdammte* skeleton, reclining by an anthill like a person who'd forgotten to come in from the sun.

Today he'll tell her. He rehearses the words as he crushes a queen bee with his boot. Another little death. But soon the new rulers will arrive by post in their customised wooden chambers. He's ordered these queens through a reliable supplier, a bloke whose Marburg swarm box was a piece of elegant genius. Stefan intended to build one himself. He has sourced the diagrams, the lumber. And the thought of this future carpentry – this bee-sorting box – calms him. The notion of arranging nuc, nurse bees and workers into chambers calls to some deep neat-freakery. He says a curt prayer for the queens he has killed, and a longer one for his wife.

Are you going to try and stop me? asks Evangeline.

Water is lapping at her chest. Jim can see the veins below her collarbones, burn scars below the left arm. Though he's only waist high, he feels the river's insistent tug. He takes another cautious step towards her.

No law against swimming, he says, screwing up his eyes and gurning in shock at the undertow.

A person can swim wherever they goddamn like, she says.

Absolutely.

He's after nonchalance, but a silent *fuck you* bubbles up. Hasn't he been warned about such reckless women? By Yusef, his best friend, who liked homely, bakes-me-an-afternoon-cake kind of girls and was always setting him up with one of these meek, rose-scented finds. Yusef who'd rolled his eyes when Jim turned up for one of their monthly dinners with Sylvie Bellamy. She'd immediately pissed off all the other women present with her bared thighs and a helpless search for matches which led her to every man in the room. Sylvie did not fade out, like Yusef's women. The hair toss, the vermilion nails tapping to some secret beat, her legs crossing and uncrossing, bra straps inching out, the smoke blown high into the air: you were always glimpsing her, whether you liked what you saw or not. Yusef had picked it right away, how needy she was, how vulnerable.

This woman, though, her regnant air, her total self-containment.

She's on her belly now, like it's a summer pool party, giving her weight to the water.

You must be a strong swimmer, Jim says. Because ... well ... the current ...

He grapples for a foothold on the slippery riverbed.

You think you can tell, Evangeline asks, when you're no longer a swimmer? The moment you become a drowner?

All right then, he says as he slides on something jagged, goes under, then comes up sputtering, arms flexed high.

Jesus! he yells. Pretty sure ... I'm bleeding ...

But she's laughing. Mesmerising, storm-coloured eyes. God, she's what – not exactly beautiful – arresting? One front tooth, discoloured. Across her temple, a nacreous scar.

Surely it's blood, pouring from his leg? Something warm and thick around his flanks.

Look at you! she cries, practically frolicking in the fast water, ducking under and gliding out, accustomed as an otter.

His lips are blue, his teeth chattering. The canopy has kept the river cold.

You're not exactly seafaring! she laughs.

He sniffs, says, Well, I'm a city boy.

But Sydney's a *harbour* city. Sydney's famously beachy. Someone must have taught you to swim?

Yes, he says, my mother insisted I learn. But not in rapids.

Veronica had sunbaked and read novels while he took private lessons in their lap pool, pausing occasionally to shout from her

26

recliner, Bravo darling! Veronica Parker with her salon highlights and her mani-pedis, doing her best to lacquer over the British hippie she'd once been. Well done with that flippy sort of thing you just did! When his lesson was finished Jim would stand, gooseforeshed, next to her hazel skin, dripping on to her paperbacks. *The Great Gatsby*, Dickens, even Hemingway for God's sake. Now Jim has a sudden flash of his small, pale, shivery self, so unaware that everything sweet would soon be over. He's exiled himself from that life, its privileges, its clannish social codes. But what has it cost him?

When I was four my father threw me into Lunar Lake, Evangeline says, moving more frantically in the current, a little breathless now.

That's … how I learned to swim. Then later two kids drowned in there.

He tries standing, reaching with his toes for a rock or a sunken root, scanning for a low branch. She's dog-paddling to keep still in the flow. They're both already downstream some way. He can only just make out their clothes. He swims closer and looks into her eyes, their downturned corners. Her hair streaming like river weed.

She ducks under. He holds his breath till she reappears.

How long do you like to stay in? he asks.

The water briefly calmer now, eddying.

You're worried, she says. Sweet! But don't be. My childhood was all about *surviving*.

Does she mean in the commune? He glances across to the riverbank. On the trunk of a huge tree he sees some bright objects tied with rope. Very small red shoes, blue patterned fabric. What looks like white boxes flattened against the bark.

When he turns back he catches her rapid look at that tree and her face transfiguring – her eyes limpid and beseeching, her jaw loose, her lips making a soundless shape. Some younger self shimmering up, primal and defenceless.

For a moment he floats; for a second, everything's suspended, the sky open through a break in the canopy, the water glass-sheer. Neither of them breathing. Only the deep current, jerking their slack limbs around. Then he anchors his feet against a rock and gets his head and chest out of the water.

> And those who are hurt will hurt without rest
> and those who are frightened by death will carry it
> on their shoulders.

He recites the lines, head leaning left, a tendency that Sylvie had photographed; a quizzical manner that she'd called *an affectation*.

Evangeline looks suddenly frightened, then says, Tess likes your classes. Of course she doesn't *say* ... but I can tell.

The current surges again. It carries them a full ten metres, her head sailing ahead of him. He's struggling now, and freaking out. He can hear the more furious water racing towards the cliff. A sheer two-hundred-metre drop. On his tongue, the metallic tang of panic.

He grabs her hands, hearing her gasping breath, feels her legs pedalling madly underwater.

Let's get out, he says, and tugs her towards him.

Her face is shadowed, her eyes clouded. But she lets him pull her sideways. He grips her elbows to prop her up while she kicks. They're eye to eye, as he surges backwards, then turns and pulls her towards the shore. To get her out he has to drag her body against his and squirm up the steep muddy bank – he doesn't want to risk letting her go first. For a second or minutes, she's on top of him. Then he rolls sideways, freeing her. They lie, side by side, breathing hard, the sky throbbing through the trees. Far off, beyond the ridge, a booming, the earth shaking. New gas wells all over the mountains.

Evangeline stays put, shivering, while Jim fetches their clothes, following the river back downstream, pausing at that decorated tree, passing the hammer and the rope. On his return he looks more carefully at the trunk. Pharmaceutical heraldry on those white boxes: standard cautions, customised type. Prescription medication. He remembers the office secretary speculating. Why does the woman carry an umbrella when it hasn't rained for months? The staff widening their eyes and nodding gravely. As if grief was no excuse for peculiarity, for a halting gait, a wary gaze, her elsewhereness. So he'd said, I hear there are cities where women carry parasols – rain or shine. Then left the staffroom to stand, unseen, as Evangeline passed down the corridor, her cedary scent in the air.

He holds out her clothes but she just sits vacantly, gripping her knees and staring downstream. He can see more clearly now, the stippled skin around her back.

Were you in that commune fire?

Evangeline shoots him a narrow-eyed look. Then wipes water from her arms curtly, over and over to the very last drip.

She's blinking fast as she asks, What do the kids in your class call the place? A commune or a cult?

Jim shrugs.

You're bound to hear the rumours, she says. Meg brings them home. Drugs, group sex, teenage pregnancy.

Well, at a school, people talk, he says.

Which is why I stopped going in there, she says. Then scratches her leg, bends forward. The broken skin on her back.

The Hive was good until it went bad! she laughs. That's how my mother put it. She was probably talking about me.

The haughty tenor in her laughter makes him think, again, of Veronica.

He looks at her steadily, the grave set in her eyes, the way she's gripping her knees. Sylvie used to accuse him of being evasive when he wouldn't get into things with her. Maybe things don't go as deep as you think, he'd said once, though he knew they could be fathomless. He'd just pretend incomprehension with Sylvie, to take the opposite side. Now, looking at this woman, naked, slick with river water, he sees he hasn't really saved her. It's herself, he suspects, that she's trying to escape. And only private acts will achieve that.

She bends her head back.

Were you ever tempted, she asks, to just go feral? How long do you reckon you could fend for yourself?

In the wild? he asks. Doesn't every kid have that fantasy?

But when I was young, she says, I wanted the city. All that excitement.

And now? You still want to escape? he asks.

She laughs again, a private mirth. It is no invitation. The pitch of her laughter veers in and out of control. Slightly mad, Jim thinks, which isn't unappealing.

Mothers don't do that, she says.

Hasn't he noticed, she tells him, a mother's leaving is never heroic or epic. Only ever betrayal. Men come and go, leave their families for war, for work, or private mental business. As if it's natural, their powerful need to flee! But mothers can't leave with impunity until they're dead.

And not even then, Jim thinks, feeling a sudden disdain. He checks the cut on his shin, still bleeding. She's imperilled him on this August afternoon. The river's a mirror, furrowed with broken clouds. The clearing is dusky and still.

Suddenly she straightens, snatching up her clothes. Then, looking down on him, says,

Yes, I was in that fire. So, what of it? No one died if that's what you're wondering. And the place was already...

Her voice, very loud, grows reedy. Another, earlier self floats up. Pigeon-toed, pouty. Just now, the early teen, he thinks. Teen Evangeline.

OK, he says. But that's pure fantasy – running away, starting over.

She puts her hand on a bare, jutted hip, sceptical.

I read somewhere, she says, very intense. A physicist. Time isn't real, only change is, she says. Something like that. Have you heard?

5

See, says Meg, flinging her lime-green Derwent across the table.
She hasn't come back.

The way she says it, Tess thinks, like it's my fault!

There's been no sign of their mother. Their father busy all day
with the bees, in the honey shed, readying his truck to move some
hives north, and laddering, as Pip used to call it when he lopped
trees or cleared gutters. He's come inside twice for some phone
calls, and medication. Migraine again. About their absent mother
he hasn't said a thing.

Outside, the darkness pours from the mountain and over their
fields till it meets the lake of light cast from their house.

Tess looks back at the table. Meg has spent the whole afternoon in
the airless kitchen, drawing trees in fog. She set out her cup of pin-sharp
pencils, her daisy sharpener and eraser and got to work, barely stirring
for hours. You could not begin to count the trees Meg's drawn these
past months and Tess learned, long ago, not to suggest another subject.
Meg, say the girls who hang by the demountables, is all about trees.

Like, you can't actually draw mist, Meg's saying. Only what
comes through it.

Sienna, the name of her sister's pencil. Burnt ochre. Bark. A field of meaning Tess is fenced off from. Meg and her mother arrived in the world just knowing how to put colours together, how to nudge them into something else. A tree or house. A field with horses. A total mystery. Light French Ultramarine, Prussian Blue, Mars Violet. Her mother once said all the old masters and the richest pigments came from elsewhere. She'd never get there, she said, and Tess didn't know if she meant the places where art began, or some scene she was painting her way towards. Her mother's brushes sit where she'd left them, stiff and dusty. All her large canvases are ghosts in the studio, shrouded in white drop sheets. Except for one, with its daubs of damp paint. Just picturing it, newly uncovered, the sheet bunched beneath it, gives Tess a queer, awkward feeling.

They hear the thunk of their father's boots.

Lina? he calls, as he treads down the hall. Lina?

Not here, shouts Meg, with a querulous pitch.

Through the window Tess watches the particular dark of the macadamias, greenish-black, pocky. She runs an eye along the Ghost Mountains – those old volcanoes, full of rhyolite and trachyte – and sees the great bald patch down the westward flank. Forest of Forgetting, Meg used to call it, when she told stories to help Pip sleep. Stories of the Powerful Owl, with its lonely *woot oot*. A bird that sleeps with meat in its talons. Tales of Pip's favourite, the tawny frogmouth, a bird so rustily mottled it seemed jigsawed from the trunk of its tree.

Sometimes Pip, in pain or boredom, had croaked, Would you both just really shut it? But Meg kept on in a lowered tone, because those Forest Stories were her own solace, they were how she brought all the extinct creatures back to life.

Little eagle, Parma wallaby, stuttering frog. Endangered or vulnerable. Tess tries to imagine a world without the barking owl or the warty Boorolong frog. If you don't keep track, things can disappear entirely. At the River School, Tess has done water watching and jerked out the death throes of a quoll in drama. She's learned about cleared streams, agro-toxins, increased UV radiation. Radiation. A word for her time. And not just because of Pip. Some people say it's killing the bees.

After a time of banging, beeping and kitchen noises, their father comes to the table. He glances at Meg's pictures as he clunks down three bowls of baked beans.

Meg drops her pencil, staring. Their mother has always laid a place for Pip, and arranged flowers there. No matter how often she'd gone off, she'd always be home by dinner, shaking leaves off her shoulders, pinning up her wet hair, placing the vase at the table. Now there are two spiracles where people ought to be, and air soughing in and out. Even their father gives these spots a wide berth, his hips swerving past the empty chairs.

What's the problem, Margaret? he asks. Would you like to be telling?

Meg bites her lower lip and continues shading with chicken yellow.

Tess spreads out the *Bidgalong Bugle*. On the front page, Geoffrey Godbold pictured with the bass he'd caught fly-fishing by Emigrant Crossing. The fish has two heads. It's an angry purple, with tarnished scales. That's from chemical run-off, say the townspeople, from the macadamia farms. It's the Carbendazim. It's the rain, washing poisons from the gas mines downstream.

That fish belongs in Krazy Town, Tess thinks. She almost tells Meg – it's become such a habit – collecting odd things for this world the three sisters invented years ago. They'd started a book, illustrations by Meg, of Krazy Town Tales. Joe Romance was on the first page, feeding his pet rat, Tuesday, a freekeh patty. Page two was Ainslie Abbott in the hot-pink toy Cadillac that her bum so did not fit.

Their father comes back in, takes the paper. Then reads aloud, *Let's keep cool heads says the mayor.*

Beside that story, a headline about fracking, methane emissions and poisoned aquifers.

Gas, says their father, it is the new gold.

Show me that fish, Papa, says Meg, one hand on her spoon.

He turns the paper around.

Will they eat it? she asks.

The Godbolds aren't starving, Meg, he says. Would you?

But we're eating beans from a tin. Bisphenol A. And you *micro-waved* them. With Cling. What would Mum even say?

He winks, spooning his beans in three minutes flat.

Tess watches Meg sketch the two-headed fish and the mayor's head inside a freezer. *Cool heads*, she writes beneath the sketch. It's amazing how she does it, making them both look so cold. But how? Something about their pinched lips, the stiff angle of their heads beside an ice-cube tray and one, stray, frostbitten pea.

Well, that is quite cute, their father says, chewing his final spoonful. You ought to send it to the paper, Meg.

Then he turns to Tess.

Pour me a drink, *bitte*. The Sloupisti. And please be giving it plenty of ice.

He cracks open the blister pack, lays two pills on the table.

When Tess returns with his *whessky* he's gone.

He'll be taking it in his study, Meg says, looking sternly back at her trees.

As Tess leaves the room, Meg calls, You going to tell him then? About that blood?

35

Tess narrows her eyes, hurrying off, liquor slopping on the hall runner. She pauses, takes a long, deep, caustic slurp.

Inside the dim room, her father is bent over his books, his half-moon glasses down his nose. *Melliferous Plants*, *The Twelve-Frame Dadant Hive*. Voirnot, Langstroth, *L'Apiculteur*. In his large, lined notebook he's writing about the bees' disappearance. She pauses, reading over his shoulder.

Hive like human home. Protection from elements. Security, food storage, resting and comfort (love?). Plus favourable place for members to communicate info about events inside and outside hive that affect survival.

By his cup, a yellow Post-it with a name on. Sgt Anderson.

Do you know, my snappy girl, he says, taking a long draught, what is tomorrow?

Tess shakes her head, leaning against the side of his chair. She has a flash of him hanging out her damp undies while she passed him the pegs. And of her white dress, which flapped off the clothesline once in a grubby wind. He'd had to climb the ladder to reach that dress, lodged high in the magnolia like a snagged cloud. He'd told a story for the next five nights, about the dress that wished to escape Bidgalong. It travelled on salty winds across the Indian Ocean, it flew over the Great Wall of China, sunned itself at the Grunewaldsee and slid down an Alaskan iceberg.

Later, like most of Tess's clothes, the dress was passed to Pip. How many times had she worn it? Once on Fair Day – the raspberry slushie stain had remained. And again, on the day the test results had shown Tess was not a match for Pip. Tess had stood in the hospital ward and stared at the dress as if the stain was her own useless betraying blood.

Now she approaches her father's desk. His coat on a nearby stool. She shuffles over, slips his wallet into her jeans as he turns.

Tomorrow, he says, is two years since Pip died. Time just passes so differently, you notice?

Tess breathes in so sharply she goes faint with guilt. She feels empty, and thinks of her mother, wandering with that empty pram. She hears the hallway clock, a sound she'd hated on those nights with Pip, willing the morning to come faster than time permitted. She'd look through her window at the stars and name them for her sister. The names had come from *The Star Book*, which had on its cover whirling pools of light. At some point Tess noticed how certain nebulae resembled some pictures her parents were given, of leukaemia cells under magnification. After that she could not look at the Angel or the Eagle Nebula, or any of the stellar nurseries, without thinking of her sister's decreating blood.

Will they go up to the Red Crest for the anniversary? That's where Pip is buried. What happens two years after? Is it like a birthday, marked every year? Or do the rituals change? Birthday is wrong, though, she thinks; it isn't a celebration, even if the funeral people said that's what they ought to call Pip's wake.

Tess watches her father gulp from his cup then set it down, very carefully, on his desk. She grips his chair to steady herself. Maybe the blood, making her light-headed. When will it stop? How will she deal with it overnight? And what about the egg? She imagines chickens, the sound they make when they are on the lay, and feels sick. She isn't ready to be a Young Woman, which you became when the blood started. Has she really even been a girl, knowing what she already does about the ebbing end of life?

I suppose that's why your mother's gone off, her father says. I try actually to work, I try to chust do what I normally do.

He wipes his brow on a sleeve, smiles, then turns back to his books.

They all used to gently correct his English. His *chust* instead of just. His *ken* instead of can, and *men* instead of man. Don't blame me for being *Cherman*! he'd say. And oh, she remembers the looks her mother cast her then, a secret sharing, reserved for her, the eldest. A radiant glance that, even in its mockery, cast no other person out. But the teasing stopped after Pip died, and the glances too. And her father lapsed into his mother tongue, as he called it, when he felt most at home.

The breath, from his talking, heady with whisky. On his desk, the Imigran, the Maxalt.

He adjusts his glasses, reads aloud,

Man may believe, if he chooses, that possessing the queen, he holds in his hand the destiny and soul of the hive … he can increase and hasten the swarm, or restrict and retard it; he can unite or divide colonies and direct the emigration of kingdoms.

Tess raises her eyebrows, wipes her nose, shucks her shirtsleeves above her elbows.

That is Maurice Maeterlinck, he says. No better guide to bees. He will actually be yours when I've finished with him, he says, tapping the old book.

Tess nods, shifting from one sneakered foot to the other. She feels the damp paper towel in her pants, the throbbing in her belly.

Her father read Maeterlinck's fairy play, *The Blue Bird*, during Pip's last summer. He'd hoped to stage it but there were too many roles for their family, so he did all the voices. He did Mytyl and Tyltyl the sister and brother, the Fairy, the forest animals, the bread, sugar, milk, water and fire. There were even roles for feelings, for STARS, SICKNESSES, SHADES, LUXURIES, HAPPINESSES and JOYS. Tess loved her father then, most of all, for trying to keep them distracted. Their mother's fear had been so tangible, her private weeping, her face dissembled by grief. The more she tried to hide her distress – the starker it became. The rest of the family took other roles in their grieving; the sisters had learned to be stoic, or blithe; their father uncommonly gentle.

Tess looks at the worn hardback of *The Life of the Bee*, handed through the Müller family. Her great-grandfather, the first to tend bees, had taken honey to his neighbours through a bombed Berlin after the war. On his rounds he'd passed burning buildings, a dead horse being butchered right on the road, a soldier sawing bread with an officer's dagger. From these stories Tess learned you could endure. Bees kept Henrik busy, her father would say, when all of Europe was in disarray. Stefan had involved Tess and Meg with the bees more than ever when Pip was ill, teaching them how to smoke them gently, how to check the honey flow and operate the extractor. How to supp feed with sugar and water.

Tess runs a hand across his shoulder, tugs the hair at his nape.

Meg comes in breathless, holding the phone.

For you, Daddy. A Detective Someone.

The sisters stare as he straightens.

OK then, he says, waving them away. Outside the door they listen in. The word *accident* so their stomachs plummet, so they think right away of their mother.

Ten o'clock. Velvety dark rims every form outside; the moon is obscured with cloud. Their father has stayed in his study so the girls guess he can't have had news of their mother.

In the kitchen Tess fills a mug with liquor, then beckons for Meg to follow. They lie on the porch taking mean little sips, pursing their lips with exquisite disgust.

Plerk, says Meg. Yuck. Let me guess. Sloupisti from Schlepzig. Single Malt No. 1?

Then reaches again for the mug, saying, My turn, my turn.

Tess feels the hot throb of liquor down her throat, like speaking in reverse. It warms her stomach and dulls that low-down pain. But how will she hold everything in if she gets like her father does, going all wordy and sad and in need of too much from everyone, most of all, their mother? *Lina, Lina, a man will stay thirsty even if you take all his drink away.* Sometimes, very late, she hears him stumbling in the front hall, or the sound of his key stabbing the lock, and knows how thirsty he has been. Other nights she'll watch his random path across the fields, his pause in moonlight to waltz with no one, conduct the stars or lie beside the hives.

The sisters, on their backs, with their eyes on the sky, soak up the day's warmth in the porch timber. They search for planets, scan the Milky Way. They watch a star searing and pick out constellations, though the world, with each sip, tips and whirls.

Are you OK? Meg asks.

Tess realises, Meg doesn't understand that the blood will happen to her too. She takes out their father's wallet. Hands Meg five dollars.

Tess! says Meg, but pockets it with a private grin. Then pulls herself up. Hey, I found it!

And there it is, hovering above the Ghost Mountains. The bright star they'd named for Pip, eighteen months ago.

They stay outside for another two hours. They drink and drink and grow dizzy and full of desire for all the things they cannot name yet. Tess losing touch with the pain in her belly, forgets the confidence required for the challenge of blood, forgets to worry about who she's becoming today.

And then, a form shimmering out of the dark. A small cobalt light, picking its way across the bee field. Their mother in her blue dress, coming home.

6

As he headed home in the coppery afternoon, Jim's skin tingled from the river, from her. Still stupefied at the feeling of her flesh against his. I'll be off then, he'd said, expecting her to follow him down the mountain. It had grown dank by the water once the sun sank below the treeline. But Evangeline had sat, nonplussed, as if they'd just had coffee together. *See you*, she'd waved him off without a glance.

On his way out of the glade he passed the decorated tree, a great quandong, its roots fanned out along the earth, and remembered the tools she'd brought with her, the fact she had some private business with that hammer and rope. As he trudged down the mountain he realised, the tree must be an offertory, some kind of memorial to her daughter.

And so, what of it? He guessed that having lost Pip, the fire was of little consequence. He stood at the tree and put his palm against it. He thought of his mother then, and of mothers throughout time. Then, ravenous, he thought of eggs, toast, butter.

He was halfway down the lane when he saw the bee. It was steering haphazardly but following the line of the road. Probably from the Müllers' apiary. The same ones, he guessed, that haloed the tangled mounds of lavender outside his cabin. *Apis mellifera.* And in the stretched seconds of the bee's approach he was struck by this transit of pollen and nectar, from his small garden, across and down the lane to the Müllers' hives and the bright, lofty home with those ethereal daughters and the candlelight by which he'd dined one evening and, after, admired the framed pictures by the middle girl, Meg, and some abstract oils by Evangeline, who'd painted so keenly, Stefan Müller had told him, for five years after the commune. She'd had amnesia, he said, after the fire. Painting helped reassemble the past. The girls had led Jim out to their mother's studio. See this, Meg said, plucking a fine paintbrush from a jar, Mama made it from my baby hair. And this one's from Pip's. And then she'd gone silent and the sisters left the room while he stayed another moment to gulp down details, half starved of such rituals – he'd forsaken his own painting since Sylvie and the pregnancy. Evangeline's canvases were draped in white sheets. Whether they were being protected or hidden, he could not say. He'd peered beneath the fabric covering the largest work. Go on, feel free, Stefan had said, coming up behind and startling him. Have a good look, friend, I don't mind. But lifting the sheets on the wife's paintings, while the husband stood by with an incomprehensible expression, was just too weird so Jim had walked out to where Tess and Meg were hanging from the massive Moreton Bay, and switched into teacher mode asking them something anatomical about bees. The woman's paintings, with their anchorless forms – horses, trees, hills, water – were technically flawed, but the flattened perspective, the naive style and the tension produced from her rapid, small brushstrokes were compelling. They had a peculiar, elusive effect. Recalling these took him back to the mountain – to what she'd said about time being abstract – this was in her paintings, disparate events layered and revised.

Stefan was a thoughtful, enthusiastic man. Jim had liked him immediately. Over dinner he described a family history with bees and showed photos of his grandfather's traditional German hives. Brightly painted, and beautifully kept, these wooden huts looked like doll's houses, as if by being part of the family the bees required a similar standard of accommodation. They were carnica bees, Stefan said. Gentle and dovelike. Really? Jim had laughed, he'd never considered any bee appealing. Ah come on, Stefan had chided, don't you think of teddy bears when you see their fuzzy little bodies?

Despite their losses, the Müllers' home was captivating, like certain lived-in houses Jim had visited as a boy. The kind of home where you lose count of how many rooms and how they lead on to each other. It was bright, cluttered and unkempt, but still essentially clean. In his childhood home everything had been slotted carefully away. In the mornings the emptied, coffee-scented expanses of hall and lounge, his mother and father at each end of the bespoke table, turning and turning their pages. In his home, bare surfaces had so reigned that objects acquired a slightly shameful aspect, intensified by how they were secluded behind nifty sliding cupboards. The eye was tricked into thinking there was nothing, when there was plenty. It had bred in him a lifelong unease about possessions and what they could mean.

As Jim neared the cabin he saw someone in his garden with a large canvas bag. For one panicked moment he thought: Sylvie. Medium height, dark-haired, slight. In the diffuse dusk he couldn't make out her features. But then she bent and yanked a clump of something from his yard. Well, Sylvie would never *garden*.

He heard a loud droning. That bee again. Hurtling directly towards his head.

He'd been too sheepish to tell the Müller family after dinner that night, as he'd retrieved his bike from the back of their house and the sisters came running to stack his arms with jars of gold blood-wood. How could he have said, after Stefan had offered, *next time we'll give you a tour of the hives*. James Matthew Parker, thirty-two, object of heated town speculation, teacher at the River School, tall, motherless climate pilgrim from Sydney, out of touch with his high-flying father, ignoring calls and messages from Sylvie, deliber-ately unwired and incommunicado in his leaky rental cabin, perpetually hungry for something and only just realising how lonely. How could he say, I am fatally allergic to bees?

He saw the stranger raise an arm at his approach. He saw the Müllers' undulating fields and, beyond the mountains, an adamant-ine sky. As he registered the approaching bee he remembered: he hadn't renewed his epinephrine since moving here, even though, he'd realised after signing the lease, he was just metres from a fair-sized apiary. Honig Farm, for God's sake. There were so few bees left in the city, he'd just stopped carrying the EpiPen around.

He thought of Sylvie, naked on the bed with her legs crossed, towards the end of their five years together, smoking furiously and diagnosing, *You're still just a boy*, though he felt he'd grown away from her. At that particular moment, he'd been a father. Then, as the bee made contact, he threw himself on to the verge and closed his eyes.

When Jim looked up, Juniper Peterson, otherwise known as Junie the Extraordinary, was standing over him. He felt his neck, he checked his breathing. He seemed to be alive.

Are you right? asked June. I saw you fall.

He sat up, blinking idiotically. Groped beneath his hips to dislodge a rock. Looked around.

It was a bee, I thought … he said.

Well, did it get you? asked June.

I don't think so.

Might've been a hornet. Or wasp, she said, narrowing her eyes. You didn't sprain anything?

No, I'm really . . . Jim clambered up.

But there's blood on your jeans. How peculiar, she said.

Ah yes, from this morning.

Really? Your blood?

Jim straightened, ignoring her.

I've been waiting, like, ages, June said, and jerked her head towards his cabin. Where've you been?

Sorry? Did we have an appointment?

He brushed the dirt off his jeans, felt welts rising on his arms from where he'd fallen into a patch of burrs and razor grass. His nose was running, his hayfever had grown worse each day with the pollen count, paspalum and the dry wind. So much for medicinal country air.

Together they walked up to his cabin, a three-roomed, hand-built place with a sagging shingle roof. A short wooden porch overlooked the square yard with its relics of a cottage garden: overgrown, dried-out grasses, leggy rosemary and lavender. On certain cool, shadowy days he imagined this yard had an artful Piet Oudolf aspect; ramshackle, unstructured, the bowed seedheads sowing their drifty spores.

On the doorstep was a large cloth bag. Jim thought right away of prisons, the great grey masses of laundry.

You left this stuff at the Red Lodge. No forwarding address is why it's taken this long to find you, June said, tapping a foot, schoolmarmy.

Stuff? He didn't understand. Had he, in his fall, lost some memory?

Clothes, she said. And another of them postcards.

She stuck a hand in her backpack, waggled it, then passed him the card.

He knew the sender immediately. Sylvie.

We thought of bringing them up to the school but Agatha said how would it look turning up there, with those? June said, and pointed to the laundry bag. People talk, you know.

Yes, he said. But what could they say about T-shirts and shorts?

June looked at him crossly. She was only eighteen but seemed much older. Papery skin, small, slight, with unbrushed hair and bitten nails. How could he have mistaken someone so tousled for Sylvie? But there was something plaintive and gutsy about both women. He'd once seen June grinning, gap-toothed, on her uncle Bo Peterson's pick-up with two hounds and a shot hog. In her hands a rifle, aimed skyward. He'd once skirted the Petersons' rambling acreage on his way home. Six horses gave off a moony glow against the green rise. Snowcap Appaloosas. Nearby there was a stream with a neat hand-built bridge, a ruined stone house on the lee side. Now he remembered, those horses, that bridge and brook. He'd seen a similar arrangement, in thick strokes of deep colour, a scene rendered mythical, alive with mysterious energies, in Evangeline's studio before Stefan walked in. That painted canvas, so large, he'd noticed, they'd have to raise the roof to get it out of there.

He looked at the postcard. Then turned it over. Weeks old. Two lines only. *Jim, please call me! There's something about the baby we need to discuss. Sylvie.*

Baby? Sylvie had never referred to the pregnancy that way. Maybe just trying to get a reaction. He hadn't phoned or written. He wasn't sure he would.

Is she going to join you then? asked June, who'd of course read the postcard, and no doubt the many others that arrived before it.

At the Red Lodge where Jim stayed for a month when he'd first arrived, June cleaned, passed him his mail and taped messages to his door. *Sylvie called 4.45 pm, 5.20 pm, 6.00. Any laundry? Breakfast at 9. Please close high window, storm coming. Magick Show in the Lounge at 8 pm.* Sometimes the postcards had been slid under his door. Sylvie, regretful, pleading, could they at least talk? Sylvie demanding he send his new number.

I thought maybe she'd ditched you, said June. But why would she leave her clothes? June pointed to the bag. Plus, they look expensive.

They're not ... Jim crossed the porch and looked inside the bag. He turned around slowly, taking a long breath.

They're not my girlfriend's clothes, June, he said. I don't ...

Jesus, he hardly had to explain himself.

I get it, she whispered, wild-eyed. You've gone and done a runner!

From the porch he could see the Müllers' cows clustered by a grove of hazel, their eruptive pisses, their flicking tails. The light was dimming. Whenever he passed they turned their deep, limpid eyes to him, torsos still as old trees. Across the lane, a fresh wombat hole, dirt mounded beside the entrance. Cockatoos posed in a nearby cedar, yacking and squawking. In the morning he'd wake to find six types of animal shit on his doorstep, as if they'd convened there while he slept. Always, and more than in the city, this sense of being watched.

I suppose you heard about the bones? June was scratching her head.

Pardon?

Stefan Müller found a skeleton near the Lower Mountain Road, not that far from here actually. Yuman, she said in a low voice.

Really? Jim said. You mean human, with an 'h'?

Now she was really pissing him off. His leg ached, his eyes were dry and itchy. He was suddenly stupendously tired. The river, the walk home, the thoughts of what that Müller woman was doing up there.

Apparently a car crash, said June. Don't you wonder who could it be?

Has someone gone missing from town? he asked, tapping his temple theatrically.

She drummed her temple with a finger. Then stared at the bag of clothes and it was her turn to laugh now, a high, chirruping sound.

What? he said.

You're meant to be a teacher. All those books in there! But you don't know anything, do you?

He studied her for a long moment, remembering the show she'd put on one night at the Lodge, the Vanishing Coin, the Magnetic Hand, various levitations – cards, rings, pencils. Her *Magick Act* was so raw and unpolished, and the audience so sparse, he'd had to hide his snarky mouth behind a VB coaster.

Pretty soon you're going to find out, she said, what went on up there. She pointed to the mountains.

I've heard quite a bit already, he said. He felt the burning itch of the co-opted to shut the busybody up.

My mother's still at the commune, she said, matter-of-fact. Then turned to his garden.

You should try companion planting, she said. She rubbed her nose, jammed a hand under the opposite arm. Marigolds will deter those cabbage moths.

He looked into the tangled vegetation.

Hold on, I have cabbages?

She laughed again, eyes downcast, and clomped off down the weedy path towards the lane, hands swinging, bruises along her narrow calves. He had a sudden urge to paint her, this figure on the verge of dissipation.

Inside, he placed the bag carefully by the fireplace. When he opened it his throat closed up, his skin began furiously itching. He pulled something out. A skirt. An odd smell, what was it? Then he realised – some pungent unguent Agatha, the Red Lodge hausfrau, had used for washing. He picked up a blouse. Its soft life, the form it had once taken around a body, had been destroyed with new, starched creases. Fucking Agatha! It was ironing as spite.

He put down the clothes and paced the small, sparsely furnished room, peered out the front window towards the Müllers', examined his shin where the blood was caked and considered showering in the dank stall, or could he be bothered filling the bath?

He glanced at the postcard. A generic scene from the Radisson courtyard. Each week they'd snuck into hotels Sylvie could have afforded. She worked in Mergers and Acquisitions with a harbour view and original Rover Thomas's on the walls. At midnight, after seeing a band or eating out, they'd stride boldly into one of those marbled city hotels and take the lift to the rooftop pool. There, under the electric haze from the ranks of nearby buildings, they'd swim. Snowy towels. Spotless sandstone pool surrounds. Sometimes music, piped underwater, to which Sylvie would drunkenly mime aquaerobics, emerging in a sudden leap with her hands in prayer above her head, a dripping sheath, marble-skinned. She'd been beautiful then, most seductive like that, absorbed in the vivid moment. They'd dived and surfaced as the traffic sounds resounded, epic, oceanic. They'd looked out to the Heads or the wheeling coloured neon of Luna Park. Now and then a scream detached from a rollercoaster or disco-ferry and floated over the harbour. At some point, for Sylvie, it was no longer pretence. She wanted a high life he could never give her.

When she got pregnant Sylvie dreamed of the child they would not have. A boy that looks like you, Jim, dark-eyed, dark-haired, she said. He's on a beach somewhere, he looks lost already. And he'd comforted her at the abortion clinic till she asked him to leave and he drove back to his Kings Cross flat so he could sit finally at the ugly, burned Formica table, and cry. A month later he'd packed his old life, and booked his flight. Three months up here now, teaching at the River Primary.

From his porch that night the rippled fields, indigo and grey. Jim looks across to the Müllers' farmhouse. Is she in there?

Some people in this town haven't forgiven me, Evangeline said as he'd pulled her from the river that afternoon. And she struggled to keep her face expressionless as they sat together on the bank.

I feel their eyes on me as I pass, she said. I stopped going to town altogether. She began to fidget and reflexively scratch her knee. She lowered her voice. There are individuals who follow me around. A woman I've wronged. A man who could reappear in my life any moment. But up here, she gestured towards the garlanded tree, I try to just think about Pip. I try to stop time.

He'd stayed beside her, the trees converting their breath to oxygen, the clouds skimming rapidly across the dimming sky, and tried not to look at her slick, bare limbs. There were no rules on how to grieve and how long, what forms it should take. He'd wanted to say this but could not. His mother's clothes so carefully packed. Her daughter's shoes and medicines nailed to that mountain tree.

Has he ever met a woman so determinedly like a poem, like an elegy announcing its grief so overtly? He decides next time he'll try to make her laugh.

Now he thinks he might sketch something of the day's events in 2D on the canvas: a woman in a river, a body in a bee field. But he'd given up painting since his canvases had become so cluttered. For two years he'd worked on stark, figurative scenes in imagined rooms, where certain objects were symbolic, charged. But he'd become unable to tell which elements pulsed with meaning, which appeared flat and inert. He'd set out to paint a bed and find it was just a bed, with no relation to the rest of the scene. His smeared palette was more compelling than any colour on his canvas. So he tried instead to sketch, working back to the assurance of outlines. If painting was, as his tutors once said, *feeling arrayed in space*, what exactly was the problem? He'd sit, smoking dope, and try thinking his way out of the dilemma until he was so far gone from instinct, impulse, flow, he could no more have painted than split an atom. He'd walk instead, through the narrow, haphazard streets of Potts Point and down past the matt grey Navy ships and the old wooden piers to Woolloomooloo. Then up into the Botanic Gardens where he'd spent so many humid afternoons with his mother. In there he could finally think clearly and he saw it was partly true what his mother said, that nature could optimise the mind. You had to squint, though, to keep the culture from intruding, you had to narrow your gaze to delimit; the Gardens were jostled by high-rise towers, the harbour was walled, its surface slick with diesel.

He glances nervously now around his three rooms. He'd worried since moving, that the deadness in his painting might infect his new home; he'd shoved all his canvases well out of sight, unsure if he'd ever retrieve them.

Through the window, Honig Farm. The farmhouse lights are comforting, the cows' lowing long and guttural through the valley. In the windows, an occasional silhouette of some passing Müller, going about their evening. When he shortens his gaze he finds his own possessions enlivened by this proximity and feels briefly, precariously content. How often does she go up that mountain, to swim naked in the river?

7

The first time we open a hive there comes over us an emotion akin to profaning some unknown object, charged perhaps with dreadful surprise, as a tomb.

Stefan recalls this passage after searching the house, the barn and fields, and finally glimpsing the bright vertical line by the studio door. He enters slowly, pausing on the threshold. Here's that mineral glow, cascading from high, grimy windows, and Evangeline, spotlit, back to him. She's standing before the huge canvas, which had been covered for years in a sheet. Seeing the fresh gloss on it, the raw strokes of black paint, Stefan thinks of Maeterlinck's words. It's something about that sudden glare, and how she seems unaware of his presence; it's the musty odour of this space, mostly unused since Pip; a queer, illicit tension.

Pinned on the wall, some sepia photos. It's these, not her own work, Evangeline's gazing at now. In each shot the same rider in dark coat and bowler hat leans into a galloping stallion. The photos form a sequence, like movie stills. They look familiar, though he can't recall where he's seen them.

Stefan watches her rocking on bare feet, a finger tracing a fetlock or tail. He senses her fervid energy, the subaudible hum of her focus. He thinks of those interludes, during each daughter's infancy, when she seemed restored to a more solid self, touching their doughy, nuggety limbs, her face suffused with disbelief and awe.

Paint drips from her brush to the floor. For several minutes he stays leaning against the buckled doorframe.

Edward Muybridge had an accident, she says without turning.

Muybridge. The photographer. Stefan remembers now, glancing again at those sepia prints.

He'd been on this... what-you-call-it? Stagecoach, she says. As it came down the mountain, the horses stampeded. He's thrown clear from the coach, knocked out.

She taps the scar on her forehead.

It's after that, she says, that he becomes a photographer.

Stefan exhales. He's heard this story, years ago. Or perhaps it just exists in the ether, like those thousand things concerning his wife that he'd absorbed without ever having discussed them.

The guy has serious head injuries, Evangeline continues. Then personality change, confused thoughts, double vision. Some years later he starts taking these photos, not just of the Yosemite mountains, but also of horses, in motion. He gets into this wager to prove that horses' hooves are completely airborne while running.

She turns to him, black paint on her forehead and cheeks, as if decorated for some rite. How she becomes when she's absorbed, he'd almost forgotten.

This horse problem, she continues, was called the theory of unsupported transit. But, see, it's really to do with time.

And so? Stefan says, then seeing that nervy flicker in her gaze, softens his tone, What do you mean, Lina?

He's annoyed. His own news still alive on his tongue. He hasn't expected a history lesson. She's still staring at the photos — silhouettes really — of horse and rider, and he looks over at the stretched shapes of her animals against the hill. He knows the real story behind that scene. A tale of two men, and a commune deal gone sour. A story for the police. But there was too much at stake to go after such people, she said.

Painting, which some called therapeutic, doesn't seem to illuminate any of it. It's more like she's sculpting, he thinks, like she's scraping away at memory. All this Muybridge business has to do with her own head injury, the Ghost Mountains, the time she stumbled, blindfolded, in a field with horses. He doesn't need a degree in Freud to recognise the elements. All of this when he barely knew her — he'd just been a visitor at The Hive back then. He'd travel to and from the commune, stay some weekends, before hitching back to the coast to surf and figure out what to do with his super-fresh antipodean life. He was still half-involved with a woman on the coast; he'd been, how should he say, undiscerning until he laid eyes on Evangeline. An interloper, Jack Hodgins had called him once, using such an unfathomable tone, his heavy hand on Stefan's neck, that the epithet had teetered between insult and acclaim.

Stefan watches the animation on his wife's face. Her slow, sensual movements. Horses can do this to her; painting can, he sighs, but he can't. A sudden hankering for one of Nora's cigarillos. He can almost smell that aged fruitiness, the bitter filament on his tongue. But no good thinking of Nora when your wife's just metres away.

She looks him over. How are you, darling? You must be tired.

Lina, he says, trying not to relish the tiny punishment in his news. Police will be coming this afternoon.

The other day, he continues, near the Lower Mountain Road, I'm finding these – ah – bones. And actually, a car wreck.

She puts the brush very deliberately down by the oils, tucks her hair behind an ear, daubing her face with more paint.

Bones?

On our property, he says. So *natürlich*, they must speak to us.

She bites her lip, her cold pallor, charcoal smudges under the eyes.

An accident, Stefan? What kind of car?

Hard to be saying. Lina …

…Well, big or small? What colour?

He looks at his feet, puts his hands at his waist. OK. A van, he says.

She stares, her voice shooting up as she asks, And the body?

No body. Only bones, he says.

He watches her swallow. He rocks back in his work boots and points to the sepia photos, asking, And so, what happened to your horse man?

She gives him a reproachful look, then turns back to the pictures.

He'd never have found his calling, she says, if he hadn't hit his head. Before the accident, the man was a bookseller. After, he chose horses. He learned to stop time with his photos.

Yes, yes, Stefan thinks. The man was shaped by his past, aren't we all? But he's really fed up thinking about it. When he looks back he can't figure which parts of his life to linger on, which parts to excise. Each memory called up seems to trigger others, more insistent for having been expelled. Each memory leads him, inevitably, to Pip. One evening he'd come in here alone, and found the sketches. They'd floored him for months after. Pip's face, all her features starkly sculpted, hollowed out as they'd looked in her final year. The pale lashes very distinct against her skin, her lips so

57

defined, the pure line of her nose. Evangeline had spent countless hours with their youngest, but he'd never seen her drawing, only sitting on the bed, holding Pip's hands or reading aloud, and sometimes they seemed to be waiting, and other times both seemed entirely without expectancy, mother and daughter in each other's hands. Some nights Evangeline would come exhausted from the room and say she wished she could reabsorb her smallest girl, wouldn't it be more bearable if she could take her back inside her own body? How would she ever let go? He was an answerless man back then, his hands blunt instruments. Evangeline's hair had just begun to curl again. Months before he'd watched her scissor it off in one swift action and pass him, without expression, the long ponytail. Why? he'd asked. Evangeline opened her other hand then and showed the much finer, golder hair. Pip had started losing hers.

Now, he thinks, it's safer to forget. No sign anywhere of those sketches. She must have put them away.

He turns stiffly so he's side on to her, kicks a boot against the doorframe. Increasingly now, this feeling of performing the farmer. A niggling illegitimacy. Certain people bring this out in him, certain gruff types around town who've worked the land for generations. Or the easeful, chunky young men he employs sometimes, short on speech but plenty secure in themselves, unquestioning.

To his left, the mountain ridges crouch behind blue fog. Above, the peaks seem very tranquil, ancient, attending. She's trying to say something about what happened to her at The Hive, about what happened to all of them. But he's done with all that. He wants pure future, unblemished, rammed with possibilities. He wants time to accelerate through every adhering moment. He's left so many selves behind. The German boyhood, the hippie-surfer shtick, the habit of father-protector which sloughed away the day of the funeral. But for his wife the past is a fever that doesn't seem to break.

You've never told me, she says as he steps out the door. Back then, The Hive fire, where were you?

You think if I am coming when I said, it would not have happened? he asks.

Another failure, not to have rescued her from the men that pursued her, from Jack Hodgins and her mother, Anita, who'd bargained with her future so they could better secure their own.

Were you with Nora that day? she asks, her voice very tamped down.

No! I was surfing. I have told you. Was only one time with Nora, and before you and I had even…

It's half a lie – because he's never spoken about Nicole Jamison, the surfer – only *his friend Nick*, a piece of sexual history he'd been slow to shuck off. Seemed no point in laying it out – he knew which woman he had a future with. Because it's half a lie and he cannot think what else to do, he walks off, very abruptly, over the square of camomile lawn. He'd sowed it years ago so that, crossing barefoot to her studio, Evangeline might absorb the calming oils. But he hadn't thought of the bees when he'd planted it, and how they'd like to visit the flowers, so that crossing shoeless became a hazard. Still she'd loved it; she'd lain, face down, then smiling said, I hope it doesn't make me too relaxed, or how'll I ever paint? He walks and walks, aware of his gait and how he must appear to her, weak, avoidant, another beast of the field. Man up, is what the young people say, what Leith, the farm-hand, says to the bulls as he castrates them, slapping them almost sexually on their languid rumps. And Stefan marvelled: how could a person know so purely what it was to be a man?

He'd been halfway up the Mountain Road, salt in his hair, sunburned and sleepy after a day at the headland break with Nicole;

he'd been thirty kilometres from the commune when the authorities flagged him down and said: go back. He protested, Evangeline was up there, either in or near that blaze. But they had not let him pass. So he'd turned, then waited at the foot of the mountains as large flakes of ash came down and the sky went bruise-coloured, hemmed with red along the lower ridges. He'd listened for news on the car radio, then, hours later, found her at St Catherine's, her head bandaged, her chest burned, in a kind of delirium. His absence had tarnished him, he'd not manned up when he ought to have struggled past the roadblocks, committed some heroic act of rescue. After that he'd promised: he'd be a hundred per cent present for crises; he'd be hers, in every weather.

Halfway across the field he can breathe. To his right the heifers, their mossy pelts, their pleasing mellow condition. Up ahead, the sky starred with golden bees. He smells honey, probably an olfactory hallucination – these often herald a migraine.

When he hears her calling, he turns back. From this distance she's a cartoon figure, arms up, framed by the studio door.

Stefan! she is yelling. But what if it's him? What then?

8

He grinds his earbuds deeper as he sings along. Lithe and rangy with a coiled, springing walk. He's headed for the chemist with the script and the letter from Dr Paulson to prove that he – Thomas Adam Tucker – is clinically depressed.

He's decided. He'll renew the venlafaxine despite the side effects. Nausea, dry mouth, genital anaesthesia, constipation, nervousness and anxiety. But should he tell his 101,253 followers about his depression? Or will this undermine the authority of his website? Facts about which comes first – plague, pandemic or comet strike, grain-shortage uprisings or nuclear blackmail plus the more immediate threat of Apian Atrophy.

Subscribers send him such questions in these End Days Times. His Twitter feed is full of doubt and certainty:

Am I, like, crazy to believe the world's days are numbered?

@Prepped you're insane if you don't believe all the evidence.

Yr totes wrong about the death of the bees!! Cuz I seen heaps in my frontyard. @NatureGrrl

Six essential knots even Moms can master!!! @DoomerMom

Dehydrated Water. A useful barter item for your kit.

His morning post:

Prepare folks. Or join the Pre-parasites, who'll prey on those who've planned ahead.

Tom crosses Greenacre Street, twisting the earphones deeper, blocking all other sounds. Human voices muttering, dogs yapping, reversing utes, the spruiker hawking two-dollar wares outside Wacky Discounts.

Sweet music. Sometimes it's the only thing to magic him through the morning.

Past the library, which makes him think of the billion trees felled to make those books. Despite being troubled by this, he's upped the print run of his weekly *Survival Report* to cater for the summer gawkers. City tourists with their market baskets of local cheese, air-dried muscatels, biodynamic stretchmark cream. So many have permanently relocated they've altered the town's original character. But who can say what that really was – something primordial, beyond all their reckoning. By the market gate he hands out his reports. And later, ten metres down the road, retrieves them from the council bin, brushing off breadcrumbs and bacon, then hand-ing them out again.

Past the butcher, the bakery, the Happy Hemp and Seed. Over there, the Ghost Mountains, getting balder by the hour. The oil and gas company have rebranded their fracking as *stimulating*. Which caused more than a few snickers and lewd hand gestures at the pub. Tomorrow, at dawn, he'll head up to protest with the Harmer boys.

When he reaches the town square he scopes it out. His new ammo belt is too small. American sizing. It's digging a red weal on his hip. When he tore it from the package, the jerky smell of leather. He'd tasted it. Bitter. Now he pushes a finger into a cartridge hole. Just wearing it gives him a swagger, despite the lack of actual ordnance. Across the road, by the Rainbow Café, a clot of mothers with their mucousy kids, their babies bound to the chest like infant possums. As the women slide narrowed eyes towards him, he holds up a greeting hand.

He's their crossing guard. Weekday mornings and afternoons. Shepherding their kids over the road to the River Primary. He's not supposed to be walking in town with a $65 Special Ops combat knife in his ankle sock. He smiles at the mums while mentally saying, *Stare Fucking Off*.

Past the Yoga Studio and the Java Nook, and into the chemist run by those radicals who refuse to sell the morning-after pill. He's slid *Sustainable Facts* under their door more than once, detailing the need for population control. Whenever he comes in, he makes a point of asking what forms of CONTRACEPTION they stock. Today, a newly sceptical look on Terri's face as she lists them.

The Pill, diaphragms, condoms, she says.

Her well-tended hair and forgotten body, the chemist uniform doing nothing for her, a sort of zippered shirt suctioned to all the unfortunate parts.

But what varieties *exactly*, Terri?

She inhales, replies, Ribbed, extra-headroom. Flavoured, coloured, studded, contoured, Space Age, glow-in-the-dark, Fire and Ice, Twisted Pleasure, snugger fit . . .

She tugs her above-knee hem, zips her cleavage tighter.

Once his script is filled, he leaves with a jumbo pack of Rocky Road, but no prophylactics, which – now he considers it – might give Terri the wrong impression.

As he turns down Archer Street he runs right into Jack Hodgins and his twins, Christabel and Aurelia. Hodgins. The self-appointed King of The Hive. Greying ponytail, wide, sulky American mouth. Jack used to be handsome. When Tom's mother could remember what country she was in, what year it was and that he was actually her son, she'd recollected, Oh yes, all the girls at The Hive fancied Jackson. Including her, he assumed.

Tom hands the man a copy of last week's *Survival Report*.

Hodgins snaps it dramatically in the air, then reads the headline aloud.

Dark Ecology. End Days Strategies. He uses a slow tone, making it sound extra stupid.

No thanks, son, he says, returning the paper. You know, he leans closer, marijuana and clove breath, I noticed lots more ads in your last issue.

Tom flinches at *son*. But – an admission – he's been read-ing it!

You say we ought to cut back on material goods, Hodgins says, counting off fingers. You call us frivolous consumers. But the ads in your little newsletter suggest we need so many items to survive the…What do you preppers call it now? The Rapture, the Quickening? Bit of a mixed message?

Daddy, sighs Aurelia. Can we exactly go please?

Her sister nods. They're in cahoots, eyes flashing like cats in the dark. Both wearing tutus with sparkly bags. Their mother had left, years back. After that, Hodgins opened a Single Fathers' Shed. But no one had seen any carpentry from there. They'd seen plenty of smoke. Seen plenty of tools, they joked, going in and out.

How's your mother, Tommy? I heard about her wandering off. Fortunate that Nico was driving by that night. Could have ended up anywhere, says Hodgins.

She just wanted some air, Tom says.

At three am? Hodgins is sceptical, smoothing his mane. Maybe it's time for professional help, son. I remember how stubborn Heidi can be.

Tom stares, recalling Hodgins, bare to the chest, with one of his mother's towels around his waist.

Stubborn, says Tom. But what were you asking her to do?

Last Sunday his mother had passed back and forth down the hall all afternoon. Ma, what are you doing? Sit down. But she'd gone on walking, with a twitchy look, making slow insect gestures at the wall. Two days later, he figured it. There was a woman in the hall mirror she no longer recognised. She was reversing through her life and he was powerless to arrest it.

On the fridge, the checklist from Dr Cheng:

• Memory loss that disrupts daily activity
• Trouble understanding images and spatial relationships.

Hodgins matches a rollie, then asks between puffs, Is it Pick's disease that she has? Or Lewy Body?

Mix her some herbs, Papa! says Aurelia.

But Tommy has never believed in my craft, Hodgins says, blowing a perfect O of smoke. Even in The Hive he refused all my remedies. We could have taken care of that stutter. Those teeth. But you're a Self-Made Man, aren't you, son?

That's what you taught me, Tom says. Anyway, she's on a prescription. I wouldn't muck with it.

But if you did try naturopathy for what's ailing her, says Hodgins, and for whatever's ailing yourself. If it worked, then you'd have to change your whole story about what a phoney I am.

Tom stands, stunned, in the silent street — *ailing yourself*! And is propelled back to those weekly gatherings at The Hive. Jack, in his wide podium stance, talking about Pureland while everyone sat in *padmasana*, hands in *jnana mudra*. The smell of that communal hall, of root-vegetable stews, body odour, bergamot, patchouli; the heady smoke of dope and incense and the drone of Jack's voice. The meditations. The hall had been built along certain ley lines. Tom always staggered out feeling sick.

Those of you who are fatherless, think of me, Jack would say. And it was hard to tell if he was addressing Tom in particular, though his mother had always acted like his was a virgin birth. He's never met his father. No other Tucker lived at The Hive, no man ever claimed him. His first memory, a smell of cedar, sun shafting through cabin logs, blocky toys of wood and wax. And Hodgins. Throwing him up into the air and jigging him. But that was his routine with all the babies, each morning when he visited the Nursery Cell. Throwing them up. As if to prove what good hands everyone was in. All the pregnant women queued to have him diagnose. Footling, twins, anterior, posterior. Once, he'd turned a breech baby, his broad palms pushing the woman's belly, his breath loud and even. The women just lay there, letting him touch their bare skin. Even before they were born, Hodgins made sure he'd handled all the babies.

Tom turns away. Remembering has made him hot and unsure and he feels the eager, absorbing part of himself that he's struggled to disavow. Across the street, Evangeline with a large basket, one hand shading her eyes. Hallelujah. Someone normal.

Gotta go, he tells Hodgins.

And watches the man swivel slowly in her direction. The extra-long draw on the rollie, the second's uncertainty in his eyes, his twins skipping off through burnt-sugar air chanting, Vanilla, Chocolate, Rocky Road.

Tom freezes for a minute in the whirling street, eyes on Evangeline. The Repentance River flows over him, the camphor-scented smoke. He's rewound, to the day of the commune fire. The clanging alarm. The infants in the nursery, the baby in his arms. Evangeline, running from the Emerald Forest with blood on her face. Flames behind her, scrabbling up the ghost gums. He'd signalled, *follow me*. It was his chance, perhaps, to prove himself. He turned to the river and started to run.

At the water, he'd waited, jigging the kid. The baby had one fist in her mouth so he could see the pearly nubs in her gums, her knuckles working against them. Finally, Evangeline came skidding down from the bush. Her shirt was burned at the back and sides. She wore one huarache sandal, the other foot was bare. Where'd she been? What happened to your mouth, your head? He started to shake, he felt liable to cry on her behalf. She took a thorough look at the baby, then leapt into the river.

Tom watched her lave water on to her chest as her shirt floated downstream. He saw the burns across her back. She was older – eighteen – but seemed, crouching low in the water, as vulnerable as the infants in the nursery. He stood, looking and loving her more in her sudden frailty. And then he remembered – he'd left his other people unaccounted for.

Take her, he told Evangeline. Follow the river track down to the valley!

But she was waist deep, arms around herself.

Tom, she said, don't fucking leave us here!

But my mother's still up there, he said, and the other babies …

When he reached the burning cabins, flames were spiring above the thirty-metre gums. The nursery was empty. Through the door, the black cut-outs of men – Arlo and Lute, Rainbow, John and Starr, calling names and checking the huts. No sign of his mum.

He found the cabin he'd lived in for twelve years. No one there. On the floor, his storm glass. He'd once been able to say from its contents what kind of weather was streaming their way. He'd once had an amateur's authority. But there'd been no presentiment for disaster – the glass was dumb to fire, flood; its drifting crystals only mastered air. Then he bolted into a rain of embers, wondering about the horses and bees, the goats, chickens and frogs. Who'd save them? And where was his mother?

Tommy!

Evangeline is tugging his left arm. She's dragging him across Baker Street.

What are you doing? she asks when they reach the kerb, her face damp and pink as a newborn.

You could have been flattened! Standing in the road like that!

He stares at her blankly. Lustred hair, smoky eyes. In a long skirt and baggy T-shirt with holes in the hem. A tooth on a silver chain round her neck. Human? Animal? *Tommy, don't leave me here*, she'd begged, back then. And where had Stefan Müller been, or Jack Hodgins when the people needed rescuing? When the End Times came at The Hive, the Real Men were AWOL. That day, all Tom had thought about was survival. And he hasn't stopped, ever since.

He has an urge to flash his belt as Evangeline shakes his shoulder, saying,

You're supposed to be a crossing guard!

Then she laughs, a curt, choppy sound he can't recall from her, though she'd once been a girl who laughed freely, and often.

Angel, he says.

Those sombre eyes. It's so nice, how she's looking out for him; it sets a peculiar warm humming in his chest. But she steps back quickly, dropping his arm.

No one calls me *that* any more, she says. Then pulls out her umbrella, launches it and races away. Seconds later, Lana Beaufort striding round the corner with her slate-coloured whippet. The dog high-stepping, too good even for the ground. Tom greets her, gives the dog a tentative wipe.

Are you all right, Thomas? asks Lana, but her eyes are on Evangeline. Best stay away from that one.

The whippet lifts its leg and pisses melodiously on to the street.

9

The forest leaves are scarlet and gold on the black tarmac. Above, winter branches blown bone-clean. It's Friday morning and the clouds are rippled with the last threads of dawn. As Meg cycles up to the Clear Energy gates she sees the three tree tripods. From further down the Summit Road these wooden poles had looked like stripped tepees. Closer, she sees Bowie and Comet, already roped to their poles.

Meg slows, ditches her bike by the road, takes a puff of Ventolin. The boys, high on their sling chairs, are lighting smokes, settling in. Tom Tucker's halfway up the third tripod, his face white and blotchy. He puts a hand to his forehead, wobbles precariously, climbs a little higher. His narrow body like a stick insect, swaying. When he used to visit, before Pip became ill, Tess had pointed it out. The dude, she'd said, is spade-arsed. After that his every posture had seemed designed to accent this feature. The sisters sat in silent, racking spasms as he reached for a top shelf, or bent to a shoe, revealing no architecture beneath that denim. Later, at the table, they'd wonder. Where did all that food go? Clearly not arseward. Their mother called it *feeding him up*, how she cooked when he came to dinner, and how he ate, as if perpetually renourishing after illness.

Today Clear Energy have brought in two cranes. They're parked about ten metres down the road. The cranes and the tripods face off, like two species of monster insect ready for battle. Five policemen are standing around, clapping cold hands in the morning chill. Marjorie Baker and two other ladies pass out sandwiches, pour steaming drinks from Thermoses, giving the whole scene a peaceable feeling. No one shouting today, no one struggling as they had last year when the graders first came in. Tess and Meg had watched the protestors then – farmers, hippies, mums and dads, even babies on shoulders wearing Frack Off slogans which seemed kind of mean because what could babies know about fracking, or even fucking, which the word was referencing, their mother said.

Now Meg watches the steam from the policemen's cups blend into wisps of mountain fog. This diffused morning light turning everything tenuous, *sfumato*. Downhill from where they stand, one holding pond has its own thin cloud line over the water. *Sfumato*, a way to hold two opposite ideas at once. Da Vinci, Meg read, had prized this skill as much in life as on canvas, this ability to reason.

Marjorie offers food to the crane drivers, but they wave her away with sheepish smiles.

Going to be here a while, she says, crossing to Meg in her lumbering gait, one hip outslung, one shoulder hunched by her ear.

She offers her Tupperware and winks, You can catch more flies with honey than mud, she says.

Meg chooses a sandwich and bites into the triangle of forbidden Wonder White. She's surprised to find not honey, but plastic cheese inside. It is a wonder, she thinks, how the bread turns almost immediately to dough in your mouth, and the cheese to paste, as if to spare you the chewing.

Last summer the boys had come up here to protect the trees. They called themselves the Guardians. And once the company started clearing with chainsaws and graders other townspeople came, including her parents. But one night Nico and Lute shot bolts in the tree trunks. The next week a company man was blinded when his chainsaw blade made contact. The girls will pass this man in town, a cheerful type with a shrub of brown hair, and a red pirate patch. He's on compo, their father says, better off than slaving for the enemy.

After that Nico and Lute were banned from the site. The protests were meant to be NVDA. Violence wasn't cool, direct action could be peaceful. It was all written up in Tom Tucker's *Survival Report*. But the loggers were violent to the trees! said Meg, reading this report to Tess. Trees don't feel, Tess replied, back then when she was talking. Even though they've got cells and blood, even if they live, die and have limbs. But they suffer! Meg said and ran through the house shouting *Timber!*

No one had shouted that when the trees fell on the mountain, there was just a whine of chainsaw, moaning wood, a leafy crash and thud. Some protestors had hugged the fallen trunks, and later planted RIP signs beside the stacked, limbed branches, as if the tree deaths were as real as any human's. Meg thought this was superpathetic. Some people, she thinks, cannot achieve *sfumato*. Their lives are too narrow, like the girls at school who'd not understood one thing she'd told them about Pip. That she was supposed to be her donor, that they would take some part of her own blood and put it inside her sister's body to make her better. There had been no transplant in the end, because of transformation. What's that? the girls had asked, and Meg, very tired that day, and not even fully understanding herself, had said to the girls, it's embarrassing how stupid you are, you better go Google.

Sometimes Comet and Bowie stayed overnight, chained to the Clear Energy gates, and Tess and Meg cycled up with breakfast made by their mother. Poached-egg sandwiches on sourdough chia, still warm in brown-paper wrapping. When the girls approached, those boys looked like two cocoons in their green sleeping bags. Just Bowie's long brown dreads sticking out and their white twists of breath. This was peaceful protest – so quiet you could do it in your sleep. By refusing to move they'd halted the fracking, sometimes for a whole day. Their mother said, you girls have helped, you've kept their energy up! So they couldn't bring themselves to tell her, *Those boys are vegan* – and that they'd frisbeed the eggs right on to the road. Seeing their mother's meticulous cooking on the bitumen had made Meg more unhappy than any fallen trees, than any wildlife drowning in the holding ponds, but being sad about wasted eggs magnified her shame and for a time she stopped going out there. It had been something to do, in that year after Pip.

Now there are twenty active wells on the mountain, topped by towering metal rigs, and five ponds of chemical waste. Meg had passed those unfenced ponds when she cycled up to the gates. Rectangular sheets of brackish water with white, salt-crusted rims. The chemical ponds kill frogs and birds. Kangaroos get trapped by the steep-sided banks, and lie in the water, their fur seeped in mud and toxic run-off, and it's disturbing to see them, beached there like inland seals. When it's roos, Helen Tarkoff comes in her WIRES ute. She flings sacks over the animals to stop their struggling, then gives them a needle so their legs buckle beneath them.

Kent Waddington, the site manager, is gliding up the crane now. You can't tell if he's calm because the megaphone bounces his voice around the mountains.

A bit much! shouts Marjorie. Only three protestors today, it's not like they're deaf!

Meg does not say that Tucker is half-deaf from the many infections he'd had as a child. Untreated, her mother had told them, except for Hodgins's poultices.

Did you hear? Marjorie turns back to Meg. Someone tried to run those boys off the road the other night. Someone's regularly tailgating the protestors.

Meg takes a second sandwich, then another, muffling her mouth with bread. She thinks of the wreck on their property, which had come off the Lower Mountain Road, said her father. An accident, he'd said, though later she'd heard Nora ask how anyone could be sure.

Bowie, Comet and Tucker start chanting, *Respect existence, or expect resistance!* from their tripods, and Meg wonders why everyone calls them *boys* while the Clear Energy workers are called men, even though they're all about the same age, some with beards and tattooed arms, and she wonders if it's a love for the earth and a willingness to climb up there and defend it like circus artists on stilts that makes you more boy than man. Or maybe it's because the boys don't wear high-viz vests with company logos. Yet Meg knows her father loves the land and, still, he's had the Clear Energy men out to the farm because he wants to get both sides of the story, he says. He's weighing up whether to let them do exploration on the north side of the property.

Meg gulps the last of her bread. The air is drier now the mist has risen, and the cranes and the men are stark paper shapes against the sky. Meg prefers the dawn smokiness that breaks up the lines between all things and Marjorie's saying under the small shouts of the men, That boy does not seem well to me, he's got the shakes, Thomas Tucker, have you noticed?

Once he'd got notice of his position at the River Primary, eight hours north of Sydney, Jim had farewelled his city friends over dinner at various houses. Homes these friends actually owned, could you believe it; no he really couldn't with his mouldy, wall-papered rental and lack of appliances.

Drunken tales unspooled at these meals about Jim's heading north, about what he was about to become Up There. A bumbling Greenie in Rasta beanie and Jesus boots, extolling soy-chai enemas. Which nostril would he pierce, the friends asked, on which flank would he get his Pentacle of Venus tattoo? Jim did his best *baleful* as he listened, while Michiko stirred her roux and Yusef skewered prawns. But this kind of talk only fired his decision to leave. Their weary superior mythology, the cosy assumption, the settling in – or settling for – city life seemed to him a kind of blindness.

Greta, breastfeeding her youngest, was especially worried about where Jim would live. She'd downloaded some photos of Bidgalong properties, which looked, printed in low-res black and white, much more foreboding than they had online. The trees and mountain backdrops loomed, so the houses seemed enshrouded by the very nature you were meant to be gobsmacked by.

But anyway, he actually liked being homeless, he'd say at someone's inner-city terrace or semi, homes that already looked post-apocalyptic: their roofs covered in plastic sheeting during the rebuild, the kitchens with wiring snaking from the demolished walls, the taped-up, resurfaced bathrooms with their heady VOCs, the muddy yards covered in tarp, and scarred by tree removals. All his friends were waiting for the rain to abate so they could finish the build. Every second house had a skip out front into which the homes appeared to have puked their incompatible contents: rusty wrought iron, old bricks, rotten plasterboard, buckled lead-light, broken flyscreens, illegally removed asbestos, excess Gyprock and last year's IKEA creations. The more covetable fixtures hovered in cyberspace – French doors, cedar-framed sash windows, decorative gables – entire deconstructed homes, up for auction.

He'd make his homeless comment and the friends who'd been burrowing so doggedly into their heritage fixer-uppers would jibe: You? Homeless – on Daddy's trust fund? But he'd not touched a cent of any family money. Sylvie would say that Jim lived as if always on the verge of leaving, his furniture scrounged from Potts Point footpaths and charity shops, things chosen without the slightest eye for vintage cool, things from the eighties for God's sake with zero aesthetic appeal. Moulded-plastic tables, an ugly mustard-coloured pouf, milk crates full of records for which he had no turntable. His fridge with its nude cheese, deliquescing cucumbers and instant pasta sauces growing new green hair. When he removed certain items, he'd sniff, then shake to redistribute any offending ingredient. Her Surry Hills garden flat was artful, luxurious, dustless. It was decorated with objects from lunch-break online shopping jags. A porcelain light fitting, an alpaca throw, wraps, shrugs, cuffs, shifts. His lack of commitment to things suggested he might be the same about people, she said. His cracked plastic Tupperware with its curry stains. His jam-jar toothbrush holder. The bed of scavenged wooden pallets. It was brutalist – no – she'd correct herself – just brutal.

Sylvie never came to Jim's friends' dinners. During their five years together the friends had not really taken to Sylvie, or she to them. They asked after each other in a vague, dutiful way. Sylvie had barely any close girlfriends, she'd always had a man, she said; and with her long working days, that was plenty.

After the jokes and the global cuisine had grown swampy, Jim would cab home in the persistent drizzle. It had rained and rained that final Sydney winter. The friends stayed inside playing Rorschach games with the mould on their new extensions. Only the parents among them were forced out, following restive toddlers across sodden parks. They staggered through mud in rainproof jumpsuits, gumboots and hoods like undernourished visitors from some intergalactic zone. They all had persistent coughs. Their kids had weals, rashes, wheezes and chronic asthma, their noses were permanently lacquered with snot, and just as the kids were up and well again they'd vomit, matter-of-factly, on to someone's shoulder, and a new virus would do the rounds so that when he rang Kate, or Geoff, they'd say, Little Olivia has caught Beatrice Mead's Slapped Cheek! as if they'd had the provenance checked in a lab.

Sometimes the women turned to him – Greta or Jane – smeared with Vegemite, teary with exhaustion and undisguised envy and said, I don't recognise the person I've become! It was impossible to prepare for children. Jim thought the acts required to parent were mythic; and seemed more noble than any of the unfinished projects in the half-life he was living. Then he'd make himself remember Geoff wearing baby-puke to the pub dinner, Andrew and Jane

77

who hadn't had sex since the kid had colonised their bed, Greta with her mysterious birth injuries.

And Sylvie had broken it off after she found out about the baby, or foetus or whatever you were meant to call it. And Jim had let her because he hadn't dared say, let's make a go of it – a kid, a house, a family, what the hell, why not? He floated through his life, she said, one week after the procedure, on her couch with unwashed hair, wearing track pants and a desolate look. She was still feeling sick from the hormones, and would disappear to vomit and return with a flannel pressed to her face. You're stuck. You can't even see it. Piss off.

She'd made the decision about the abortion, it wasn't his pain to feel. But he'd allowed himself brief fantasies of himself as a father, of a small hand inside his. And for weeks after he'd left the clinic, the faint impression of footsteps shadowed him. How could he have said he wanted the baby more than anything then, he just hadn't wanted her?

Back then, as his friends became fathers and he visited them in the busy wards, watching them bathe their infants more devoutly than he'd seen them do anything else in their lives, a painful longing for family had stolen up. As if a child could return him to what he'd lost, animating some genetic thread; perhaps even lead the way back to himself. He'd told no one about this feeling, which seemed unmanly, mildly shameful – he'd never thought genetic connections important. He'd imagined adopting, or fostering, unfazed by blood links, biology. Try as he might he could not deny their appeal, these babies, so rapidly absorbed into lore, their presence creating the family, a thing he longed to restore, but could not, or would not with Sylvie.

After five years together it wasn't the first time they'd broken up. But by moving to Bidgalong, Jim had made sure it was the last.

On their final date in the harbour-side restaurant Sylvie got speedily drunk on dirty martinis. She ran her hand down the menu with eyes closed, and opened them on five sea textures and a celery-heart salad. When he looked at her frankly he remembered the roots of his attraction, how some frightened kid shimmered up behind all that posing, how her sensuousness was bound right up in need. Behind her, through a massive window, the ocean, seagulls passing, a chain of cars crossing the Harbour Bridge. A parade of tourist brides, stuffing their white skirts into limousines along the quay. Further south they'd pose for wedding shots beneath a bridge pylon. Say Cheese! *Chiizu! Kimchi! Patata!* Pepsi! *Ouisttiti! Käsekuchen!* The tuxedoed men beside them, drowned by tulle and chiffon. Was this what she wanted?

Sylvie examined her naked hand, adjusted the thin strap of her dress where it lay over a sharp collarbone. She was six weeks pregnant. By the time the oloroso caramel arrived, they'd decided. But – she was drinking heavily, hadn't he noticed? She'd made her mind up already. He'd take her to the clinic in two weeks, after that it was over. The pregnancy was all that bound them. Ending it would extinguish their connection. But, he said, quietly horrified, there is memory. And she turned, very grave, liquid-eyed. Do you think *remembering* me made my mother and me any closer? I'm only doing what she should have, thirty-two years ago.

She rode off on a ferry, her pale face a small full stop. Jim walked beneath the train line and stood on the kerb. At Circular Quay the taxi drivers pulling up chose you. The buses waited for no one. He thought about getting a motorbike and driving recklessly north or south, about becoming anonymous in some other place. He thought of his mother, gone before she was gone. Drifting on OxyNorm and Sublimaze while he read aloud to her. In her last months at home, she'd become very keen on Hemingway. She

79

needed his clipped manliness, she said; all that austere coldness made her feel she could cope with her pain. Jim read the birth scene from 'Indian Camp': the native woman labouring without anaesthetic, Nick's father attending and deaf to her cries of pain because – as he tells his son – they are of little consequence. Jim had read aloud while his father sat in the kitchen with the *Fin Review*, putting his head around the door every so often, it seemed to Jim, for Veronica's permission to continue his life downstairs.

One month after the abortion Sylvie came to the airport in a shiny car that wasn't hers. She smelt of leather – upholstery? after-shave? – and was doing her best to seem jaunty, but was breathless, high-coloured. Her mascara was smudged, a stray pin abseiled from her hair. Jim remembered her late-night calls, early in their relationship, when she'd said she just needed to hear him breathing down the line.

She sipped Pellegrino at the airport café, sallow-faced, puffy, still recovering perhaps from the pregnancy. The problem of what to call it – their child, embryo, incipient being – seemed to grow in Jim's mind. Outside the nondescript clinic he'd passed the religious fanatics. On their illustrated sandwich boards, tiny hands, bodies floating inside their mothers' atmospheres. Jim had deliberately shouldered one man then stared at his slogan: *Your mother gave you the gift of life, pass it on*. He realised then how Veronica really would disappear once his memories of her were gone. This baby, who'd hardly seemed to exist at all, had already utterly changed him.

Sylvie, watching the planes, could hardly look at Jim. Why had she even come?

Jim felt murderous and grateful – he was leaving. Through the huge window, an Airbus climbed the sky.

He took her cool, thin hand, but she was way off, jaw tight.

You get to escape, she said finally, turning, her right eye quivering. To clean air and mountains, rivers that you can probably even drink from.

Now, in Bidgalong, eight postcards stacked on his desk. In each, Sylvie's clipped sentences track a new phase of their separation: anger, regret, remorse and spite. Today's card: gnomic. He has, writes Sylvie, no idea what he's lost and what he's left behind. Her words insinuate themselves within his evening's mantra, as he sits on his broken porch and tries zoning out, tries not to turn towards farm or mountain. The air is balmy, scented with mint. The clouds are shredded along a carmine horizon. He's so utterly shit at meditation, he realises, because his focus is only repression; it is no letting go. And what leaks out tonight, between each attentive breath, is Sylvie's plaintive voice from postcard number four, her *something about the baby we need to discuss.*

You could think of the weather, said Tess's teacher in yesterday's class, as a gateway between the earth and sky. So Tess is giving it more attention, gauging the atmosphere for pressures and risings, collecting cups of sooty rain, scouting the escarpment for shreds of fog. Today one cloud, thick and striated like a skinned shank in a medical book. In the morning, mist, rolling down Fox's Lane like stealthy mountain spooks. In the quiet lounge, curled on the sofa, she opens her notebook, scrapes her fringe sideways, yawns.

In class they'd listed words for winter climate. Raw, nippy, dirty, thundery, chilly, foggy, foul and sharp. Mr Parker had written them up, then turned to Tess. He no longer addressed her directly but waited, with a lifted brow, in case she decided to speak. At lunch he took her aside.

If she didn't feel able to talk in class, she must at least keep a journal, he said. Or risk failing.

Tess had shrugged, then boredly scanned the walls and ceilings.

So, he continued gently, what would a person write in such a book? Since our subject is Landscape and Identity, I want you to write about your particular weather. How is it connected to your family? How is the atmosphere part of who you are?

Tess had looked around at the posters. The British Turners, and the intricate landscapes of Petyarre, Napangardi and Kngwarreye they'd discussed for Conceptions of Land. Bugs, stick insects and butterflies motionless in jars by the window. Last week they'd watched Olafur Eliasson's *Weather Project*, an enormous sodium yellow sun, rising inside a London hall. Pale English people lay on the floor, glorying in the light, as if they'd never seen sun before.

We can't exactly avoid the climate, can we? Mr Parker said. When it's unpleasant, when it's raw, dirty and clammy, how do we get through?

A cold tremor passed through her. She stared at her feet with her mouth slightly open, forgetting to breathe or swallow. She knew he wasn't talking about weather. She jammed a finger in her dark hair and wound it. She began to kick the leg of a nearby chair, unwittingly, over and over. How could her teacher know her mind, and what her thoughts were running from?

All those people entranced by Eliasson's fake sun reminded Tess of how she'd once calmed her sister during the long drive home from St Catherine's. In the backseat Meg was slicked with sweat; she'd already vomited twice by the roadside and was chewing Bach flower lozenges. Her damp hands trembled in her lap. On her arm, a tiny bruise from the last time they'd taken her blood. Tess leaned over then and wiped a circle of fog from her sister's window. *Look Meg*, she said – and as the world outside appeared, a frosted cameo under her hand, the sisters remembered, for one second, how it was to marvel.

That was the day their parents told Pip's doctors they did not want a technological death. Not long after, the social worker visited. She politely surveyed the kitchen, the bedrooms, the study.

Looking for signs of a crazy hippie diet? said Evangeline, very loud. Just because I lived in a commune the department thinks I'm anti-treatment! Why don't you test the water by the old well fields? That's where all of this started, she told the woman.

She believed she'd become contaminated from drinking there years back. Five other kids in town had developed leukaemia. The national paper had called this *a cluster*. The social worker wrote everything out in a book that snapped shut with a built-in elastic. She spoke in a gentle voice used for a child, lighting Evangeline up with fury.

Maybe her teacher is right, maybe there is a kind of inside weather, Tess thinks as she scans the lounge and the sepia cones of light in the hall, remembering how the house felt when they returned from St Catherine's, how she can tell, without even looking, if her mother is home, whether her father has taken his first drink for the day. How the bedroom felt the night after Pip's death, even though she'd been away from it many other times. The room had throbbed with a different order of emptiness: blue-tinged and total. The girls had warily eyed her clothes and toys, and then looked away. Who did they belong to?

If the weather is, as her teacher says, a gateway between the earth and sky, where is Pip, who was said to have ascended to a higher plane?

Tess puts her head on her arms as memories come, storied, simultaneous, dreamlike.

On another drive home, past Harper's Bend, she'd watched an eerie shadow slide over a field of bright canola. Then, not far past the escarpment turn-off, something began hitting the roof. Soon, the car windows were smeared a glassy green.

Tess sits, smooths her book then writes it all out:

'Locust plague!' your father yelled above the noise. He turned on the wipers to clear the windscreens. It was the big rains that made the insects fat and restless. 'They'll cause an engine to overheat,' he said and pulled into a Mobil. Beside all the bowsers were hills of gross dead locusts from the other cars' radiators. Your mother really needed *to go*. But crossed her legs tight. She'd rather wait. She hated petrol stations, and the gasoline smell. Her eyes would go empty. The other thing was that sometimes she'd retch. She stayed in the car while your father poked the locusts from the grille. The world was greasy yellow through the killing windows.

Towards the end, Pip was only allowed liquid out a straw. Her hands felt so strange in hospital. Like she'd warmed them at a fire. 'What must Pip think of us?' your mother asked as your father propped the bonnet. 'We can't go on, just leaving her in there.'

Sometimes your mother stayed over in the ward. You could make this type of bed from a lounge chair. Your father packed the morning lunches and laid out school clothes. Washed, dirty, did it matter? You had odd socks and inside-out shirts because of stains. You had butter sandwiches for ten days. You had dinners left by other people at the house. Your father served them in their weird flowered crockery. Sago and macaroni cheese. Pumpkin soup and strawberry sponge. Everything soft, so your father said, 'They think already the Müllers have forgotten how to masticate.' There was food from Nora especially, and you weren't to tell your mother but this always tasted best.

On the night of the locusts you waited for Meg to finish. Then you climbed into the cold bath. Most things look better underwater. You held your breath till it felt like your chest would tear open. You found your mother's razor and shaved your legs up to the knee. When you wiped the steam the long mirror showed a person wearing beige socks below dark-haired thighs. Blood ran from the nicks on your calves.

Another thing was that Benjamin Davis from 5P had sent the family a sympathy card. It had a lopsided love heart in one corner. You felt a bit sick, looking. How had he got your home address? You hid it inside your pillowslip.

Next week the weather turned very clear. The house echoed and the edges of the doors and windows seemed straighter than before. On the day your parents brought Pip home the sun barged in. The house timbers sighed in the heat. Your legs were itchy and the many cuts had turned into silver lines, or scabs where you'd sliced deepest at the ankle.

Tess has used her best cursive. She stretches a hair elastic around the notebook, so it will shut with the same snappish authority as the social worker's.

One week later she stands by her teacher's desk, her matted hair absorbing the light. In the hall some girls are waving, very urgently in their nearly imperceptible style, hands low and close against their thighs. Tess dully remembers how it was to have a friend. The living weight of Amy's head on her shoulder; the gooseflesh pleasure of linking arms. Her spontaneous, airborne playground hugs. It is this exuberant physical force of friendship that she misses most, and which had dwindled when she'd stopped wanting to talk any more about her life.

Finally Mr Parker, tidying shelves, turns around.

Ah, Tess. Hold on, he says, shuffling papers. Then hands her a catalogue. On the front: MATTHEW BRANDT, *Lakes, Trees and Honeybees*.

How about this guy's art! he says. See those – they're real bees. Brandt found a bunch of them dying on a lake shore. So he printed his photo, using emulsion from the bees themselves. And then soaked the print in the lake water for months.

Tess breathes in sharply, pushing her glasses up her nose. Art from dead bees. She stares at a lagoon beneath what looks to be a rain of fiery snow, the photo paper damaged. Above the *Sylvan Lake* is a spooky cloud formation, like a rent in the universe. What are you supposed to think – an artist making ruin into beauty?

She wants to say, I'm not artistic. He has her confused with Meg, or her mother, whose paintings he'd stared at one evening after he'd come for tea. And yet this singling out has warmed the slight sense that she's truly worth attention.

Mr Parker returns her journal, then leaves. Inside are some small ticks. He hasn't said whether her writing is good or bad, he has not graded it, only: *A powerful account of place and memory. And where are you in the story, Tess? Which of the 'you's is you?*

It's around four pm when Jim hears the footsteps. She's already on the threshold and then she's inside before he can whip off his mother's gown, before he can hide his habits of loss.

Evangeline. Her lips cracked, her brow glossy with sweat. A drumming pulse at her temples, her great gusty exhalations.

That morning he'd climbed the mountain again, pausing at the spot where he'd found her undressing three weeks before. The river was glassy and calm. The bush smelt of loam, rotting leaves, eucalypt. When he reached the tree she'd decorated he thought of aboriginal *djurbils* – those beseeching rituals for more plentiful possums, for increased echidna, emu or kangaroo rat.

Evangeline had performed her own, secular rite on that tree. But what exactly was it for? He'd examined the white boxes nailed to the trunk. The faded labels, the cardboard pocked and holed by weather. Must have been there a while. He could just make out the girl's name in black type. Pippy Müller. Evangeline's youngest. A memorial then. On one of the red sandals, roped to the trunk, the small shadow of her sole. He thought of his mother's empty shoes in the cupboard, signalling the time before she was ill, when her living weight had left its traces. Then remembered the day his father had discovered him.

Usually, hearing the muted swish of the Saab door, Jim would put away his mother's things and retreat from that room where her smell was fading, where he'd stand before her mirror trying to bring her back. But that afternoon his father was already by the door. He lowered his briefcase, lifted one large hand. Jim, seeing it headed fast towards his face, tried not to flinch. But his father just cupped his ear gently, pulled back. In his open, extended palm – one of the gold clip-on earrings Jim had forgotten to remove.

In the bedroom, Veronica's things were dangling from cupboards and drawers – a shirt arm, a jeans leg, one shoe aimed at the door as if trying to flee. His father, absorbing all this, had said, This isn't the way, James, then trudged slowly downstairs, leaving the stunned boy alone. It had been a ritual of sorts, Jim supposed, to covet everything she'd once worn against her skin.

He was a tall and broken fifteen-year-old then. Clear-skinned, bean-thin. Top of his class. A brilliant sprinter with an oiled, compact stride. Every morning after she died he bolted around the neighbourhood till his knees buckled, then waited, his ear pressed to the grass in Centennial Park, then ran again, motherless, with a father gone mute but for business things. He ran and it was like swallowing the world in great, racking gulps of air. And all the Paddington streets made him wretched with their boutiques and bars and clots of shoppers with their vintage fucking bags and shoes and their chain-store accessories for slummy cool. And their animals with all the dogness bred out of them.

Sometimes he'd wag school and drift through the city, the scene of their many outings – down Art Gallery Road past lunchtime joggers, where once they'd watched paramedics working so long and violently on a man you thought they must be doing his chest more injury, and down into the Gardens. In the winter ponds the dried lotus stalks stood broken necked and all the trees had lowered their coverings to the earth. He'd stay until dark and listen to the industrial noise played in the defoliated trees to keep the five thousand bats away.

Towards the end he'd often crouched outside his mother's room just to make sure she was still breathing. She'd often caught him at it. Oh darling, I used to do the same when you were a baby! Come here. He'd climb on to the bed and they'd sit folding origami while she talked of Akira Yoshizawa, the famous Japanese master of folding, who'd decorated military patients' beds during the war. She'd learned some basic origami as a kid watching Harbin's TV show in East Sussex. They liked the fantastical beasts best: the Hippogriff, the Cerberus, Pegasus, winged lions. She'd often fall asleep in the middle of a difficult fold, and Jim would complete the animals, lining them up like Yoshizawa had for his patients, at the end of her bed. Not wanting to keep her awake, Jim's father had taken to sleeping on the fold-out couch. His bed, utilitarian, unmade, in the downstairs lounge, gave the whole house an eerie feeling of impermanence. Worse, though, when the cleaner had finally folded it away. That mattress, soundlessly sliding into its recessed place, an echo of his mother's coffin gliding.

In the Ghost Mountains, beside Evangeline's tree, Jim realised he'd had none of this woman's resourcefulness in grief. After Veronica's death he'd found no solace in river, forest, mountain or lake. The funeral was formal and restrained, curated by his father, or his father's secretary more likely. At the wake, the seven distant British relatives had congratulated them on the tasteful service. One played discreet, bland music on the baby grand so Jim felt like he was at one of his mother's department-store functions. Upstairs he found the London cousin zammed out on Veronica's leftover Sublimaze, reading *Harper's Bazaar* in the empty bath.

Jim, still Jamie among his relatives, had retreated to the garden where the pool was covered for winter. He slid the canvas back and climbed inside the empty cavity. Thin currents of light sieved in from tiny holes in the fabric. Why burned not buried? He lay down in the cold pool and wondered about the difference between ash and dirt, about the confounding word cremains. He'd never returned to the place where his mother's ashes were interred, that wall of niches, oddly ordinary like the PO boxes at the local PostShop.

That woman's offertory, in a glade by the wild Repentance River, was so primeval and so much more suited to loss than the militant ranks of spruce at the Northside Crematorium.

Hello, she's saying, right inside his house now and crossing the floor, her hair down her back, arms bare to the shoulder. Lina, was that what Stefan had called her? A different woman maybe, to this haughty Evangeline.

I was out walking, it's hot. Could I beg for a drink?

He stands, embarrassed, unlooping the scarf from his neck, uncording the dressing gown. Beneath it, the ripped knees of his old jeans.

Very stylish, she says neutrally. Silk?

Not mine of course, he says, I just ... Sometimes I ...

But she's looking around at his spartan quarters.

He takes off the gown and tucks it out of sight. Then fills a glass with cider. He clears the table, pushing aside books flagged with Post-its. *Walden*, Solnit's *Field Guide to Getting Lost*, Bill McKibben, Bruce Chatwin.

He gestures, says, Sit.

When she puts her elbows on the cracked wood, he sees it. Poking from a pile of labelled folders. Sylvie's latest postcard. *Jim, when are you going to stop avoiding your past. Call me, please.* He jabs it out of sight.

Somewhere on the mountain, axed wood starts groaning and splintering; his floor shudders when the trunks fall. He'll sometimes imagine, after a joint, that his cabin boards are sighing, he'll imagine the very sap in the wood stiffening in empathetic horror.

They sit drinking, in the quiet. Very weird, trying to act like he hasn't already seen her half-naked. But now he supposes it's his self that's been exposed.

She pulls out a page from his notes. He's taken the kids on field trips into the mountains, sketching and photographing, gathering evidence of the changes wrought by climate.

She reads it slow and haltingly and he notices, for the first time, an intermittent throatiness in her voice.

What is the message that wild animals bring … ? What is this message that is wordless, that is nothing more or less than the animals themselves – that the world is wild, that life is unpredictable in its goodness and its danger, that the world is larger than your imagination?

Her forefinger moves over the page like a child new to reading, her hair slipping around her face.

That's true, she murmurs, the world is wild.

He swallows, nodding, recalling the notes the younger kids took on their first field trip. Wombats are so cute, one boy had written, but only from afar. Wombats rub their bums on trees, they jump a metre in the air.

Do children really understand? she asks. Life, unpredictable in goodness and danger?

Probably more than us, he says.

Does she talk in class?

Tess? he asks. No. But still, she's taking everything in.

Doesn't tell me anything. Doesn't talk at home, either, you know. I'm told that's unusual in selective mutism.

Selective mutism? He hadn't been given any special term for Tess's silence, only told by the school it was part of her grief.

I blame myself, Evangeline says, standing, forefingers pressed to the table.

At The Hive, she tells him, there'd been a distrust of technology. She'd been raised to believe in the healing powers of crystals, ley lines, tinctures. They'd tried them all, along with the conventional medicines that devastated Pip's body without destroying the disease. But once Pip went into transformation the doctors confirmed – no machine, no medicines could save her. They decided then to bring her home.

He waits, aware of his jerky breathing, her grey eyes dulling.

She crosses to the window, puts her forehead on the glass.

I didn't think I could save Pip. But I knew where she belonged. Perhaps I was wrong, though, to put the others through it.

Jim remembers the long afternoon in the house after school, when his mother was taken to the hospice. Each empty room had contracted around his fear. What was a chair, what was a couch, what was home without her in it? All the objects turned very rigid and immovable. Each designer item repelled him. He'd gone for a run, every step like he might alight from the crooked suburb. Everything in him stopped up, so he didn't hear the car that felled him, coming around the Pike Street corner.

You think that's why Tess isn't talking?

She shoots him a quick, uncertain smile and he wonders if it's a disguise for shyness, her demeanour. She shrugs and looks back out the window. What must she make of his clear view of her house, over the lane and across the fields?

He takes a long sip. If she was so thirsty she could've walked the few metres further to her own kitchen. So then, was she here about Tess, or something else?

Was it just your decision to take her home? he asks. How about Stefan ...

... Oh Stefan's ... agreeable. Let's say *he'd* found me, the other day, in the river. He would have just let me alone. Whereas you jumped in, she laughs, her gaze cleaving the air between them, as if you could rescue me.

He drains the bottle, trying to work out what she means about her husband, and how he is with her.

Seems like you're angry, he says.

She brushes her palms together.

Oh don't do that, she says, frowning. The counsellor thing. I can't bear it.

She comes closer to where he's sitting at the table. Curriculum documents, photocopies, assignments. Her daughter's journal somewhere in that pile. It's very important, he sees, not to move an inch in any direction.

You have Tess every week. How's she doing? says Evangeline, tucking a hand under each armpit.

I think she'll be fine if you are, he says, exhaling.

Then in three swift strides she's right before him.

Well, she says, I just want to be ...

She pulls his hands on to her waist.

... lost.

94

He stays very still, his mind racing. The Cusp Fold, the Swallowtail, the Butterfly Crimp. With her hands holding his fingers flat against her hips, his skin jitters with memory. In the futureless weather of his mother's bedroom, from those coloured squares, they'd folded themselves into another dimension. The world, larger than your imagination.

Do you think that's possible? she asks.

Then she leans down and puts her mouth against his hair.

Two

... they will have no time now to visit the
gardens and meadows; and tomorrow, and after tomorrow,
it may happen that rain may fall, or there may be wind;
that their wings may be frozen or the flowers refuse to open ...
Maurice Maeterlinck

I

When Stan Baker of Stan's Water Divining and Swarm Removal Services Inc. drove up in his small brown Honda, Tess was out checking an empty hive – the honey super, the brood box, the tiny bee door – not one insect left. She imagined the black clan soaring over their neighbour's house, above the green creek and along Fox's Lane though it was too early for swarming season, and there were no signs of what Tucker called pestilence.

Now Stan sits with their father on the back porch, stretching out his dicky leg, the good one propped on a rickety chair. He's come to help solve the mystery of the bees. Tess perches nearby, swinging her feet in the mid-morning sun. From inside the house, the sound of her sister's practice, the ladder-notes of her scales and arpeggios, the deep full boil of the sonata. Tess is not musical and Meg's playing fills her with an awe purified of envy. Meg, all grace, full of unaccountable artistry.

A lyrebird dashes out of the bush, its bum wagging. Tess makes a note in her journal, logging the path of nearby animals, their behaviour, their sounds. What if wilderness is just an idea? her teacher had asked. What if there's no such thing? And Tess had wondered if any inch of the earth remained untouched by human industry. Fifty-five butterfly wings found on the forest path. Each wombat she's seen lately afflicted with mange. For three days the roos have not come down at dawn or dusk. Are they moving to higher ground? On the radio the other day, a woman yelling at the local member. *Stop refining nature's obituary! Do something, just please do something!*

You're not the only beek around town with a problem, Stan's saying to Stefan.

Five prime swarms, six secondaries and one absconding colony just this week, Stan continues. Maybe this fracking? It's upset the water table. You seen George's place, on the rise? The company finished their drilling and left. He's got wells on his land you can light with a match. Gas coming out the ground, out the kitchen spigot. Orange-coloured, smell of old socks, says Jean. Three of his palominos got sick from the water. His cabbages grow rotten from inside out.

Ah, Stefan says. But George is coming richer for it, so they say?

Rich from the gas company? Stan asks, scratching an ear, looking doubtful. Maybe, for your bees, try magnets. One at the front, one at the rear of your hives. Bees like a strong field. Or, move your boxes.

Tess watches her father stand, twisting his stiff chest left to right. She thinks of his face above the opened hives, radiant with bee-light, and how he'd taught her to detect the sound of piping. A high, repeated G sharp. That's the queen, he'd say, his green eyes shining, signalling to her rivals.

What's this rumpus with the police? Stan is asking now.

Stefan freezes, looks away.

It had been in the paper. The car wreck and the unidentified person who'd died right there on their land. The body there for more than a year. A police hotline to call with information.

Any ideas, Stan asks, who it could be?

They're just bones, says Stefan, tucking his workshirt into his trousers.

How about the chassis number? That ought to do it, Stan says.

Stefan holds out the veil, the helmet, asking, You want to suit up?

Stan pulls his hat over his long earlobes and says, No thanks — I ain't getting that close.

He levers himself from the chair, his tanned legs below grey work shorts, thick as timber. The lined backs of his knees like cuts in the grain. He gropes in a pocket, clunks his battered phone on the table.

Stefan doesn't believe in divining — it's Evangeline who'd phoned Stan for help. But Stefan hadn't protested; he'd indulge her everything if it brought her happiness. Anyway he approved of Stan's holistic methods. Stan, who speaks at town meetings about over-farming, mite pressure, eutrophication. Stan, who's bequeathed his land for conservation to make sure it won't be cleared when he's gone.

As the sun dips behind the mountains the whole family wanders out to watch Stan dowse. They stop in the bee yard in a line that still seems one person short. But as Stan works, this feeling shimmers, then fades.

Evangeline's in a worn summer dress, her skin still pale from being indoors, her body filling out after the hard years. Tess looks at those strong legs, at her mother's broad, sandalled feet. It's as if she's finally returned to earth. Around her neck, that pearly incisor on a thin silver chain. Stefan touches her lightly on the shoulder.

She smiles, but keeps her gaze on Stan, saying, He can detect water sources to two hundred and seventy-five metres.

There's something about the way her mother speaks, and how she gets mesmerised watching Stan work. She prefers the old ways, Tess thinks, because of her childhood in The Hive. Though sometimes she'll say it was primitive, the way they treated injuries or ailments, how some women gave birth with only Jack Hodgins attending, their screams resounding across the valley. She blamed the old ways for Tom's deafness, for the death of June Peterson's mother who ought to have been treated at St Catherine's. She'll say the old ways are a load of fucking rot, that only men like Jack could believe in them. They'd strived up there for purity through nature, but this had cost the women and children most, she said.

Stan uses L-rods for divining, held out from his body. Some use forked sticks. Others, like Ken Baines, use a pendulum. Baines made his from a gold bullet and witched five wells on the Johnsons' farm, his bullet swaying over the site of potable water. But Baines got the fever. Works for a mining company now, mapping gold in the ground.

Stan slaloms across their fields, transfigured through his work into grace, despite his gammy leg. But it's not water he's divining, it's ley lines. Bees are happiest on intersecting lines, slower to swarm, less aggressive, the varroa mites stay away.

At some point, approaching the hives, Stan calls, I'll keep my distance, don't worry!

Stefan holds up questioning hands.

I have very powerful electromagnetic fields, Stan shouts. Too much for bees!

Meg starts to snigger. With his back to them Stan adds, Ask the wife!

The girls erupt, hands over mouths.

Shush, says their mother, but even she is smiling. It's true, she says, Marjorie's told me all about it. Guess how many wristwatches Stan's destroyed?

★

Later that afternoon Meg curls up in the wingback chair with *Peter Pan*, though she's already read it twice. A boy with all his baby teeth, a boy *clad in skeleton leaves and the juices that flow from trees*. They loved hearing their mother read this, on those sleepless nights when Pip had first come home. She'd spent so many hours with them then that this block of time, though layered with grief, was cherished. It was only later, when their mother receded, that Meg and Tess realised that time had been for Pip alone – and after, when she had nothing left for any of them, they blamed themselves for not knowing how to lure her back.

Peter Pan. Sometimes their mother's voice had stumbled and cracked in the reading: *To die will be an awfully big adventure*.

Another expert with his theories, says Stefan, walking sock-footed through the kitchen. He quarters an orange, jams a wedge in his mouth.

You don't believe him? Evangeline asks.

Stan says we should flush the hives, get rid of the remaining bees in case they're infected, Stefan says, spitting seeds into his hand.

Hany had a lens-cleaning company radiate his boxes. Either that, or burn them, start over again.

Evangeline stands with the spoon from the pot. Passata dripping to the floor.

But, she says, he isn't saying you should ... ? Radiation, Stefan? I don't understand. Her face is red and filmy.

The girls grow alert at their mother's tone; at this word, radiation, which takes them back, again, to Pip.

Their mother has always believed the bees were delicate. She says you've no business getting close when you aren't in the right temper. Now she's rummaging by the stove. She whips out a brochure, *Clear Energy*, a letter with Stefan's name typed on, and waves it in the air.

Did you tell Stan what you've agreed to?

Meg, trying to ignore the rising timbre of her mother's voice, sketches a picture of Stan and his dowsing rod. Hands it to Tess.

He's so magnetic, whispers Meg.

Tess laughs, covering her mouth. Then below the picture writes, *Just ask his wife!*

Stefan says, They only have an exploration licence. I haven't promised anything.

Your famous promises, Evangeline says. When were you going to tell me?

Tess and Meg look up, and their parents gaze back with slight awe, as if they've forgotten them. Tess thinks of her teacher's house down the lane, the patched roof, the knee-high weedy garden. Through the doors she's glimpsed a worrying lack of furniture. Is this what it is to be poor? Without the bees, without their cattle, how will the family survive?

And what about the car crash? their mother is saying. Is there news?

Their father stomps from the room.

Evangeline unlatches a window above the sink; her eyes follow Stefan over the paddocks. In the far corner of the top field Tess can see the depressed heifer, its head bent. Since her calf died of paralysis tick she had not stopped lowing.

Once her father's safely gone Tess can read this week's *Survival Report*. She leans against her bed, legs crossed, flicking the pages with a damp finger. In his report Tom Tucker tells how to keep meat in waxed calico tepees, what goods to lay in for your doomsday bunker. There's an alphabetised list of Preparedness Tasks:

B is for Barter. C is for Combat Skills, CB Radio and Command.

All because of the approaching Greater Depression, which is something to do with weather, and also, Tess knows, an atmosphere surrounding her mother.

She reads the tips on building shelters, tracking, hunting, making clothes and tools. At least our family has land, Tess thinks. Though this might make them a target of what Tucker calls *Pre-parasites* – people who'll prey on the more organised when their own resources run out.

I sincerely believe in charity, Tucker writes. We should not just Prepare for our families, but make sure we can distribute to the less Prudent, the Doubters, the Lazy.

Tess feels a heady chill. Who are the Doubters? Maybe it's us, she thinks, with their leaning, termity barn and the back acreage left bald and unplanted, their meagre tinned supplies and mouse-chewed bags of local grain, with the infested fruit trees, the old bantams their father can never bring himself to kill, his gentle hands making beeswax candles and, lately, a silly peacock topiary from the pittosporum, designed to buoy their mother up. But perhaps this makes them the Lazy. Beef, eggs, honey, how long would that last in an End of Days Scenario?

Mountain House freeze-dried entrées, Security Seeds (open-pollinated), KIO3 Anti-Radiation tablets (medical grade). Five-hundred-round case of Federal 5.56mm-grain FMJ ammo.

But Tess knows there's more than all this to surviving. You can sit in a cold hospital ward and lose nearly everything that matters. You can watch your mother cross lawn and paddock till she's a sinuous shape by the wall of pines that hold the forest back from the fields. Your mother way off. Your sister sketching bare winter trees. Your father, burying cow horns on a day determined by the stars, out in hard rain, not properly dressed for the weather.

When the foraging season has finished, the worker bees will kill the drones to spare them from starvation.

Tom Tucker has too much time on his hands, Tess thinks. They've already survived the indescribable: named the stars to distract a sister, stood very still as her coffin hovered. They'd lost Pip and a fellow feeling. They'd lost the mother who'd once been fearless, who'd led them to the sea each summer and, gripping their hands in her own, pulled them through the glassy water. I've got you, she'd say to each girl as they kicked, their small heads glistered with brine, and turning them on to their backs she'd ask, do you think this must be how it feels to lie down on the moon? Later, she would *bake them in a pie*, covering Meg and Tess to the neck in hot sand while Pip built moats and trenches. Then she'd ignore them, idly reading a magazine as they writhed. You're only medium rare, she'd say, I'd prefer you all very well done.

Tess looks back at *Survival*, its shivery italic font. Throbbing most urgently beneath Tucker's reports is something unspoken. What is it, Tess wonders, that we are preparing for?

Today the air is clear of everything. It has no knowledge except of noth-
ingness. And it flows over us without meanings ...

Evangeline reads aloud. Wallace Stevens, the book flat on the
table. The long, sturdy bones of her arms. Her neck bent in
concentration.

Jim pulls her towards him.

And there's another problem, he says. I like your husband too much.

What? she laughs, a saddening sound. More than me? And she
takes her blue dress off in one movement, clear over her head.

Jim looks at her heavy breasts, the squarish hips and round belly.
The feeling of her body beneath his in every way opposite to
compact, nimble Sylvie. Her earthy solidity and drifty air, how she
appears to abide by some other, more urgent frequency.

Outside, all the forms are trimmed with final light. But in here
the cabin lamps project a woolly, dispersing glow.

She lies down in a sturdy-limbed way. Oddly meek, but sullen.
He feels flushed with power. She's cut herself off – from the town,
from the daily routines that might bring about contact – in order
to live, and now the consequences. Tess, refusing speech. The

townspeople, she claims, cool towards her. Some woman she'd known from The Hive, and wronged, still pursuing her; some dodgy men out to ruin her family. This history of vengeance is so biblical-sounding he thinks it must be partly delusional. At night he watches the mists descend around her house. At night, from afar, it seems to possess its own private climate.

It's been more than two weeks since she's come around, but now her husband is off, trucking his bees towards a fiercer heat, following the honey flow. Sometimes on her visits, the hour passes in near silence. She's a lesson in now and this and yes. Their bodies working boldly because of their futurelessness, because both want, just there, and like that, and ah this, to forget. A pragmatism in how she is with him – so direct, so unenthused by any romantic, delaying gesture. They're snatching time, they are grabby.

After, he crosses to ashtray and papers. Rolls a joint in that residual, sexual quiet. She's saying the poem over again. She's on her stomach, one leg crooked at the knee. Her ashy, falling hair. Her hipbone. Her frank nudity clashing with how she hides her self. Sometimes she calls their meetings *her tutorials*, then utters a short, unhappy laugh and he sees how unpractised she is, at inhabiting a place she does not belong.

I used to be really good, she'd said, the third time they were alone together, at being what other people wanted me to be.

And what was that? he asked.

In The Hive I was this little know-it-all until maybe thirteen. Once I started up with local boys they called me a wildcat – but I knew what they wanted and I liked knowing it. And, well, you don't want to hear what they called me later.

He was thinking on this *started up*. Then he said, Ah, the free-love ethos.

But you were only free to love within The Hive, she said. Not to just sleep around. Unless you were a man. Women paid the price. I didn't understand how you could be what the boys wanted, then hated for it after.

What was the price? he asked.

She looked up, confused, and said, Well, pregnancy. The oldest story in the world.

Then bent down, quickly strapped her sandals, and left.

So he made her promise to make demands of him and not squander or undermine them. He said, Be honest when you're here or how else will I know who you really are? She thought this was hilarious, she fell back on the bed silently shaking and clutching herself until he continued. For example, he'd said, do you like this? How about that? And here?

You're one of the good ones, she said, very fondly to him once. He turned red then, and restless. Wasn't he the mysterious stranger, riding through town with his own intriguing secrets? All the more macho since he'd removed the jaunty plastic basket on his Malvern Star. He hadn't fancied himself as the mild neighbour, doing her bidding. Sometimes, he thought, there are only two choices — you're Hemingway, or Derwood from *Bewitched* whose woman masters all the spells. You are your father — corporately priestly and aloof — or his louche, unravelling opposite.

Now she's holding a palm up as he offers the joint. No. She doesn't like marijuana's dislocating effect, she's already floating off from everything rooted, she says. Even the scent makes her uneasy. There'd been a time when she'd smoked it a lot, she said, a time after Pip. But she'd grown suspicious of everything she'd once been certain of. She began to white-ant every relationship, she picked at all the strained seams of her marriage. She'd fallen out with her only friend, who'd had it coming, but enough about Nora, although, I suppose she's your supplier? she asks.

Jim stays quiet so she says, Anyway, there are other ways to slow time, and runs a hand across his chest.

Jim likes being suspended, he likes staving off the emptiness that will furrow through his cabin, after, his forehead against the window, his eyes following her path back across the lane and fields and further out until she's a blue chimera vaporising by her white front door. In the distance, the cattle drift, clockwise around the Müllers' farm; even corralled they're governed by some primeval trait, *Bos indicus* tracking sun or shade, ley lines below the dirt.

> As if none of us had ever been here before
> And are not now: in this shallow spectacle

After she's gone it's rekindled. The poem she'd recited, each line driving through his head. And it amazes him, how a woman so resolutely stuck has transfigured his world so completely.

> No thoughts of people now dead,
> As they were fifty years ago,
> Young and living in a live air,
> Young and walking in the sunshine,
> Bending in blue dresses to touch something.

THE WEATHER INSIDE

By Tess Müller

Hail

One afternoon, about her fourth week home, Pip said she wanted to go back to St Catherine's. Outside there was a dog wind, whining and yipping. You told your father. He rubbed a finger on his glasses and he said, 'No need to go telling your mother.'

The sky that day was far. It was clear. The planks on the house were creaky. When you came back Pip asked, 'What did they say?' You pretended you'd forgotten something and went out again. You were starting to leave her alone.

It was sometimes easier in hospital, Pip said, because your mother's sadness came and went. Plus there was Esther Goldfinch, she was sharing the ward. But when you pictured the hospital room you couldn't remember any Esther.

Your mother was at the kitchen window. 'Hey look!' she said. You stood beside her and watched white stones fall from the sky. 'How about that, Tessa Jane!' She put her cool hand on you. She hardly ever called you Tessa and mostly saved her touch for Pip. She asked, 'What is it, honey?' But how could you tell her that Pip wanted to return? Your mother had been marking off the days till she came home. On the nights before the hospital she'd whizz about. She was always searching for what Pip might need, or cooking something to bring her hunger back. You would watch and feel so hungry yourself or maybe empty.

'Come on,' your mother said. 'Let's go!' Outside, the lawn was turning slowly white. Leaves and twigs were tearing down with the hail. The world was becoming something new but you didn't want to see it. 'What, Tess? You're scaring me,' your mother said but she was smiling. So you asked her. 'Rhesus positive, what does it mean?' That's your blood type, she told you. Then she asked if you felt bad because you had not been a match for Pip. You said nothing. You started thinking very hard about silence. She took your hands and pulled you close. 'You're mine,' she said, 'don't forget.'

'Esther,' Pip had said and started up angry. 'Don't you remember her, in the bed by the window?' But that bed was totally sheetless. It was really completely bare. What kind of surname was it anyway, Goldfinch?

Actually Pip wasn't interested in the hail when you bought it in. She picked up a hailstone. It melted double quick. You took her hand. You said, 'You're hot, maybe you have a temperature.' But Pip snatched her fingers back. 'People forget it's only water,' she said and she shook the stones on to the floor, 'just because it has another name.'

Stefan wanders over, pretending disinterest, but a wild swarm could be very useful. A wild swarm's usually strong and disease resistant. Five apiarists and several hobbyists have already gathered in the Brookmeyer Forest by the time Stan arrives for the swarm removal with his truck, ladder, bee box and broom, his clippers and smoker. The beekeepers form a horseshoe, heads cricked back, gazing up at the natural hive.

Behind them the sluggish, algaed Olver River, lined with smoky green casuarinas. On the ground, the trees' beaked conifers, fallen prematurely.

Stefan looks at the broken cedar, lightning struck, cleaved in two, its top branches reaching skyward. Ten metres up, on a thick limb, the bees on their hive form a huge, brassy pendulum. He remembers as light pours through the canopy, keeping bees, *like the direction of sunbeams.*

A wild swarm. It's like striking gold now the bees are disappearing.

He puts a hand on the fallen tree; what was that Midrash his grandfather taught? *When God created the first man he showed him all the trees in Eden and said, See my works, how beautiful and praiseworthy they are.* Some consolations, he concedes, in memory.

You lot beekeeping with ladders now? It's Nora, laughing and shaking her head, dragging on a cigarillo.

You think this is your swarm? she asks. Seriously, Stefan?

Put that out, he says.

Geez, those bees are boiling, I hope Stan's feeling chilled.

It's how Nora smokes the bees, shooting her cigar breath right into the hive – he'd seen her do it, brazen, suitless, just as Hodgins had taught her.

Forty thousand or so. Looks about right to me, Stefan says, trying to stay calm around her. But the cigarillo is making him queasy. This morning, in the bee field, he'd watched the sky and forest flickering like a badly tuned TV. Every sound amplified, each noise a clamour. These auras, which still fool him with their total lack of pain. He ought to appreciate the warning. And the Imigran numbing everything now but his nausea.

Those are wild bees and you know it, Nora says, dropping the butt, doing a boot-twist to extinguish it, a slow-mo dance move.

And that also, he points at her waistcoat. Take it off. Who wears suede to a swarm removal!

Anything else you want me to strip off? she asks, moving close. So sweet, how you're protecting me, she says, slinging an arm around his shoulder.

Stefan sniffs, nods at Stan who's dragging the ladder towards the tree. He ought to help the man, but feels massively indolent. He'd rather lie on the forest floor and have a what-they-call-it, kip.

She takes a long stare, says, Headache?

He nods.

You've got that smeary look around the eyes. You tried the fever-few, the butterbur?

Stefan toes a hank of moss, swats a fly.

Don't you remember? Nora says. Hodgins wrote it all out for you!

Ach! Stefan waves an arm. I would listen to that lunatic?

You didn't used to think of him that way, Nora says. I remember a young man in total awe, I remember a surfer in search of a guru.

Stefan reddens, then both fall silent watching Stan meticulously adjust the ladder, moving it around the roots of the tree.

What did you decide then, Nora says, to do about the bones?

Up to the police, he says. They've taken them away.

Aren't you worried? she says, then calls, Further to the left, Stan, no, *left*! Then up, that's it!

Nein, says Stefan. Why should I?

Nora gives him a piercing look. I heard there was a van.

Stefan shrugs, stays quiet, trying not to stir things up, for his health's sake, and to keep Nora and half the town from beaking around his land.

When did it happen, this accident as you like to call it?

Maybe a year ago, or two? says Stefan.

Strange, don't you think, Nora asks.

No, I don't think, he says.

You and I both know who used to drive a van, Nora says, leaning in. And you know their plantation was around those parts.

Stefan turns to check on Meg and Tess, metres back. Then he realises that Nora is dumbstruck, that beneath her swagger she's stricken in some unfathomable way. She sees him clock her shaking hands, and plunges them into her pockets.

José Torres staggers over, wheezing. A belly fold on grey KingGee's; a spartan combover through which his pate is shining. He lives right by here, a migratory beekeeper with a huge pollination operation. They're definitely his bees, he says.

No way, says Nora.

José sucks a Nicorette from a blister pack, then offers the pack to Nora. You want?

How will you know if they're your bees? Do you mark your queens, let's take a look at her then. Nora folds her arms.

They continue arguing as Stan climbs higher, dragging his bad leg up the ladder, one hand on the smoker, which he's stuffed with pine needles and dry twigs. Nice cool, dense white smoke. So calming, Stefan thinks, just to watch it curling out the spout.

How many colonies have you lost? Stefan asks.

José kicks the earth with a cowboy heel, downcast.

Let's just say, Stefano – I'm getting very comfortable with death on an epic scale.

Stop using the Fumagilin for a start, Nora says to José. Plenty of natural tinctures you can try...

Stefan tunes out. He stands beneath the cluster, barefaced, hot and pissed off, arms exposed and already host to five bees. He breathes steadily through his mouth to avert José's cologne, the oily smells of hair and skin that become, mid-migraine, so magnified. Then turns to his girls again, safe enough in shorts and shirts. Meg taking photos of the cedar's great unearthed roots.

Stan and some others have bee suits on, or have at least tucked in their trousers and unrolled their sleeves. Nora, from the commune, does not dress for bees. She doesn't mind a sting, it's insurance against arthritis. She's started supplying a Brisbane practitioner with venom for apipuncture, selling pollen in cellophane bags for salads and smoothies. She's started packaging her honey in corked glass test tubes. *A Suite of Distinctive Single-Varietals.* The tourists clamour for these at the market, though it's nearly impossible to verify if your bees are feeding on biodynamic clover or the herbi-cided lantana two properties away.

Stan makes three deft swipes with the stick before the swarm drops into the box and then it's locked, strapped and loaded on to his ute.

Late that afternoon, at the Wounded Ram, with its psychedelic, gummy carpet, tufted vinyl stools and massive new flatscreen, they continue drinking while figuring it out. The bees are in the car park. Stan will bee-sit till they decide who's getting them. Halfway through Stefan's fourth or fifth pint, just when he's thinking about switching to spirits, in strolls Tom Tucker with a stack of *Survival Reports*.

Here is coming the Fourth Horseman, says José. He shoos Tucker with a flapping arm as he approaches.

Look man, José says, I come here to forget about doomsday...

Oh leave him, says Stefan. Half of what the kid writes is true. Does he do any harm?

Tucker surveys the group, taking in the empty glasses on the table, the red-rimmed eyes, the alcohol shimmer around them. He knows this chancy imminent feeling; at The Hive no one ever knew what was about to happen.

Nora drains her Erdinger.

Light, spicy, with some citrus hints, she says, holding the glass up. Perhaps a hint of peanut in the nose and mouth?

Then she jigs down to the bartender. The men's eyes following her. Those legs. That skirt. She bends very deliberately over the bar.

José gets up silently and disappears into the back room.

Stefan can't walk or piss straight, let alone reason with himself. Whisky, or vodka? He eyes the rack behind the bar. Nora's shots glisten on the counter. Then remembers the Imigran. Probably not smart to mix things. He's tipping over, ruled by chemicals now and no other order.

Tucker intercepts some newcomers, hands out five copies. Stefan feels for the kid – well, he's a man now, but his naive, deluded manner makes him seem delayed. He'd been a plaintive sight in The Hive, a wispy boy with a crippling stammer and a palpable crush on Evangeline. It had shocked Stefan to discover that a commune kid could be so outcast. At The Hive the cult of alternativism had not been inclusive, it turned the place into a dysfunctional parish. The weekly gatherings had all the hallmarks of stricter faiths – the burning of incense and candles, the upturned, open faces, their man at the lectern telling them how it will be. And Jack Hodgins, naturopath and midwife, had the fugitive demeanour of a man with a clandestine life. It was peculiarly Australian, Stefan thought, how nearly everyone in the commune adopted this foreigner's cosmology without question. But hadn't he too been susceptible, to starting afresh in a wild environ? Hadn't he, for a short time at least, looked to Hodgins, a man in every way opposite to his own father, and credited him for that alone?

You want one, Stefan? Tucker is flapping a newsletter at him.

Chus, Tom. Listen, will you stop giving them to my girls?

But she always asks for a copy, Tucker says, turning back to the table. Should I say no?

Who asks?

Tess, Tucker says, his eyes darting to the flatscreen.

How's the girl anyway? Nora sways exaggeratedly over, keeping time to some suffering jukebox cowboy. Talking yet?

But Stefan's fixed on Tom. How does she *ask* you exactly?

Sticks her hand out every Saturday at the market, Tucker says.

Stefan looks him over; the kid's jumpy, as if over-caffeinated, very zealous. Eyelids twitchy, lips cracked. In The Hive Tucker's mother had struggled alone with the boy; she'd left the older son,

Peter, elsewhere with his father and asked to keep their whereabouts from Tom. Heidi had nothing after the fire. What The Hive collective hadn't factored was the cost of re-entry to urban life – there'd been no assets to distribute, no insurance payouts. But when people started kvetching Hodgins claimed you were well resourced. You had your survival skills, he'd say, you could grow your own food, cannibalise a broken-down car on a roadside, make a solar oven from cardboard, foil and glue. But these were negligible abilities once you descended into town with your highwayman beard and your rennet-free cheeses to face the supermarket plenitude, the families divided and ruled by devices, the people gazing into monitor glow, backs turned to each other.

And now Heidi Tucker, with her early-onset dementia. Late one night Stefan had found her wandering the Mercutt Oval. He'd slowed his ute, crossed the sodden field. The puddles, floodlit, dark mirrors. The mud, dragging his heels. As he led Heidi back beneath the goalposts she'd asked wonderingly, Where are we now? as if those posts were a gateway to a new reality. He tried manoeuvring her into the truck, to drive her home. But she'd refused, called him Peter. When he'd finally got her home he'd warned Tom, best she forget Peter if she wants to avoid trouble. And Tom, blinking in the mothy porch light, mouth ajar, had said, Peter? Who do you mean?

Stefan had not replied, Peter of the hydroponic grow house and the dismantled drug lab on Lucerne Hill. Or told how he and Evangeline had once been the beneficiaries, via Nora, of Peter's summer harvest. Just a bag of dope now and then, nothing entrepreneurial. This is what he has rehearsed in case the police should enquire.

Every family in this town, wormy with secrets. Stefan takes a final gulp of ale. Now Heidi's deterioration, just when Tom had the better half of his life ahead. No functional relatives to help the kid out.

Why would Tess just go silent? Nora's saying. Parents keep secrets, but kids ... ?

She looks Stefan over, hands on hips.

Sooner or later someone will tell her, she says. Better if it's you.

Tell who what? asks Tom.

You are the expert now, on childrearing? Stefan says to Nora. Funny!

Buy your own fucking whisky. Nora turns, blags a smoke from a passing trucker and tromps back to the bar.

Well, stuff me, says Stan coming in from out back. Someone's nicked our bees!

In the car park Stan's empty ute gleams under surging orange neon. The beekeepers stand confounded beneath the pub sign spruiking Murder Mystery Dinners.

Something for your little bulletin, Tom, Nora says. The effing bees have disappeared again!

And have you told them all, Stefan? she says, lurching towards him and poking his breastbone.

Stefan found human remains, she announces. A crash! And what if it's Pete? Did any of you even think?

But the others are headed for their vehicles, keys jangling. Nora stands, in the sherbety neon, and begins openly weeping. Stefan dimly remembers now, that Pete had started up with Nora. It had marked the end of Nora's friendship with Evangeline. Then the man had disappeared. When they'd realised this, one day at the market, Evangeline had wordlessly taken his hand and squeezed it. He'd nearly died of happiness. They'd bought croissants, and had a picnic, toasting the future with soy-chai. A Peterless future, or so they'd thought.

I know, Nora is calling out, he wasn't a saint...

...We didn't know him like you, right, Nora? Stefan says, turning back.

Bad for business, we understand, says José. Your supplier's gone.

He was funnier than you lot, Nora says, and cleverer. You mightn't have liked him but if it's him that's dead in that field show some fucking respect.

The men look away, slightly chastened. Cleverer? Jeez, that had hurt. There's a long, ticking car-park silence.

Who are you talking about? Tom asks, his eyes flashing at Stefan.

Fuck you all! Nora says and strides off.

And Stefan has a moment's remorse. He hasn't done right by that body on his land, regardless of who it is.

Come on, Stefan, Stan says, patting himself down for keys. I'll drive you.

Halfway along Fox's Lane, Stefan's house comes into view. An umber glow through the draped front windows, the mist furling around the barn, the Charolais clustered under a hazel and the miniature village of the hives filling him with such *verdammte* relief. For a second he really believes in the promise of rural homeliness. Stan punches his shoulder as he stumbles from the car. Buck up, Herr Müller, he says, and winks, I hev *güt* feelink about zose bees.

So much for their socialistic upbringings, Stefan says later in the kitchen.

Anything going free in this town you can be forgetting love thy neighbours, he says.

You can't really believe they were our bees? asks Evangeline.

She's sitting very upright at the table. He rolls two bottles from a lower shelf and comes up banging his head on the pantry door. Ginger beer, Becherovka. He shoves the bottles back, offended. Ginger, cinnamon! What are we running, an apothecary?

Maybe you've had enough, she says.

My father used to hide his liquor, Stefan says. He'd rip the heart from a butter lettuce and stick a *Schwarzbier* inside, then shove it back in the cruncher, the crispy, whatever that vegetable home in the fridge. You want me to resort to that, Lina?

That's why your mother moved you boys to Munich. Your father's love of salad?

He gets on the floor and sticks his head below the bench, gropes an arm under. Some other bottles there. Pear fucking cider. But, hang on. He rolls something over the flagstones. A dusty bottle of local Merlot.

You'd think they'd struck gold the way they all raced over, he says. *Make sure you get the queen, Stan, don't leave her up there. I wouldn't clip that branch, Stan, if I was you, you'll spook them. Nag nag naggedy nag.*

He rolls four more bottles from under the bench. Incredible! How they've genied out of floor dust. Whips the cork from one, decants wine into a mug. His face is flushed, his eyes are veiny, the knife in his head starts cranking again, then suddenly the whole thing seems hilarious. Why struggle so hard against nature? What's the point? A bee in the hand will bite you then die. Pests will spread on the wind despite your companion planting. GM crops will contaminate your biodynamic paddock. Certain men in the pub will always turn when a woman passes. *Those who are fatherless, think of me.* Men will spread themselves around, Hodgins would say, it's natural. But what is *natural* anyway? There are sicknesses that no substance on this good green earth can remedy.

He glances at his wife, at the table with something under a tea towel. Very still. Knitted fingers. Serene, desolate face.

And what are you doing, up so late? he says. Is a mystery.

I have some unmysterious sourdough, proving.

Such a woman, she makes bread at midnight!

He takes another swig, says, Or maybe you just got home?

Because, you're allowed to stay out all hours, but I'm forbidden.

He picks up a hank of her hair, sniffs it. But where do you wander, Lina? Pretty risky, mountain climbing at night?

More than Imigran, beer and Nora Roberts?

And how you get such a bruise, right here, another whodunnit. He lays a finger against her neck.

She whips her head out of reach.

It's not just the bees in town, I hear, he leans very close, travelling far from home for honey.

She stands fast, pushing him backward with her chair. He grabs her shoulder, tight.

Some of us just can't forget how we were raised. Sharing everything. Isn't that right? Isn't that actually what Hodgins taught? Love thy neighbour.

You're the one who thought the commune was *Paradies*, she says. Shall we pretend I was the first woman you slept with up there?

Pretty clear that I wasn't your first, Stefan says.

So what does that make me? Come on, say it. A commune whore?

I have never said...

...No you're nothing like the others. They will say it aloud if they think it, she says. Then she pulls the tea towel from the bowl and plunges her fist in the leavened dough.

Who are you comparing me to? Peter? Hodgins? Your mother? he asks. Suddenly these schemers are all so much better than me?

You're drunk, go to bed.

He tips the mug back, his tongue recoiling. Ugh, the Merlot, balsamic, fit for salad.

Lina, he says, I stopped all that when we met and you know it. I thought you had too...

...How is Nora? Can she still keep up with you at the pub?

Am I holding your history against you? he asks. Don't forget that you were already... that when we met you were...

...My history? You mean a child? she says.

And he instantly wishes his tongue had been knifed from his mouth. He longs to reverse the past twelve hours, the hazy morning, the nasal spray, the topping up at the pub. He wishes away fresh bees, fallen cedar, Nora running her cold hands over his neck at the pub, saying *reiki*.

You are the only one for me. And the girls, he says, quietly now.

Right, her voice very tight in the teeth.

Then she walks down the hall. The bare, regal back of her neck more reproachful than anything she can say.

Later, in his study, he tries switching off. Turns on the lamp, opens his notebook. How is it that a one-night stand he barely recalls means so much more to his wife?

Drones often maligned as being lazy... But they don't have the body structures possible for work – no wax glands, no stingers and their proboscis so short they can't reach nectar. But they are very efficient sperm machines. Isn't that enough?

In the morning Meg slices the warm bread as Stefan drinks coffee and turns the newspaper. Snap, thwack, snap. The loaf is dry and overcooked. Their mother had put it in the oven and then gone out, leaving the girls to guess when it was done. Meg had knocked on the loaf, then held it against her ear.

Daddy, were they our bees? She passes him slices, a knife, butter.

His cracked palms, his nails chipped. Farmer's hands. Except for the morning shaking. They still surprise him.

I can't say I know what belongs to who any more, Margaret, Stefan says. The bees are belonging to the earth and then came the interfering of man. We should give up trying to control them.

And everything that I created, I created for you. Be careful not to spoil or destroy my world – if you do, there will be nobody after you to repair it. He can recall the whole Midrash now, and how his grandfather told it, lightly, and often, but mostly when they were strolling about his Neukölln allotment.

In the forest Meg and Tess had stood far back, because they weren't equipped. Their legs were bare and their arms exposed, but they were not afraid and did not hold their breath like their mother around bees. They had such trust that came from … he could not say where, a self-containment he could credit neither parent for. They'd seen him lift a swarm from the eaves one summer with bare hands, carrying the weight of some twenty thousand bees and wiping them off his arms like mud. When he came into the kitchen after, bees in his hair, Pip had started laughing. It's the latest super-cool look, haven't you heard? he'd told her. Everyone's all abuzz, he said, and he danced around Pip's chair, trying to keep her laughter going while her thin hands pawed the air, in case a bee was heading her way.

Now Tess comes in gesturing, goes out again with Meg. When they return, Meg leans towards their father.

Papa, she says, there are sheets on the couch.

Ich war kalt.

You slept there? Meg purses her lips.

Meg, the little mother, always neatening the world around her.

How does it looks like? Stefan frowns, then pretend-reads the business pages.

He catches Meg and Tess eye-rolling. Their colluding makes him briefly content. He'd encouraged this sibling camaraderie, and they'd maintained it despite, or perhaps because of, the fracturing opposition.

Stefan squints at the kitchen window as if he might see, from here, the mahogany krasnozem soils on the mountains. Nutrient-rich with a deep profile, and clay minerals. Or he might spy beech, black bean and coachwood where lava once flowed. From all that heat, fertility.

Where's his wife? Which field, which road, which mountain path? Whose home? When he'd come into the bedroom that morning the sheets were cool and empty. He'd plunged his face inside them, inhaled her woody scent, then retreated to the couch. What kind of a man ignores rumour and fact, so as not to create more disturbance in his house? Cuckold, a word he'd heard in the back bar one afternoon. He'd had to look it up later, thinking it a type of rooster, and will still picture lurid tail feathers, the word cock, when he hears it.

In the corner the girls are bent over the computer.

Meg laughs, and says, Dad's reading cow porn again!

But he's engrossed now, smoothing the paper across the table. An arsonist has struck again, destroying forest near the Beauforts' place. Stefan thinks of Heidi Tucker beneath the goalpost crossbar, mistaking him for Peter. Peter, rumoured to have burned three properties years back – drug labs or warehouses for stolen goods. And what had become of his forest crops, sown not far, Nora claimed, from the farm? Stefan thinks of those bones, what they could mean. He must try harder to right everything that's gone askew.

The Charolais Online Semen Catalogue, Meg says, very poshly, reading aloud from the screen.

Tess beside her, laughing without sound. Tess, slight and lean, olive-skinned; her dark hair and eyes, her judicious expression, reminding him of how she'd come into the world. You are mine and not mine. It's never mattered to him. But does it matter to her, even if she doesn't know it?

Classy, Dad, really nice, Meg's saying.

Later, she'll draw a spectacled cow in an armchair. It holds the *semen catalogue* between its front legs. She'll sketch a pool of lamplight on florid carpet, and inside this the cow's hoofs crossed tidily at the ankle. It's these feet that will floor him when he finds the sketch. Those hoofs, so humanised. An anthropomorphism so totally Meg, who cried and cried when the calves were separated from their heifers, the time the mothers trampled three fences and the new deck in a desperate search for their newborns.

The phone. It's Stan, in chipper morning mode.

The bees are safe, Stan says, don't worry. You should have seen Marjorie when I got home. Incog-bloody-nito in trenchcoat and hat! Stan chuckles. Stuffed her back, though, lifting those bees off that ute.

They seem to be disease free, he tells Stefan. Come get them anytime.

Stefan hangs up, feels himself relax. He has a project. And he thinks of his wild bees, how calm he becomes among them, his ears attuned to their resonant droning. His thronging insect communion.

5

James Parker is standing by the chai tent, chewing a currant bun. Long-limbed, broad-chested with a suspiciously even tan. A straight-toothed movie smile, his head tilted left.

James offers a hand as Tom approaches.

I know your type, Tom thinks, as he slows. The sort his mother calls *a charmer*.

Thomas? he asks. Aren't you the lollipop man? At the school?

Name's Tucker, Tom says. Then salutes him, ignoring the hand. And I prefer *crossing guard*.

It's market day, the whole town's come out in the coppery light.

James, also known as Jim, had arrived from the city months back with only two bags. One full of women's clothes. A fact gleaned from the excellent sleuthing of June Peterson. On her shifts at the Red Lodge, June will spy on the blow-ins. Then, when she comes to look after Tom's mother, she spills:

- James Matthew Parker, formerly of Kings Cross, Sydney.
- Receives postcards from a person called Sylvie. Girlfriend, former wife?

- Reads small-print books about Early Australian Man. Plus somebody Solnit, *The Wild and the Domestic*, someone Lorca and Thoreau. Poetry and anthropology.

Jim also has a bike. Rusted and secondhand. Rides in the dark without helmet, reflective vest or headlight, does not seem in the least Prepared, though anyone from the city's a likely Climate Pilgrim because when the End Days come, the cities will fall first. Frequents the southside chemist, probably for prophylactics, snugger fit. The women look at him, sometimes even mothers at the market with babies in tow. Hungry. People think the women round here are loose because they wear tie-dye, because some were raised in a commune with its fluid midnight community. But Tom knows they're reluctant.

Tom, surveying the market, turns back to see Jim's left swinging towards his face. He intercepts with an open high karate block and Jim backs off, hands in the air, a spasm of terror marring his face.

Hey man, relax! Jim's saying. You had a bug on you, that's all!

I'm the type of person, insects just don't bother me, says Tom, giving silent thanks to Sensei Jeff of Wednesday night dojo. Sometimes during classes Tom is floored by students he must greet the next morning at the school gate. Teenagers, chucking a zenkutsu stance on the zebra crossing.

I see you two have already met.

It's an umbrella, talking. No – it's Evangeline, magicked up from behind a tree. She tips her brolly back, revealing a flushed and eager face.

James, she says, breathless.

Tom inserts himself between them. We've known each other since we were kids, he tells Jim.

Evangeline flashes him a look, says, James is one of Tess's teachers.

I thought you didn't like it in town? Jim says as if he actually knows her.

She looks into the distance, touches his arm.

Are you keeping tabs on me? she asks.

And she's laughing again, which is notable. She'd once been the liveliest kid at The Hive, the only one to challenge Hodgins's pronouncements, to outright scoff at what she did not believe. She'd disappear for days, then come striding back up the Summit Road in the same clothes, *a new woman*, as she said, though she was really just a girl. Everyone grew up faster in the commune, though Tom has come to think they were in so many other ways stunted.

We've come to get our new queen bees. Evangeline gestures towards the post office.

You're importing queens? Tom asks. Better to get yourself a wild swarm. Mite-resistant, hardy.

Hard to come by, though, says Evangeline vaguely.

That depends, says Tom, on your connections, right?

Then he rolls his sleeves down because of how Jim is staring at his burns.

If the bee disappears from the earth, man would have no more than four years to live, Tom says.

Evangeline sighs. How depressing.

That's Einstein. Tom rushes in to distribute the blame.

Tess appears, holding a large cardboard box. Tom feels his breath change, he forgets to swallow. He remembers her as a newborn – dark-eyed, beautiful. She probably has no idea how well he's known her. Used to sing her to sleep, had maybe even saved her. He's done nothing quite as majestic since that fire, and probably never will. Then, an odd thought drifts in – that she has survived, and he hasn't.

Come and look, Jim. Stefan ordered them online, says Evangeline.

Tess unwraps the small three-chambered box.

There's the queen with the yellow mark. And that's the queen candy, says Evangeline.

Jim starts walking slowly backwards, saying, You've already named her?

Evangeline laughs, winking at Tess.

No, Jim, *candy's* what the queen eats while she's in the post.

He takes another step away.

Tom examines him. *James Parker, apiphobic?*

Jim's changed his mind about the market. Claims to have forgotten something. He says his goodbyes, lopes off.

Evangeline, watching him leave, has a pinched look on her face. Tom supposes he's considered handsome, cycling in his languid, unsweating way around town, slowing and throwing one leg nonchalantly over the still-moving bike. The way he *leans* it so trustingly against a lamppost when he enters a shop. As if this is a town where you don't even need to lock up your treasures. A town small enough for trust. Tom supposes he has assignations; he's seen him riding late one night when he was searching for his mother. A person who reads poetry in the rain at a bus stop. He has seen him sometimes, outside the school gate, a minor rock star, mobbed by mums, high-fiving tweens with his clean, bookish hands.

Later, at the market, Tom tries remembering what his mother has asked him to buy. Everything jumbled, her nouns unintelligible. *Turn on the people box, Tom, go check the wall-watch will you?* Asks him to tuck in the tablecloth after he helps her to bed. She's unlearning and he's supposed to – what – teach her again? Sometimes, sponging her face after dinner, her eyes so trustingly fixed on his, he has a surge of pre-emptive grief. He will rub her face harder then, to remove the expression.

Appleberries, was that what she'd wanted? But did she mean apples, berries, or some other mutant fruit? He'll choose her favourite; perhaps the mouth will recognise what the eyes regard with doubt.

Three kids skate past in a dusty whoosh of urgent air and he envies their brand of childhood – knowing, cool, bent on intensity. Full of possibilities. Once at the commune, a Polish woman had appeared. A scar on her neck from where her thyroid had been removed. After the winds blew from Chernobyl, all the young girls in her village grew ill. She was his first brush with noteworthy environmental disaster. She'd hiked to the commune with a backpack full of white bread and Nutella and each day made him a slice. White flour and sugar – outlawed at The Hive. She helped out in the crèche. I can't have kids, she said, tapping the scar at her throat. He must have been ... twelve? Gone weak-kneed at Eastern European girls ever since. Irina was tender and poked fun at the residents. You notice, she'd say, how Nico always goes missing when is sewage-pump time? Help! I want to flee to forest when Starr gets out his pan pipes! My *Gott*, when I see Rainbow dancing I nearly phone for paramedics. When you grow up, Thomas, leave! Travel, then you decide for yourself.

But what was he supposed to decide? Since his mother's illness, he doesn't have to know any more. There's only one place he can be.

Now the high, broken voice of the market busker, Peony Skelton, who holds the mic against her chest between verses, as if to amplify through beaded muslin, the sound of her young and desperate heart.

6

Meg flexes her fingers around the Staedtler Triplus Jumbo. She's bent over the page, tongue out, kneeling on a kitchen chair. She's attempting a tree recalled from two years back, a tree that captivated at her sister's funeral. She takes her line from the base of the page, turns it smoothly right. But when she looks it over, her drawing arm frozen in the air, she sees a line flawed by tremors, wavers, uneven camber. She sighs, sinks on to her shins, blows her fringe from her eyes. Probably her faulty grip – she'd never mastered the Tripod despite a sheet covered in fingers sent home by Ms Myers. She had not been granted the Pen Licence given to every other girl in her class. And ever since her pencilled marks grow fainter by the day. Perhaps tomorrow she'll complete her homework in lemon juice.

At school today her friends decided which singer they loved. Then said, *you can't love her also*. Gizelle Lee Powers. A tawny-haired wailer who stalks the stage in spike heels and prairie skirts. Her YouTube clip features a nervy fawn in a forest and Gizelle in lace corset, silhouetted against a lightning sky. Meg's father, nursing a mug of whisky, had a laughing fit when he watched it. But the sisters leaned into the screen, enraptured, their cheeks pressed together, their breathing shallow, till Gizelle, among toadstools and moss, vibratoed her final note. Stefan banned the CD, blaming it for a vomiting migraine. So now the girls listen with dual headphones, lip syncing and knowing more than Gizelle possibly could when she sang, *I'm losing you*, their eyes bright, their faces afire with memory.

At school, though, Meg cannot openly love her.

Love is something permitted, she sees. It does not run free as a golden river like Gizelle says. Love's a *bossy word*, like run, chop, throw, sleep, hold, listen, slide, push, put and beg. What the f— does Gizelle know anyway, Meg thinks, remembering how her father said that lace bodice, so cinched, must surely cut circulation to Gizelle's brain.

Meg's best friend Sharon likes to play Twins. So Meg had braided her hair that morning. She rolled – not folded – her white socks at the ankle. She'd followed the previous day's instructions, issued by Sharon on a Hello Kitty Post-it. But Sharon, thinking on it for the whole of lunch break, decided they couldn't be sisters. Meg's plait was a normal fishtail, hers a labour-intensive mermaid. Plus Meg's shoes were *totes* wrong. Vitally, Sharon said, as she often did, her shoes buckled, but Meg's Velcroed. At Sharon's Tudor-style home in the new development, Meg has learned that thongs are bad for growing feet, that there are three species of apple juice, that mince isn't considered meat, and nor is a toilet the loo. At Sharon's there's a preferred word for fart that her family invented aeons ago, but it's spoken in such subaudible tones that Meg can never quite catch it. Sharon prances across the playground with a high-necked head, her luxury plait swinging, her lunchbox full of contraband: cheez-stix, froot roll-ups and yogurt inhaled from a bag. Meg rubbed dust from her school shoe with one saliva finger. She saw they were actually quite orthopaedic, as Sharon had said, so lobbed them in a hawthorn hedge on the long walk home.

She doesn't want to get like Tess, wandering round the school basketball court with no one, her hair unbrushed from three days before and totally full of flyaways. For a while after Pip died Meg had tried spending lunch with her sister, both girls gnawing sawn chunks of charity rye from the neighbours. But Tess didn't seem to care about being alone and Meg really, completely did. So now she hides in the library and reads about insects that eat their own young and how to tie a tourniquet. She borrows to her limit, every book about horses, and stashes the rest in Astronomy, a subject Sharon calls *lame*. At home she snaps the arms off one of Sharon's dolls and flushes it. It will not go under. It floats, freaking everyone in the house when they need to wee.

This afternoon, Meg had checked if she had two holes and not just one as Sharon claimed. Sharon, who hated being naked because she believed her parents had a spyhole in the bathroom wall. Sharon, who wore a cozzie in the bath that time she'd slept over. Sharon, who Meg cannot stop loving, even more now she knows how vitally wrong she is about anatomy.

She tries to be a hater of the horses Sharon favours. Lists them all now, in her tiniest hand. But soon after, tears it up and watches the white paper drift through the kitchen. As she sketches the stately head of the white Camargue, she knows these creatures hover far above human pettiness. If you were a horse, which would you be? Sharon had asked her once, risking her immaculate braid by leaning it on Meg's shoulder.

Equus ferus, Meg had answered, or Przewalski's wild. They were the true wild, along with the tarpan. Most others considered wild came from domesticated horses – brumby, mustang, the New

Zealand Kaimanawa. So, what's to love about those Polish beasts? asked Sharon. The Przewalski, once endangered, now thrived in the zones where humans couldn't live. Meg recounted this history, recently read. But the nuclear disaster that shadowed this story left Sharon blank and mistrusting. She did not like to dwell on dark events, or wild places. She liked steady-tempered Hanoverians with their pretty manes tightly knobbed for dressage. These horses excelled at showjumping and eventing. What could you do with a feral horse? It'd simply run away.

Meg dreams of fires and her sister's body on the final night of her life. Meg had been the one who'd found Pip, then run into the fields and told. Her parents were standing, hand in hand, peering into the unlidded bee boxes. After Meg reached them their fingers let go and they tore back across the fields. The sight of them, sprinting over the vivid grass, somehow both childlike and much older than their years, has become as indelible to Meg as the image of Pip, so still. Her parents, running, seemed like people from another time. And her sister, in the bedroom, was Pip, and not Pip at the same moment. Her face unguided by any Pip-ish spirit, her body so suddenly loosed from pain.

That day a thought had stolen in and never gone away: *I'm the youngest now, I'm the youngest.* Is Pip still her sister? Or something else like air, water, clouds over valley? Meg had asked Tess after Pip was gone. She'd fidget in bed. She could not sleep. Where was Pip really, what would happen to her body? Tess had stood in then for their mother, who was not to be disturbed. Tess had answered what she could and then one day burrowed deeper into absolute quiet. When there was no one left to ask, Meg began to draw.

It's been a long while since the family has even glanced at her pictures of trees. They line the floor around her bed. They sprout in her schoolbooks and grow on the walls in her study nook.

People trees with arms in the air. Plaintive trees, weeping willows moping into brooks. Trees morphing into houses to protect the small people she sketches in her faulty grip, crouched and huddled inside. Suitable trees for steep slopes. Trees for koala forage. Swamp mahogany. Flooded gum, whitish and columnar. Grey ironbark. Bunya pine, the kauris. She keeps a notebook under her pillow, and must draw and draw on the nights that she wakes in darkness, her heart pounding, the bed soaked. She'll peel off her wet pants and sheets and huddle, naked, with only pen and paper to help her find a way back to herself.

Putrid trees, Meg mutters, scrunching paper. Today's drawings souring in the swiftly closing light.

Sometimes a person can paint a picture so large it must stay for ever where it was made. Meg had helped her mother prime the canvas. She'd sanded till it was smooth as paperbark. Maybe she can become useful like that again? Meg's longing, recurring, desultory, clogging up her days.

Her mother had left that huge painting dressed in a sheet. Meg goes in some nights and stands underneath, peering at the horses painted on the green hill. They gallop, encircling something unfinished. Only the dark ashy outline, and charred grass around it, waiting to be explained with contour and shading. Meg stares and tries to figure the breed and pedigree. *The Hanoverian is characterised by an elastic ground-covering walk, a floating trot and a round, rhythmic canter.* Such facts have colonised her head, learned by heart one fervent evening, when she'd stayed up till star blackout, taking notes from *The Equine Compendium*, desperate to win back the cooling heart of Sharon.

FU Shaz, she writes. Then, emboldened. PUCK YOU!

She looks out the window. Sheer cliff faces of rusty red. Rock pinnacles exposed by erosion. And three great patches on the east and west flanks of the mountains. Every now and then a massive tearing. She used to imagine the forest advancing at night, the trees shuffling closer to the house. But it's really the opposite. One day she'll find a barren brown mound strewn with the bones of northern blue box, blackbutt candlebark, nightcap oak. The trees giving way for new mines. At school they're writing a song on it for final assembly. Sharon was asked to rhyme a word with *methane*, but her father, who worked for Clear Energy, sent back an excusing note.

It's time, said Nora Roberts, Nico and Lou Perkins at the Saturday market meeting. *It's time to start triaging nature.*

Here's her mother. Coming up the drive, pinning straggled hair back into its knot. Meg, overcome with a lonely passion, clings to the sight of her, knowing that she cannot be enough for any of them, not even for herself.

Her mother lifts an arm, waves, turns her umbrella back into a stick. Then goes inside her studio. It should be enough that she's returned before dark, that she'll be there at bathtime to cocoon Meg in the white towel, to kiss her forehead as she anchors the bedsheets and promises that the morning will be better, renewed somehow by darkness. There is one second's haven in this ritual, when her mother bends over, her long hair surrounding both their faces so it must appear as if they are joined. Meg gazes into those grey eyes and her mother looks back, very steady. In this tiny, curtained privacy she breathes the sour, milky smell of her mother's breath; she remembers, it is enough to simply be alive. After this she will try not to follow her solid shape across the bedroom and out into the hall, the heavy way she walks and pauses by the empty bed to put one hand flat upon it.

Our Pip, Meg writes in decorative cursive beside her best sketch, her most resolutely arboreal tree. Chunk-trunked, frankly branching, shrubby at the canopy. Its tiny rosulate leaves, if anyone should look closely, love-heart shaped. But she cannot picture the real Pip any more. Only the pale shadow that passed through their house, always in pyjamas. *Our Pip, there are such trees* ... When she runs out of words, she draws her way back to Pip.

7

Glories

Cloud streets, parry arcs, updraught turrets. Horseshoe vortices, whales' mouths, billows. Meg's favourite section is haloes, rainbows and glories. She's stared so long that when you even touch it the book falls open *abracadabra*! at those exact pages.

Your father had *The Weather Book* for ages. Then he gave it to you. He'd bought it secondhand when he came to Bidgalong Valley. Back then he had long hair and flappy trousers. You can see them in the photo he used as a bookmark. His chest is bare. He is smiling on a cliff.

Beside the different kinds of weather he'd put a tick to say what he'd seen. Mostly on the mountain, when he'd visited your mother. You can sort of imagine him, staring at a light pillar, castellanus, floccus. But you can't recognise the woman he describes.

'She lives up high, among the clouds,' he says. 'She comes floating from the Emerald Forest escorted by bees. In her hands, fresh honeycomb; in her hair, purple flowers. Your mother is a forest being, with a leftover wildness from her time on the mountain,' he says.

One afternoon she stood in the doorway. She had dark smudges under each eye. 'The town's gone quiet,' she said. 'It is very very still.' You felt scared so you turned back and started reading out from *glories*. In China they call it Buddha's Light – a coloured halo, said to come upon enlightened people. In science it's light backscattered by a cloud of identical raindrops. It's easier to spy a glory from a mountain or tall building. And on a plane you might see your craft's shadow below you, spotlit against the cloud. This is called the Glory of the Pilot.

Meg asked, 'Why are you shouting?' Your mother was sitting beside you. She was really listening hard. The heavy book was open flat. The glory looked like a rainbow-coloured target in the sky. 'We do not know what to believe in,' your mother said. Her voice was small. She held your hand. You were surprised to see that your palms nearly matched. It didn't seem possible that you could be growing. It felt like time in the house had stopped.

Also you did not understand why some people said Pip was now of the earth and heavens. After the funeral came some mighty storms. In the wet it was hard to tell what was river, what was rain, when the dry earth turned to mud. All the lines between things became blurry. Meg worried at night about the coffin in all that rain. You did not know a thing to tell her. But Pip, you knew, was wholly here among curtains, chairs, carpet and table. Pip was part of the weather inside.

8

How go your bees? asks Jim, fists clenched in his back pockets.

On this first dry Sunday he'd come to the market, hoping to find Evangeline. He hadn't been with her for weeks. Minor floods had blocked the lane, cut off access to her house and swamped the road to town. The rain had been gentle but unrelenting for twenty days.

He stands now at the family stall: *Honig Farm – Honey, Wax and Candles*, a small booth on the sunnier side, with a jaunty orange and black striped awning.

How to compose himself in public with her? He hadn't considered this when running a hand through his three-day growth and glancing that morning, for a second, in the cracked mirror above his sink. He'd made an effort, pulling on the least torn jeans, a shirt that Sylvie had once favoured, shunting his sleeves to his elbows. But his undisciplined face would betray him, his brown eyes grow keener the more he strives for nonchalance.

Evangeline, hands on hips, with damp half-moons under each arm, blows hair off her face. She's pretty unkempt, he sees, and feels reprieved. It's more real, what's between them, he tells himself, without the usual primping, without the first-date posturing.

We're trying a new hive, she says. The People's Hives, they're called. Invented by a French monk. Stefan's ordered a dozen.

What do you think's causing it? he said. This Bee Rapture?

He's tried saying it without emphasis, the throbbing word, rapture, but his chest goes tight.

She wipes her forehead, shrugs, reaches into a gumboot to scratch a shin. She isn't meeting his eye. He looks around; no one close enough to overhear, though the market's thronging, everyone stir crazy after the rains, and the floods, everyone embracing like they've been away and just returned, checking the stats about their properties – the stock and crop losses, the tracts of ruined fences, if their power has returned.

Look, he says. I can't just come over, can I?

He'd like to grab her by the arm and pull her home with him.

Not now please, she says, shaking her head.

Then he realises he'll make her miserable in every location but the neutral zone of his house. Even there he suspects she's performing a self, and who is this performance for?

Evangeline tugs her T-shirt lower, stretching it. Shifts from one foot to the other. This skittishness has nothing to do with him, he thinks. It's the rains that've kept her from coming around, that's all. But their meetings, so sketchy and infrequent, have taught him barely anything about how to read her. Sex gilds the illusion of understanding. And as for intuiting each other's thoughts? Just a trick the mind plays in the afterglow. Chemicals, neuronal firings. He'd cadged that psychic sensation often enough from local weed. So it was hardly remarkable, was it?

He looks about. Tess and Meg are standing with some school-kids near where the market fades into cow fields and meadow. There's a huge ash where the stalls end, casting a circle of welcome shade. Something odd about that tree. It's seething.

Then he sees: the branches are crawling with kids, even in the highest twigs.

He picks up a jar of honey and reads the label. *The first honeybees came to this country in 1822 on the convict ship the* Isabella.

Convict bees? he says. Christ.

He swats an insect hanging around his neck, gazes at her, separated from him by a line of jars along the stall table. Someone approaches, peering intently at the small bowls with their samples of honey. Evangeline casts Jim a look that would silence a stonier man. He waits as she serves the customer, wrapping three candles in yellow tissue, applying a bee sticker.

Now she's scanning the market, standing on her toes. Could you find ... Can you see Stefan at all? I'm so tired suddenly.

Eva, I've upset you.

It's this rawness that he loves after all, despite her efforts to hide it. Now, though, she's closed up, looking every direction but his.

It's only for seconds he can pretend she doesn't have another life. When she's moving above or below him, his fingers in her hair. The way he searches the sweep of their land, their house at night, smouldering below the mountain, surrounded by cows and rusting machinery. Sometimes when the mists billow the place seems to drift, majestic and huge; it appears to throb with a secret power. In the frank daylight, cycling by, he sees it is merely a house, run-down like most others round town, the paint flaking, roof tiles missing, the decayed, detaching guttering.

Once, through his cabin window, he thought he saw the silhouette of a man, as if Stefan were looking directly back, his gaze travelling over field, fence, verge and road. But Jim knew it was a trick, or a desire to be caught, was perhaps even his own reflection in his own glass. And which was a lonelier sight? Part of him wants to finish it. There's Tess — sitting very still in his classroom or aimlessly drifting around the playground. Her presence makes him feel more compromised than when the husband waves from across the fields, or passes him on the main street with that quizzical eye, singing out his *Chus*!

Jim despises the man he's become, carnally knowing his neighbour. Is this happiness? It's so chimerical, it is something deeply dredged from a dream. It is perhaps nostalgia, a forgotten feeling of home.

She hands him two unlabelled jars. This is goodbye for now, he supposes.

Here, she says brightly, Patterson's Curse.

Ah, possibly thanks? he says.

She musters a smile, holds out an ice-cream stick swizzled with honey.

Farmers might hate the curse but bees love it, she says. We give it away for free.

She puts the stick in his mouth, then pulls it out. He feels the sweetness on his tongue, the rough wood scraping his gums. Then forgets to taste, and to swallow; his eyes on hers are a challenge.

Even bees, the little almsmen of spring-bowers / Know there is richest juice in poison-flowers, he says.

Oh yes, she says, Shakespeare.

Then reaches over, wipes a finger across his chin.

You have … honey, she says, then puts the finger into her mouth and sucks it clean.

And now he sees it. The line of her belly against the loose T-shirt. A curve he hasn't yet felt under his hands. Unmistakable in Sunday's vigilant light. She's pregnant.

9

Tom Tucker's recurring dreams embarrass him on waking. In these his father wavers up, a giant crossing a primordial landscape, sweeping trees from his path, wading through lakes as if they were puddles. The man is always headed right for Tom through over-saturated jungles, fetid swamps, limitless canyons. A superhuman, impervious to pain and weather.

These dreams leave him doubly haunted – first by the father who never catches up – then by the penumbra of loss after waking. He snorts salt water from a neti pot. His sinuses get purified, but the dreams clot, sticky and persistent as ectoplasm. He'll walk out to find his mother spooning Milo into the teapot. He'll cross the kitchen and butt his head on her bony shoulder over and over saying gently, Stop, Ma, please just stop.

Even before she started forgetting, his mother had always been vague about the details, getting strident whenever he asked about his birth. *It was natural* was all she'd say. You came out smooth, without a squeak. She'd arrived at the commune with three-year-old Tom, this single mum from two towns away, and soon got devoted making candles, sewing calico bags. She was deft with wicker, and weaving. I love you, she'd say, isn't that enough? He ought to be grateful, she wasn't always sure she'd make it up here, a woman alone, she'd say, trembling and marring the wax or breaking a line of cane, so he'd stop himself asking. Who is he then, my father? Where does he live?

Occasional men had come to The Hive and paid Tom small, thrilling attentions, teaching him to whittle a stick into an arrow, build the ziggurat shape for more powerful fires, or how to catch cod in Repentance River, ravelling the guts and cleavering the head. And there was Jackson Hodgins. Good as any father, always there for you, said his mother, biological or not. But asked to play football, or to join the kids on a bush quest, Jack would say he didn't have time for *small details*, so Tom, pale-faced, whey-haired stutterer with rope to hold his shorts up, started to believe he was one of them.

When he was eleven Tom was sent up the escarpment with a new resident, Evan. *Gather rocks for the frog pond* – that was Hodgins's mission, his morning koan, whatever. Evan Perske had been detoxing since drifting into The Hive two weeks before. He staggered from the Calming Cell, blinking at the sunlight like a wintering mammal. A twenty year old going on fifty. Beside him Tom, stalky, fine-boned, looked newly born.

At the summit Tom surveyed the great silver bales of mist that covered the poky towns and settlements. He could not even glimpse the treetops. This plane of white air had a tension, like the surface of a lake.

The fucken view! Evan flopped down wheezing, and rolled a joint. Where the bloody hell is it?

Tom squatted, stuck out a hand, his eyes fixed on mist. He took a long draw, blew two expert smoke rings into menthol air.

Then Evan's hand was on his shoulder, his gravelled voice inside his ear. Forget the rocks, man. Let's just enjoy the day.

But Jack said . . .

. . . He ain't your dad, Tommy, Evan said. Why take orders from him?

Tom shrugged.

Which one's your father anyway?

Tom turned slowly and scrubbed his head, realising. How would they get the rocks down? They couldn't carry more than two at once!

It's going to take us all day, he said dully.

You think Hodgins didn't consider that? said Evan.

He likes to set challenges, Tom said, thinking hard. It's character-building.

Evan wheezed, hawed, burped. Tom realised this was laughter.

Once Hodgins had said, *go collect sticks for the fire*, but only a certain type of wood. It had taken Tom and Juno all afternoon to come back with five branches. Cedar. Hodgins liked the scent it gave to evening festivities. That night, Lute had told Tom those trees were almost entirely gone since the cedar cutters cleared the land. But how Lute told it, Hodgins's challenges were still important. What they tested, Lute said, was your doubt; they were supposed to *awaken* you. Rare timber. Juno had only been six years old. How was he supposed to know box gum from beech?

Tom felt the grass take effect, his limbs drifting from his body. The clouds were looking fully impressive, super awesome in fact. It was tempting to step out on to that white plane of nothingland. He did a little mountain dance. One leg in the air, weaving his hands over his head, his hips jerking left and right.

My theory about Hodgins, Evan continued, the less fathers in this place, the more he's admired. Women love that commitment. He's all Mr Reliable and shit.

But Tom didn't want to think about Jack. He was swaying in the soft breeze. All the living things from the forest floor sounded amplified, as if whispering to him.

You don't know who he is, do you? said Evan. How about your brother?

Tom inhaled sharply. What brother? What could Evan know with a brain fritzed by chemicals? Tom felt his limbs turn hot and cold. He jammed his fists in his pockets and took air through the nose like he'd been taught, to settle anger in a peaceable way. Then reached for the joint and sucked it direct to ash. Sometimes, he had an urge to destroy. When he was rostered to work in the Laundry Cell he'd snipped nicks in Hodgins's jeans and T-shirts. Just small enough so no one could say if it were man or moth that'd damaged them. Some weeks later they appeared in his mother's sewing basket; she'd been tasked to darn them with her beautiful, invisible stitches. Tom had watched her bent over, tying off thread and biting it clean. He'd stayed in the corner where she could not see his tiny torrid misery. Hodgins's jeans, in her hands.

Had Hodgins chosen her for mending because he knew what Tom had done to his clothes, or because she was handiest with the needle?

If he hated Hodgins so much, then why come here? Tom asked Evan. Why not The Ferns where they had naltrexone and an actual doctor who oversaw your withdrawal?

I'm neutral about Jack, said Evan. He's letting me doss down, that's ace. And, the benefits! Up here Jack Hodgins is a king. If he lived in the town, I'm telling you, he'd be just a man.

Tom clenched his back teeth. There was something intrinsically lacking about being just a man. You ought to be a god, or a fucking foam-flanked stallion, as the women called certain men in The

Hive, heads bowed in the Weaving Circle. Evan was right, you had to be so much more than yourself. How else to get noticed?

Tom looked at Evan's sepia skin, his nails so deeply bitten there was a line of dried blood above each one. Evan smelled sharp and sour, like the sap from an injured plant.

People in town think you're all nuts, Evan said. The Hive's a great place to offload some grass, grab a quick fuck. Probably what happened to your mother. But why stick around? Mountain rocks! I did less work in juvie.

Tom stood. A dank taste coated his tongue. A mean shrunken feeling inside.

Sunlight winnowed out above the clouds. Then shoaled down very hard and bright. Once his dizziness subsided, he saw – across the milky lake of mist a great elongated man.

Check it out, he said. And as he pointed, the giant's arm ascended in greeting.

Evan stood. Man, what the fuck?

Tom, reeling his awe back inside himself, flicked hair from his face, and said casually, No one told you about him?

Tom lifted his arms and the figure responded, its great limbs waving in the warming air. The boy stood on the cliff edge, swaying and gesturing, as if engaged in some grave rite, his arms outstretched, head thrown back. The shadow responded, rippling and sinuous, backlit by the sun.

Rare phenomena, son, Hodgins told him that night when Tom described the figure. Tom hadn't said how Evan had fled, or about the abandoned stones which didn't seem to be required any more.

But that was just *yourself* you saw, said Hodgins. Your shadow projected on to a cloud. A Brocken Spectre.

He sounded almost impressed.

The next week Hodgins knelt and folded Tom's fingers around a gift, his large hands swallowing the boy's. A storm glass. A lidded jar filled with boiling steam and crystals to predict the coming weather. Hodgins knew a guy in the valley who made them, he said. Camphor, ammonium chloride, potassium nitrate, rectified spirit, distilled water.

Tom went speechless with gratitude. He clutched the jar against his chest and scampered across the native garden. He kept it on a high shelf in his cabin, and at night watched the vapours swirl into new formations. Each morning he warned his mother of coming winds or rain. He took the jar into the Nursery Cell and showed the infants what these swirls and flares could mean. Overnight, he'd become a kind of diviner.

Clear liquid – bright weather.
Crystals at base – thick air, frost in winter.
Dim liquid with small stars – thunderstorms.
Large flakes – heavy air, overcast sky.
Rising flakes – wind in the higher regions.

One morning, Tom woke to find Hodgins standing over him, shirt off, towel around his hips. He was holding the jar up to the light, his loosened hair muzzy from sleep. Tom could hear a distant sound. A minute before he worked it out. It was his mother, singing.

Some weeks after the day of the rocks, Evan drifted back into a neighbouring town. Tom would see him on the main street with his paltry collection of broken things and his GOODES FOR SALE sign. With his afflicted skin and hollow cheeks Evan seemed in the grip of drugs again. Tom would give him honey, some sourdough from The Hive. But Evan didn't care for food; though he looked like the hungriest person alive, he'd rather you gave him dope, or the cold hard ducats.

Once he was with a young girl, playing a cracked guitar. As Tom passed the honey to Evan, she grabbed it. Stuck her whole fist in the jar of Raw Redgum, then let the syrup run into her mouth. After fastidiously sucking each finger clean she began to strum and sing in a heavy accent. Her voice soared, breaking on the high notes. Tom stood spellbound as she stopped and started, over and over. Then he sang along in perfect, unstuttering harmony, his good ear cocked towards her.

How's your father? Evan interrupted. Tommy? You find him yet?

Tom ignored him. What's your name? Tom asked the girl.

She glanced from one to the other. Then gave Tom a wide, solar smile.

Marta, she said, and began singing again.

This kid, Evan interrupted, if he's real lucky, he's going to grow up to be just like me.

As he heads out to protest at Clear Energy Tom considers Evan's prediction. It's true he's become ruled by chemicals not of his own making. And in this has violated his own *Tenets for Natural Survival*. He swears that when he finds his father, he'll come off the antidepressants. They're merely a prop, he thinks, an adjunct for some primal thing missing in his life. A father will round out starveling parts, a father will nourish enough to shake off dream dads, world-ruining phantoms, any nightly visitants. Now from a treetop, the yark yark of a cockatoo, a sign of assent, though he'd have preferred a less jesterly messenger; a stately swamp harrier perhaps or falcon.

Today, on his way to the two pm meeting, Jim is overtaken by a powerful, leaden tiredness. As he crosses the barren playground he recalls the wonder tamped by the monotony of teaching. Phrases feather down from mezzanine rooms, *big elephants can always understand small elephants, il pecola rosso, five sixes are thirty, is Jupiter a planet?*, and now a listless child, shepherded across tundras of field and concrete to sickbay, and a mother, ferrying some vital item – lunchbox, library bag, mulberry leaves for 3P's ailing silkworms.

And here comes memory. Jim's schoolboy self, loitering by a playground paperbark. A hot Monday morning waiting for his best friend to arrive and wondering how he'll say to Matthias, my mother is gone – no, not *back to hospital* – gone *for ever*. How to say *dead* in a place where the word was traded daily, denatured, detached, dehumanised, *you're dead, Jamie Rogers, dead right, dead wrong, that's deadly, dead heat, it's a dead cert*. His mother's illness had distinguished him – for months at school he'd become arrayed in sombre light. He'd always been popular but after her death deigned not to be, turning aloof and scorny and superior. He realised now that losing her had realigned him – he'd drawn much closer then to the teachers.

All this rises up on his afternoon journey from Block C to the staffroom to discuss with Jordana Blastic the *Patterns of Place and Location* lesson plan. Specifically, *how religious and other belief systems affect the way groups interact with the environment*, his mind circling back to Evangeline and that tree she'd festooned, to her daughter's unbending silence in class and then to his favourite professor who used to rock on orthopaedic shoes at the rostrum as he said, *ignorance is a kind of forgetting*.

Was Tess's silence another way to forget?

A teacher with unexamined beliefs, the professor had said, must be broken down to blankness.

Jim sinks on to a cold silver bench and thinks of what he's doing and what he's done. *I bless the rains down in Africa-a-a-a, seven sixes are forty-two, you will die, 3.10 pm at the back gate.* From the music rooms he hears a single violinist saw some unearthly tone from rosined gut and oiled wood, *violin makers prefer wood from old-growth trees cut during the cooler months and left to season for a decade or more*, and he listens, fingers splayed on his knees. He stays very still in a long current of dappled shadow, chills along his forearms. He swallows hard. And what have you refused, the music seems to ask, what parts of yourself were discarded in grief? And then, it's just music again, suffused with effort, more touching in this raw form than any practised sound.

Wasn't it for all of this that he became a teacher? The distillation of effort, the bright hope for each child's potential before it hardened into myth. He pictures his students' faces and tries to summon that rare feeling of a class expertly flowing; a pure love for each kid in his or her incomparable glory. In a school, after Veronica's death, two teachers had rescued him through their steady, abiding attention. They'd not turned from his grief. They'd neither rushed him nor lingered over it. They'd simply named it with the correct degree of consternation and more than his father had managed. It's this getting at the fundamentals that he works at in the classroom. But how much must he know of his own self, before he can possibly enlighten another?

As he thinks hard about Tess and her mother, he grows radiant with regret. Then has a mighty hunger for a generous spliff, a ride by the lake, a run. What kind of a teacher are you now? Can you really hope to help or save anyone but yourself?

In Tess's notebook there's part of a poem her teacher had read aloud. Listen, he'd said.

> …When we love
> A sap
> Older than time
> Rises through our arms
> …
> we love inside ourselves…
> the fathers who lie at rest
> in our depths
> like ruined mountains
> and the dry riverbeds
> of earlier mothers…

Tess had copied it out. And then, when she read it over, her mind went straight to The Hive.

Now, as she climbs the Ghost Mountains trail, she thinks of her family growing smaller below; her father castrating the bulls, her mother reading, or wandering, Meg finishing her farm diorama. She'd begun it a week ago and it had taken rapid shape; it had trees, hives, animals. Best of all, said Meg, gluing matches to build a fence, the weather here's always the same. Today's forecast: fine, dry, an occasional breeze. Tess thought that sounded deathly, life in such a static atmosphere.

It's maybe why her mother took to walking, Tess thinks as she clambers through thickets of ash, brown kurrajong, weeping fig. When you're walking the view shifts and changes. Walking's a form of hope.

Tess peers through the lean, dark trunks, the snarls of strangler fig and bower vine. She hurdles the plank buttresses of huge trees, past ferns and orchids, the sun much lower than she'd thought. About an hour left of daylight. She speeds up, leaning forward on the slope, parting knitted branches, this old track nearly overgrown now no one has much use for it. Her chest is tight, the air colder inside as she climbs.

As Tess rounds the first burnt building she sees a white horse tearing grass by a stone wall. It turns one glossy eye, folds an ear in her direction. Beyond it, the hexagonal footings of the old hall, its leftover walls overgrown with woody lianas and saplings. In the dwindling sunlight, against these blackened ruins, the horse is like something dreamed. It meets her gaze then continues tearing tussocks.

It's oddly quiet – no – it's just still. There *is* a sound, an almost inaudible hum. She tries imagining her mother here, learning to cook and sew and birth a baby goat. She knew how to build fences and put out spot fires with The Hive teams that were called on in emergencies. She'd learned piecemeal about the world beyond the community, a place of wars, hypocrisy, ecotoxins, corruption. From Jack Hodgins she learned to shun man-made things that poisoned the good green earth and the wide, amazing, innocent sky. Electricals, battery-operated items whose guts did not decay for aeons, computers that revealed the world in random ways with impure consequence. But inside, she'd struggled. If the commune was Pureland, as Hodgins said, why had she felt so suffocated there? She'd run to other hamlets, in search of new friends. You're better off, she told the girls, having lived your lives in the valley. Some nights the sisters will catch their mother in the green glow of the Acer laptop, poking inexpertly at the keyboard, her neck craned forward like a species of bird they've seen, her lips silently moving. The excitement on her face, the way she shifts and rocks on her chair like a kid in class, keeps them up, speculating. She will say she is a backwoods girl badly needing teaching. At the Ghost Mountains school her periodic lessons were accompanied by stamping and clapping. This way they'd arrive at their deskwork for Gratitude and Nature Stories with hearts and hands enlivened.

She'll read their schoolbooks hungrily and copy some parts in her own spiral notebook. She'll carry the radio out to her studio, wholly immersed in news of elsewhere. In the morning they search the laptop browser but its history is always erased.

Tess wanders deeper into the commune ruins, hearing the horse snuffling as she passes. Which cabin had her mother slept in? And where had she tended the hives? To the right, a makeshift grave-yard. By one of the larger headstones, fresh flowers and leaves. Tess listens hard again to that sound. Insects? She turns to the horse, and sees it's tethered. Then straightens, feeling a cold intimation. Where has she seen that particular horse before? Snowcap Appaloosa.

And there, high in a tree festooned with strangler fig, is Juniper Peterson, watching Tess intently, her bum planted on a tapering branch. Tess looks back at that horse and flowers, then up to the placid sky as June launches herself to the dirt.

That's my mama's grave you're looking at, June says, righting herself.

Tess stares at her own feet. June lives with her uncle, Bo Peterson. It's rumoured he has tunnelled under his property, that he's a survivalist with a well-stocked bunker, that he deals meth and gambles. That young men come and go from his place. At All Hours. Others say he's decent – hadn't he taken his niece in when she had nowhere else to go? June was the only orphan Tess and Meg had ever met and this lent her a special radiance. They'd see her cantering round the town, or leading Tucker's mother, Heidi, to the GP and the charity shop. They'd once sat through June's Magick Act at the school fete. She'd sawn the library teacher clear in two, then tweaked a pretend skirt for a curtsy.

Tess picks a hangnail till blood jewels out. It's getting cold, the sweat from her climb makes her shiver. The sun low, the shadows furtive.

You and I were only little, says June. No way we can remember what it was like living here.

Tess smirks. Fail! She's never even lived at the commune! She tips her chin up, narrows her eyes.

June gestures to the smaller graves. Those two bubs, she says, they died at birth. She makes the sign of the cross, eyes shut. Then burps.

Some women had free-birthed on the mountain until Hodgins forbade it. People did some foolish things trying to live by nature, Tess's mother said. They forgot that nature can be cruel. The world is wild, she'd said, and life is unpredictable in its goodness and danger. Tess had heard this before – maybe those words had come from her own schoolbooks.

I like it here, says June, surveying. So quiet. No one ever comes, not even to visit the graves.

Tess scans the billowing trees, the empty rock circle where the pond once was, the ordered shapes of cabins and hall. Through the majestic mottled trunks, past the settlement, there's a wedge of coastal sky, the lit, staggered lines of ocean. The land Jack Hodgins chose.

Tess, turning back, sees June's mismatched eyes, one flecked green, one hazel.

My uncle knows who set the fire here, June says.

It was lightning, Tess thinks. Everyone knew that. She puts her hands on her hips, but a worry ticks beneath her ribs.

He says the individual's still in town, says June. Knows all about that car wreck too – the one on your land. And who was in it.

Big deal, Tess thinks. She feels queasy. Maybe hungry, or tired because she'd stayed up reading Tucker's thing about Apocalyptic Signs and then finishing the class handout on Thoreau and Bruce Chatwin. Her hands are sweating. June's horse whickers, insects whirr above the squally mountain breeze.

Lucky Tucker rescued you, said June with narrowed eyes. Some other babies nearly burned in that fire. He left them all in the Nursery Cell! What made you so special?

Tess shakes her head. She hadn't been there to save or leave! She hadn't even existed!

June whips out a pack of cards, fans them.

Pick any card, she says.

Tess tugs one out.

Queen of Hearts? June asks, tapping a foot.

But Tess is remembering something overheard. *Time to stop pretending*, her father said to her mother one afternoon, *that she belongs entirely to us*. She'd thought they were talking, back then, about Pip.

Well? June yanks the card from where Tess has it pressed against her chest.

Scheherazade! I was right. With magic, she says, the audience knows you're tricking. They wouldn't just let a person cut another in half. That's called suspension of disbelief.

June straightens, shaking a leg. Tess thinks of a golden dog she'd once known, its air of solid, dumb assurance, and is seized by a violent hatred for June, believing any rumours.

You OK? June pats Tess's shoulder, bending to look into her face.

Tess, folded over, gripping her knees, brushes June's palm off sharply. No one must touch her, it's all she can do to keep from puking. She remembers her mother saying, *my milk had nearly dried up after the fire, then you started to refuse the bottle* and how she'd stood up suddenly then and left the room.

After the fire? What had she meant?

Now the sky is smoky purple through the canopy.

Come on, says June. I'll show you something.

She trots across a clearing towards a crumbling wall, cards falling from her pockets. Queen, Jack, Spades. Queen, Queen. Queen.

Trick pack, Tess thinks. And feels a dim misery because she cannot tell any more which people in her life are pretending.

Tess follows, muscles stiff from the climb. That sound getting steadily louder, the livid air pocked with busy insects. Closer, inside the dim cavern of that ruined hall, the noise is unmistakable.

As her eyes adjust Tess sees what's hanging from the ceiling and jutting like lichen in thick, creamy layers. They protrude from the walls and fan from the corners. They garland the roof beams. Great waxy chandeliers lit with yellow bees. A massive natural hive.

June has thrown her arms wide as if showing a buyer a remarkable home.

Nearly a gazillion! she shouts. Maybe more!

But are these wild bees or have they swarmed from someone's apiary? You can't say if they've come from man or nature. You can't determine without capturing a queen to see if she's been marked. You think of your father's stolen bees and the new queens that cost him two thousand dollars. You think of how he'd said the honey would only trickle in this year. He'd driven off to check the two hundred hives set out for contract pollination, but came home from the avocados three days later. Half the hives had been stolen, even though those boxes were fire-branded with his code.

Tess knows what she's looking at, but can hardly guess its worth. Some things get their value from being owned.

Dear Jim

Every teacher knows that teaching is never just the conveying of infor-mation, but rather a way of joining, at a distance, the families of all the children they teach.

  Why haven't you called? At least let me know you're OK.

Sylvie x

13

Today Evangeline says, I can't lie on my back any more. The vena cava.

They sleep for a while, then wake. The rain has come and gone, the day ebbing fast. Through the cabin door they watch cockatoos unpicking worms from grass like thread from fabric.

Jim stands, pours a long draught of cider.

You'll never leave them, he says.

What would you think of me if I did? she asks.

Tell me. Then I can decide to stay or go.

He drains his glass, his tongue perfumed with pear. He's learned with her to drink lightly, and rarely. When he takes out beer, or the vodka, she practically backs across the room.

You'd really leave? she says, eyes widening. This house, or the town?

Would you care?

His need for her makes him feel debased. The plain lack of small talk, their hurtling directly into ardour, turns all their conversations lurid or grave. To say it's hot might mean: take off your clothes; to mention darkness conjures those they've lost. By choosing her he hasn't escaped his grief, just walked headlong into hers. Does he love her? He can't name the feeling. It's stealthed on him like panic. She lies in his cabin asking for nothing. After her body, she has nothing else to give.

I can't watch you from a distance play happy families, he says, inverting his cup on the table.

Don't watch then!

She stretches her legs, circles an ankle, moves further left so their bodies are more distant.

Hold on, she says, you think I pretend?

You love us both?

And he instantly sees his mistake: neither of them had said the word yet. Now he has.

Through the smeary window, distant swallows swoop and career in their intuited formation. In his yard, bees fuss over lavender and climbing rose, siphoning nectar. When you open a hive it's clear how promiscuous they've been, all the multicoloured pollen from the many flowers. Bees. He wishes they'd just fuck off.

Evangeline examines her nails with distaste.

He moves towards her. Eva, he says.

There's a long, blank moment.

No one calls me *Eva*, she says. Is that what you've been saying all along?

She turns side on. Her breasts, which he'd first seen eight months back by the Repentance River, now heavy with milk. She opens the book of poetry.

If only I'd studied, she sighs.

Your daughter's bright, he says. Her writing's …

…Writing? Evangeline sits. Then she stands, and stares at the corner table where his schoolwork is piled.

What does she write about?

His dread deepens. Somewhere in there, Tess's journal. If they were at school he could bring it out. Show the daughter's work to the mother. But here, in his house, the mother fresh from his bed, wasn't that a violation?

Why don't you ask her? he says.

Evangeline has crossed the room. She lays one hand on the stack of exercise books.

In here? she asks. Show me.

He walks over, takes her arm, saying, Don't. It just makes everything more complicated.

She pulls her head back, breathing slowly, her eyes glassy and unfocused.

Let go of me, she says.

He loosens his grip, but keeps his hand on her forearm. Puts the other one on her breast.

Ah. That old trick, she says. But what's to hide? Or does she write about me? And she lets out a choked laugh.

No, he says. I'd say it's about grief.

And he feels her muscles liquefy beneath his hand.

When Stefan met me, she says, I was already pregnant.

Jim swallows.

And now they want to tell Tess, she says. About her real father. They'd planned to years back, but because of what happened to Pip ... And after the funeral, they hadn't the strength. The risk of losing another girl. But lately they've tried to figure out how to say it, and when.

Jesus, he says. But why tell *me*?

She'd been supposed to adopt Tess out, Evangeline says. She'd been so young. She hadn't wanted anything more to do with Tess's father. A badly chosen fling. So, Jack Hodgins and her mother decided she should give the baby up. There was a woman from the valley, Lana Beaufort, desperate for a child. But as the time approached Evangeline knew she could not do it.

Jim paces, the cabin suddenly stifling, very low-ceilinged and dingy. His own disloyalty strikes him painfully. How can he encourage what's blocked in Tess now he's co-opted into this family secret?

I can't do this any more, he says.

She stiffens. Then he sees it, a marvellous aquatic undulation beneath her belly. He puts his hand there, feels the nub of a fist or foot connect. Go on, let yourself think it: something of yours might belong to her.

Is it mine? he asks.

His thousand imaginings of being a father. It will encompass him, it could be so simple. But he knows from how his Sydney friends withdrew and bunkered down, from their whispers when he'd phone at the Worst Possible Time, from the background howls and the declined invitations – that he's only in thrall with the idea of kids, and how far can an idea carry you into the routine and grind, the sickness and healing, the sublimation and sacrifice, the burden of making sure your child survives their own childhood?

She knows, so much better than he, what this new life might cost her.

She bends, retrieves her dress. Just a woman, her hair bedraggled from their time in bed, her face flushed. Swollen-ankled, mouth-breathing with a greying front tooth. No sign of the particular aura she'd had when he'd found her by that river. His compulsion to rescue, he realises, just deflects his own inner peril.

He catches sight of himself in the window, what's so special? She might have chosen anyone. He has no idea what he can mean to her.

Don't look at me like that, she says.

What?

It makes me feel anonymous.

You're like no one I've ever met, he says. But, this baby, he points, is part of *your* family. So I'll be …

Like the undead, he thinks, roaming, restless, unable to connect with some fundamental part of himself.

You can't just go on pretending with me – or Stefan, he says.

Until I met you, that was my life! she tells him. She pretends for her family. That she wants to keep living in a house where everything reminds her of what she's lost, in a town she never willingly chose or belonged. She pretends till it feels just a bit real. She has tried to remember the person she was, but even that young woman, she realised, had been entirely invented.

Are you so scared to think of another kind of future?

Yes, she mutters. I'm terrified.

He remembers the Xanax packet hammered to the mountain tree. Her name typed on.

He bends towards her, gently moving her hair from her face. She tugs her dress over her stomach. Then tries and fails, with trembling hands, to fasten her sandals. He kneels, takes her foot, secures the buckle.

When you chose me, she says, you knew what you were getting into. I can live day by day. But I can't afford to sink.

She pulls her foot from his grip then says, Stefan knows, OK!

He absorbs this.

Now she's beside the door. One hand in her hair as if to re-assemble herself after dissembling. It sinks deeper: Stefan knows.

Have you really never travelled? he says, handing her the other sandal. Jesus, have you been in this town your whole fucking life?

I chose you, she says with a dull laugh. For once in my whole fucking life I've been entirely selfish.

14

Dented filing cabinets. Scuffed vinyl floor. A Japanese fortune cat, swinging its pendulum arm. Evangeline in the grey police station crossing and uncrossing her legs. She felt her baby undulating, hopped up on shared adrenalin. At the last appointment the midwife had been approving. You're all baby, she'd said, as Evangeline stood in her faded underwear.

Some pregnancies had liberated her. There were weeks when she'd receded as the baby pushed closer to the world, her mind becalmed and hazy.

But now, in the station, she swallowed a bitter, greasy taste, knitted her puffy fingers. Thursday morning, 10.12 am.

On the desk beside her, a computer with astronomical screen saver. Stars. Moon. Some ringed planet twisting in orbit. Onscreen at home she'd browsed the images from the astronauts. She'd read their posts on the world's lonely splendour. Oh the puny travails of humans viewed from afar! Oh the cities, lit up at night like new constellations! She scrolled the photos and thought of that outmoded diminutive *earthlings*, which seemed to refer to an earlier, more elemental species. From space they were mapping disquieting changes: ocean vortices, widening gyres, dislocated tracts of polar ice. Still, the cosmic perspective was soothing. After, she'd click towards the physicists. There exists no proof of the past but memory, no evidence of future but our belief in it. She'd read and reread this, gently ruined. When she shared it with Stefan, he said, That's a convenient theory, if you're after absolution.

He hadn't recognised it as a simple hunger for new knowledge.

No time now for the cosmos. It was the hour of uniformed men with their stricter currencies of what and who and precisely when. There they sat in vanilla air. One sallow and gaunt, the other handsome, acne-scarred. A pinky ring, the tail of a tattoo below shirt cuffs. She absorbed their holsters, their Tasers, the sheen on their uniform pockets. The taller man's gun seemed more worn than the other's, more used. Had she ever, in her whole life, touched an actual weapon? She had a sudden unholstering urge and a hazy sense of where she could take aim. She felt an old, reckless seam that she'd never tamed to her advantage. No one had ever taught her the difference between an instinct and an urge.

They asked about her time at the commune.

I can't remember much from then, she said, taking quick, shallow breaths, like a person surfacing.

Her arms were frozen to her sides. Her feet seemed not to belong to her legs. She remembered in the hospital after the fire, her mother had read aloud from her file, pausing at the word, dissociated. They were transferring Evangeline that day, to another unit. But Stefan had materialised in a cone of arctic light, then signed for her release.

You once lodged a complaint, said the handsome one, waving a file. About some men in a van. Peter George Tucker and Gus Van Loon. Sergeant Becker handled it for you. Why did you withdraw it?

Wasn't this supposed to be about the accident on their farm? Weeks back she'd gone out to inspect that lonely patch of scrub. By the barricade-tape she'd found a cross from old fence boards, and bunches of sunburned flowers. Stefan's work? When he confirmed this later, the shame. She walked around the property then, picking burdock and hypericum, cat's claw and kudzu, thinking of a man she'd once known, keen-witted and sensual but at his core, very harmed. She made the weeds into a rough bouquet and laid it by the cross.

The broader policeman was waiting, flexing delicate, tapered fingers. Odd, wasn't it, that the same type of van ended up on their land years later?

Evangeline looked up, her eyes unfocused, and asked, You think one of them is the dead man?

Was it before or during the commune blaze, the broader man asked, that she'd injured her head?

I had amnesia, she said. The whole thing's still a blur.

She fingered the scar at her temple. Painting was how she knew fact from feeling. Outlines defined the touchable things. Objects, adjacent, produced the emotion.

Then she pointed at the taller officer asking, What kind is it?

He followed the line of her gaze to his crotch.

Your gun, she said, side-eyed.

It's a Glock.

And she laughed, then fenced her mouth with fingers and grew deeply intrigued by a sticky patch on the floor. What she remembered most starkly was that time in hospital, after the fire. The pain from her burns as if she'd been struck by a thousand immortal bees. A keening that persisted, hour upon hour, and gave every proximate thing a peculiar, pulsing glow.

Where was she located when the fire started? This was Sergeant Entsch, sterner now. All the reports say you hadn't been seen for hours.

At first, she'd found it ridiculous – those boys, coming to The Hive to threaten her. Pete was so shambolic and incapable she couldn't believe he was pulling it off. Plus they were both high. But when they dragged her into the van and tightened the blindfold she thought, this is no game. Even now she can detect the oily, vehicular odour, which adhered for weeks after despite Sulfamylon, debridement and hospital bandages – a sumpy stink that would make her for ever avoid petrol pumps, mowers, tractor tanks and any car with its bonnet open. She'd groped blindly in the back of that van as the men drove. She picked out shapes with her hands. Wrench and spare tyre, jack, zippered bag, torch and lighter. When she called out and heard their affectless answering tone, she'd pocketed what she could.

She looked at the policemen, blocky shapes shimmering in the air.

They drove me around, then took me out by the falls and later in a horse field, while they sat nearby, smoking and laughing.

She did not tell them Peter's threat – that he'd come to claim what rightly belonged to him. Or that she'd replied, She's breastfed only. How will you feed her?

At the news of her pregnancy Peter had become very fervent, crowing around the district. His childhood had left him with a fantasy of repair; fatherhood was a rapid route towards it. But he was homeless, shambolic, a drifter making do – she'd called it off, but kept the baby.

Later, on the friable grass, she'd watched as the commune bees, abandoning their hives at the smell of smoke, passed overhead in a black mass. The men had gone and the forest was dense with the sound of burning. When she tried standing, dizziness felled her. Her temple throbbed from where it had hit when they pushed her against the van. She reached for where her forehead ought to be, and someone else's fingers came back covered in blood and ash.

She came to think the fire was blessed. Maybe even cleansing. A secret part of her was glad the commune was destroyed. Wasn't she newly forged in that fire, hadn't she become another person entirely?

But after, in the hospital, even the gentlest nurse wore a look that said – you're just another hippie homeschooled from a curriculum of no consequence. Evangeline thought she'd known some things well – how to properly pin a cloth nappy, how to swaddle her baby, that raw aloe and calendula could soothe raging nappy rash, impetigo, eczema – but at St Catherine's she'd learned she had not. Because of the burns to her chest she could not breastfeed and when the nurses put the bottles to Tess's mouth, Evangeline heard The Hive women who'd always said, boob is beautiful and best, formula is fucked, even though her supply was low and she'd constantly worried in the commune that Tess was going hungry. When Tess cried, the nurses barely stirred but said, She'll teach herself to settle. Later, when Stefan showed Evangeline the new farmhouse, she'd thought, He's teaching me to settle. But was it for their new life in the valley, or for him?

How about once you reached the river? the detective asked. Why not proceed to safety? Why stay near the fire and endanger your baby?

His forefinger tapped the table. His smell, cigarette clad in spearmint.

I was waiting for Tom, she said. I couldn't go down the mountain alone.

Her hands were twitching, which was noted with looks. Her skin was burning again.

Why not? they asked.

She turned to the grimy window, and stared past the station hedge, starred with flowers. Green lawns. A man jumping furiously inside a rubbish bin. A white dog running up a dry brown hill. A boy jogging by with a huge balloon, filled with many smaller balloons in pearly blue and white. There were worlds within worlds, she thought. The whole time we were on that mountain the town went on without us. Another dissociation. And which was more real? The Pureland steeped in benevolent nature, or the clamouring valley hamlet? She'd looked down on the town every week of her life: the lake's mercury smoulder, the rippled plots of wheat and lucerne, the ordered geometries of road and house. Once, a skywriter and the cloud-word *Virgin*, drifting apart.

The station fluorescents flickered. Her fingernails left bloody crescents in her palms.

I couldn't go down alone, she said. I didn't know what kind of men might be waiting there below.

The policemen swapped low-browed glances. The fair-haired cracked his notebook.

Evangeline felt the baby revolve. In her throat the tang of vomit and ash. Soon she'd paint it all – the giant preying bee of that fire; horses dissembling under her touch; the gas company's steel rigs, arcane pyramids on the denuded slopes. The time that had stopped time. Wasn't it so outright unholy, wasn't it an act against all living sense, disinterring what ought to stay fixed underground?

At the hospital, the mental-health worker had wanted to dig. But Evangeline had not been willing, or able. And she'd kept it together now, for so long, hadn't she? She was determined not to grant those men her suffering. In the end, it was guilt and secrecy that had done her in.

As each thought floated up, her eyes darkened, welled, then took on such a terrified cast that the officers grew kind and hushed. One fetched water and handed the cup while the other quipped about baby names, his own father named after a frickin pub! Then, whenever she's ready, they said, tapping the photo.

She tried to organise her hair which was still flossy and snagged from sleep, tried pulling her face into some mild expression. She thought of Pip, and how everything had ebbed after her death. How people seemed unconscious actors. And yet, her life before and after Pip ceaselessly called for a reckoning.

She looked at the van; well, maybe she knew it. But not from the outside. She knew it blindly, by fingertips and smell.

A DNA sample would determine if the van at the farm was the one in which she'd been abducted. They passed the consent form. A buccal swab. She wrote her name without recognising the hand or the words it left behind.

Only three people knew what had happened when that fire started, and one of them, it seemed, was dead. She became very grim, thinking of the consequences for all of them, but most of all for Tess.

A few more questions and then, free to go. Beneath her clothes, the old burns pulling tight. Outside, on the footpath opposite the station, a stranger affixed a blue hat to a dog.

Closing In

It was after Pip's funeral that your mother started carrying the umbrella. Sometimes the sky was clear and threatening nothing. You didn't like seeing her in town that way. Her face was so shaded that the umbrella looked like it was walking on its own. Sometimes she came home with wet hair in the dry weather, and still you heard that sound of the brolly folding inside itself.

Your father was often away, following the honey flow. Ironwood at Caster's Creek, Salvation Jane on Hussaini's acres. In the northern chemist, you queued with the scripts because your mother would not come in. Two women stared through the window. 'Is she preserving her skin with that parasol?' one asked. The other said she was hiding. 'With artists, there's a fine line between eccentricity and just plain barking.' You ran out so you wouldn't shout. The Maxalt, Xanax and prednisone rattling in the bag.

The next year, Meg said, 'It doesn't make you invisible.' You'd been silent for just two months. She said it was the opposite.

You and your mother were drawing attention. People began to call you shy. They poked you as if you were deaf. They didn't like how your silence made them feel. You stood outside the headmistress's office. You brought the crested envelopes home and your mother ripped them open. At first she said, 'You'll talk in your own good time,' and threw the letters away. Later, she spiked them in the study. One day she said, 'Tess, it is high time for speaking.'

In the school counsellor's office your father could not explore your silence. His right hand was red and swollen from bees. He asked Ms Byers if she'd ever tried propolis for her gums. It's a vegetable mastic gathered by bees from bark and flowers. It keeps the hive clean, he told her. On the gums it prevents decay. Ms Byers closed her mouth then and hardly said a word.

Meg had asthma trouble. She played piano louder and louder, one foot jammed on the brass pedal. She wheezed between chords. Your mother said, 'She's wasting her precious breath, speaking for you all the time.' Meg started sketching her trees bent with top branches growing like roots in the ground.

Stefan hears the bee, butting itself against the screen door. He's been stung twice already and his forearm is voluptuously red; the skin has a shine, as if buffed. He applies the bag of frozen peas, checks the swelling, then walks the hall. Are his reactions getting worse? He knows two beekeepers who've given it up after becoming dangerously allergic.

Evangeline's in the bedroom sleeping. She must have returned while he was loading the hives on the ute. Tomorrow at dawn he's off to Parson's orange trees.

She's onion-belled now with the child, pouchy around the eyes. Her nose seems wider, changing the whole aspect of her face. Pregnancy can do that. Maybe a boy? He thinks of how she'd let him touch her before the fire, and then after. Her burns were still fresh but she'd moved his hands over all the parts that could still register his fingers, her eyes closed, her face turned away. Before then he'd been stunned at her openness, at how she gave herself with a frank pride, a manner he'd never found before in any young woman. After the fire, though, she was newly wary.

Once, at the commune, he'd wandered into the Nursery Cell and found Tom Tucker singing in astounding choirboy soprano. The babies – how many? – were quiet, their hammocks all in a row. He'd thought straight away of *The Life of the Bee*.

On all sides, asleep in their closely sealed cradles, in this infinite super-position of marvellous six-sided cells, lie thousands of nymphs, whiter than milk, who with folded arms and head bent forward, await the hour of wakening.

All those infants had caused him concern. There seemed too many for the handful of women he'd seen at The Hive and the even fewer men, and he'd played a game with young Tom trying to guess who the parents were, while the boy stuttered out the names. Just listed the mothers, as if they'd all been born fatherless or maybe Tom didn't consider fathers part of the equation. Tess was asleep in a corner hammock. He'd pointed, asking the boy, How about this one? But Tom had shrugged as if he really didn't know. And soon Stefan considered the child his own as he planned a future with her mother.

Evangeline shifts, one arm under her head. Is she really sleeping? Maybe even this, pretence. Had he taken advantage by choosing her when all she'd known was commune life? By loving her he'd also freed her – she might have been claimed by another; if the commune hadn't burned she might have got stuck there for ever. But was he any different, really, from Hodgins? Putting limits on her life, bringing her here, not even far enough from her past to forget it.

She reaches for the paper and, without looking up, says, Four letters?

Through the bedroom window, the towering gums at the edge of their property, their rusty ribbons of half-shed skin snapping in the breeze. The fresh stump of the camphor laurel, which he'd slaughtered, just because he could not figure, one afternoon, what else to do. The next three days Meg helped stack the wood as he'd corded it. Now we have plenty to burn through winter. It's good you murdered the tree, Dad, the roots get into the water table. *If a trunk is under tension, prevent the saw from binding by first cutting a wide notch in the inside of the bend. Saw a little at a time, slowly, until the trunk breaks. Be ready for kickback.*

Lina.

She looks up, smiling vaguely. Black pen on her cheek. Her shampoo smell. Ylang-ylang, some peppery note, bergamot. Beneath that, her raw woody scent.

Four letters, she says, creasing the page into narrow sections. Beside the bed, in a green folder, are crosswords scissored from the paper.

He stamps a socked foot. Itches his throbbing arm. Bee venom and some other vague pain inching to a crescendo. The room turning bright and unfocused, as if someone were opening and closing the curtains.

The police had visited again that morning. They'd asked him about The Hive fire. And the young male from the van who was yet to be identified. What did those two things have to do with each other, Stefan had asked. And they'd replied, very smartly, What makes you think they do?

What is the clue? Stefan asks.

She looks at him dumbfounded. How will he love this new baby, fired from loss? Reminding him of the time that preceded it, when he'd lowered his youngest into the ground. But babies, he knew, were easy to love; babies were small enablers.

When she shifts, a yellow glow courses into the room. He holds his smarting forearm over his eyes as he thinks of the virgin queen, everyone busy around her, while she sits at the heart of the hive. Through the window, way off, the leaky outline of Parker's cabin, backlit, the sun getting low. Even from here so plain to see who comes in, and out. And maybe she likes it that way.

Despite the tenderness in his body, and how he just wants to lie down with her, he grits his teeth. A neural pain shoots through his head, and merges with that other, persistent smoggy ache.

Lina, so actually I'm trying to understand. It is some kind of punishment?

Huh?

Something missing...

She puts one arm over her stomach.

...in your life? he asks. This affair...

...You think this is about replacing Pip? She shuffles upright, kicks the covers off her bare legs.

I did not say about Pip! he says, one hand chopping the air.

She looks down. Maybe ashamed. He can't tell any more.

Don't yell, she says. The girls...

He shucks his muddy socks off. How can he argue with the spectre of Pip between them? He rolls one sleeve down, then the other.

We can talk about why, he says, trying to sound reasonable. Why this particular man. A schoolteacher. Maybe he knows some things I don't. But think about Tess, he says. Think of Meg.

I don't mean to hurt you, she says. But when I look at your face I see Pip. So, I look away.

He ought to be shocked. But he's briefly relieved. It isn't hate, or some other feeling between them then. It is at least love that averts her.

We're both unfaithful, she says. Isn't your drinking a way to escape? You don't like talking about the past. OK. But she's part of it. I don't want to forget, even if I have to remember things I'd rather not.

Total despair, in his eyes, in the downward shift of his mouth. *Unfaithful*. This word throbs most acutely. He chases down his anger but he has a right to feel it! He thinks of his brother expressing everything, and of himself struck dumb before his father's casual violence. Compared to all that – his mother's black eyes, the broken bones, the hours in the hospital making up new stories – this is nothing. Isn't it, so, so minor? And yet, pain and despair sneak up when he goes about unmedicated. Mersyndol. The new script on his desk, waiting to be filled.

Just tell me about this one, Lina, he says. Is it mine?

Jim, heading for town on his bike, brakes, skids, digs a heel into dirt as they pass. She's in the back of the ute, between Meg and Tess. Stefan at the wheel, driving slowly down the Old Mill Road. Seeing Evangeline, ensconced with her family, makes his stomach turn.

As they pass, she looks determinedly ahead. Meg's head is bent. Tess offers a wan smile and Stefan places one finger against the windscreen.

Jim rears back. Some kind of accusation? He remembers Evangeline's *Stefan knows*. But surely the man's just defending his glass against loose gravel.

Still, there it is: Stefan knows. Once the man might have waved, he'd invited Jim into his home, left jars of honey at his door.

Jim takes the longer, shadier route into town, then pedals warily into the frank light of the busy main street. Mums and dads pushing prams, filling hessian bags with supplies, pensioners under canvas outside the cafés. You can see from the particular make-up of the crowd that it's Thursday, when the benefits go into the accounts and back out through the ATMs, all the small businesses busy. Kids ride by on bikes and rollerblades, finally liberated by weather, and the spring break. One waggles a finger at his teacher as he passes. Stay out of trouble, Mr Parker.

Three kookaburras start up on an overhead wire and for a second he feels he's the object of their hilarity. Just a bit paranoid, and now regretful about this morning's spliff. His regular anxiety's bad enough. Somewhere in town, the Müllers. He isn't in the mood for another encounter. His breathing short and shallow, his heart palpitating. It's October the twelfth. Happy birthday, Veronica. You'd be fifty-nine today. He ducks into the nearest shop, greeting June Peterson on her way out.

Inside a fug of mothball, and damp wool. Across the large room, Heidi Tucker, leaning towards the shop assistant and shouting, Excuse me!

The Unity Mission is packed with musty clothes, shelves of cheap knick-knacks from the deceased estates, old, dented plastic toys, rows of outdated shoes. No vintage treasure here, Sylvie would say. The poorer towns yielded so little.

Would you please direct me to Hi-Fi? Heidi asks.

The assistant – Marlene says her badge – is peering over half-moon glasses. She takes Heidi's arm and leads her to a plastic chair.

Sit, we'll take you up in a sec.

Is it too much to ask for proper music? says Heidi, agitated.

Good question, Jim thinks. There's a terrible furry sound coming from badly wired speakers.

Let's look at some gloves while you wait, says Marlene. I put a lovely cerise pair away for you.

Will there be dancing?

Of course, Heidi, says Marlene. But you haven't got your hopes up? It's been a long while since we've seen him.

Jim ambles off through the camphor air past a rack of ties and belts that conjure the men he sees, sitting out their final days at the Hillsdale Home by the river. He picks through the broken-spined hardcovers with their faded dedications, the scuffed picture books, the liver-spotted Penguins, and spots two volumes of Neruda, a dog-eared *Robinson Crusoe*. A nice companion to the Thoreau he's been reading the kids.

Then he climbs the stairs to a mezzanine. Veneer cabinets, old suitcases and a keyboard jostle in the cramped space. New music, louder here. On the shelves, Skyhooks and John Travolta posters in cracked plastic frames, teddies gazing benignly through glazed eyes. As Jim sidles by a glass-topped table he hears John Lennon's voice swelling, then sees, by the row of encyclopedias, Heidi Tucker swaying, face upturned, eyes closed and singing.

She twirls, pink gloves out, terror and longing on her face. Jim immediately sees that this is some deeply private ritual, and steps quietly back downstairs. *Mother*. He recognised the song, he'd learned it himself on the guitar as a kid – Lennon had written it for his mother, Julia, who died when he was seventeen.

Is she OK up there? he asks as Marlene lines up knitted booties. Eight miniature feet.

It's her favourite song, Marlene says. She comes in every fortnight.

Jim hands her the paperbacks, some coins.

Poetry! Marlene says. Well, no one ever, unless it's Pam Ayres!

Then she leans in closer. I suppose I can trust a person who reads poetry.

Heidi used to meet her son in the shop, she tells him. Not Thomas – the older boy, Peter. The staff soon realised she was giving him her benefit because he always came Thursdays. But he hasn't been in for more than a year. There were rumours about police trouble. He was always a bit furtive, that one.

We play along, just for Heidi, Marlene says. We've pretended ever since that he might still turn up. It's the ritual that counts most, after all.

She bags the books and counts out change.

His daughter lives round here, Marlene says. *Estranged* was what he called her. But he was always saying how very keen he was to get her back.

Later, in his cabin, Jim drinks vodka and reads the dog-eared Defoe. Every now and then, glancing up. Lights blink on at Honig Farm. But he forces himself back to the book, thinking of Lennon, who was said to have never recovered from his mother's death. He thinks of Heidi, waiting for her son amid the cast-offs. And of his own young, feeling self. What to do with all that emotion? He looks at the glass. Drains it. Still thirsty, and breathless. Still restless. He turns back to the book and starts underlining:

> *I went up the Shore and down the Shore, but it was all one, I could see no other Impression but that one, I went to it again to see if there were any more, and to observe if it might not be my Fancy; but there was no Room for that, for there was exactly the very Print of a Foot, Toes, Heel, and every Part of a Foot; how it came thither, I knew not, nor could in the least imagine. But after innumerable fluttering Thoughts, like a Man perfectly confus'd and out of my self, I came Home to my Fortification, not feeling, as we say, the Ground I went on, but terrify'd to the last Degree, looking behind me at every two or three Steps, mistaking every Bush and Tree, and fancying every Stump at a Distance to be a Man ...*

Defoe, on his island, haunted by footprints, by signs of strange habitation. Heidi, waiting for the son that will not come. Jim's feet in his mother's shoes, trying to figure out how it is actually possible that she won't be coming home. He tightens Veronica's gown around him. Then starts idly sketching on a scrap of paper. A mountain; a tree; a child's sandal roped to the trunk.

You girls know how to do eggs? asks Nora, parking a basket on the porch table.

Tess and Meg squint into razory sunshine, both in pyjamas, their stomachs churning because they've forgotten breakfast. Now it's nearly noon. Tess, scratching her head, yawns. Three days into spring holidays. Bored already.

Thanks, says Meg. But we have chooks, so ... plenty of eggs.

I bought them for your mother's lying-in, says Nora.

You're way too early for that, says Meg. Besides, she's at the clinic.

Anyway, says Nora, how exciting, girls!

Tess, watching with pursed lips and folded arms, slowly shakes her head.

Nora wriggles on to a porch chair.

Omelette, scrambled, fried, poached, frittata, she says. *Huevos rancheros*. A real favourite at The Hive. So nice to cook from your natural larder, eh Tess?

Tess looks at her blankly. Her mother hasn't eaten an egg since she found the fourth duckling among the chickens, henpecked to death. Tess had found her after, filling the tiny duckling grave, in sudden need of a hug. But Nora, who's been coming around more often, wouldn't know that. Nora only appears when their mother isn't here.

So, will it be a brother or sister? Nora asks, her eyes very eager. A boy might be nice.

The girls stare with closed, hostile faces.

I'll never forget the night you were born! she says quickly, tapping Tess on the head.

Tess frowns, scrapes her hair into a ponytail, tipping her neck right back. She yawns, she's got more urgent stuff to do than listen to Nora. Their mother's left a list, things to be washed and folded for the baby. Clothes from a trunk stored in the attic. Last worn by baby Pip. When their father saw these, piled on a chair, he said, Put them back – we'll buy new ones. When their mother asked, what with, he'd said, the last of the honey money. But the clothes stayed in the lounge because no one had it in them to return them to the ceiling.

At The Hive Birthing Cell, Nora's saying, there was boiled water and clean sheets. But no epidural or gas, just marijuana and meditation.

Your poor mum had an awful time. We all heard her, clear across the common ground. At first the moaning, later came the screaming...

Meg turns her mouth down, then disappears, disgusted, into the house.

Well, you ought to know about it, Nora calls after her. Specially if she's having it here! There is pain, girls. There'll be blood.

Tess looks back through the shadowy house. Meg taking her time, clanking things in the kitchen. Tess feels cold in the chest; she clenches her fists and sighs loudly at Nora.

First June's stories and now Nora's. I was born *here*, Tess thinks, a home birth. Just like Pip. The doctor won't let her mother risk that now, even though she hates hospitals, and says, Well maybe I won't make it in time, considering St Catherine's is three hours away. Maybe I'll just lie in the barn like Mary did with Jesus. How's she supposed to travel that far in labour? She must book in early, the midwives told her. But there's just no way, says her mother, she's not spending another week in St Catherine's.

Nora settles on the porch chair, crossing a thigh. When Meg comes out with toast and tea, Nora asks,

What's the due date?

Out along the lane a white goat is wandering. Tess looks across to the bee huts, where her father's trialling Demaree swarm control, confining the queens to a lower chamber with the brood on top, though he's almost given up rehabilitating these particular bees. She sees his blue denim back bent over and feels very sorry for him. Should she tell him about those bees on the mountain? If you stumble on a secret, are you bound to keep it to yourself?

Still not talking, Tess? asks Nora. Plenty of folks probably think you're rude. But I understand. She helps herself to tea, tipping some into her saucer then lapping at it like a cat.

Tess glares at a heifer in the front field, crosses her arms more tightly.

But if you want to ask the hard questions, Nora lowers her voice as she eyes their father, hammering propolis, *you should*. Don't spend your life wondering, she says. Once your parents are gone, all their stories go too.

Meg brushes the grubby table with the side of her hand. Everything lately, silted with brown. Dust rolls across the dead-grass fields and wafts inside, dulling the floorboards. It aggravates Meg's asthma, so their mother damp-mops every day just to get her off the Flixotide. Whenever Meg has an asthma attack Tess hears her mother's words, *wasting her breath speaking for you*, and feels responsible.

After the endless autumn rain – six weeks now of dry.

Nora stares at their father, his face a mystery beneath the bee veil.

Everyone on the commune was so excited when you arrived, she says, turning to Tess. A young woman's first baby is always auspicious.

Nora helps herself to Meg's buttered toast.

So, she says, chewing, everyone at The Hive was counting down the days and when you finally came there was panpipes and drumming and Jack just couldn't wipe the grin off his face. He hadn't the first idea about babies, though. Even if you were asleep he'd pick you up and joggle you. He had to have you awake, see. Then he'd throw you into the air like he'd seen someone do, way back, some memory of dadness. He throws you up, you scream – you were too small to be thrown, anyone could see that, your scrawny neck was loose, you were only good for swaddling, you certainly had no idea about *fun* ...

...Then why do it? Meg asks, foraging in her pocket. Three pencils clatter on to the porch.

Jack did what Jack liked, says Nora. No one questioned him. Except your mother but even she turned quiet after the baby deal went sour. He chooses you for his favourite, OK. Decides you're the one for reaping, you for peeling potatoes and you're for beekeeping. Yes sir. Throws a newborn in the air ... Okey-doke.

Meg takes her cue from her sister's face. It's all closed up with that violet tinge her skin gets in the cold.

After I was sent to fetch Lana Beaufort, Nora says, Angel never forgave me.

Meg, still scowling at Nora, asks, What do you mean, *baby deal*?

But Tess has suspended the facts because, in this story, she sounds a bit special. Even if a lot of Nora's *tales*, as their mother says, aren't true. Even if Nora's heading perilously close to Krazy Town. Not because of the rainbow hair, or the very short skirts and shorts she wears in all weathers. Not because they once watched her at a town picnic drunkenly dance towards their father and trail a scarf around his neck while their mother looked on very pinch-mouthed and sceptical. It is something about the expression she wore when their father pushed that scarf away. It's how she surveils the family's land. It's how, when their mother is here, Nora magics into another, apologising person. The girls cannot reconcile that she and their mother were ever friends.

Tess wants, more than ever, to cry out. She clamps her jaw, pulls her ponytail headache-tight. What had she heard that day, careening down the mountain on June's Appaloosa? Its muscles moving so sinuously against her own that she felt herself becoming a new creature. *You and me were too small to remember what happened up here. We have to rely on other people.*

Leave me any tea, Nora?

It's their father. Dust-caked, sweat-runnelled. In one scratched hand, a metal hive tool refracting bright shapes across the veranda. The bee helmet with its black mesh. When Tess feels his palm on her shoulder she starts to breathe freely.

Guten Tag, Stefan, Nora says.

Meg, still glancing at Nora and Tess, says, But you must mean some other baby? Because Tess and I were born *here*, not in the commune. Right, Dad? Tess wasn't even …

… Everyone remembers the past differently, says their father, shooting Nora a stony look. And if actually you're a drinker, you're looser with the facts.

Nora stands, tugging the raw edges of her shorts in a waggle-hipped movement that makes Meg and Tess stare at her bum.

Expert advice from you, Stefan, she says.

You came all this way with rumours for my daughters? he asks.

Eggs, she points to the basket. For Angel's lying-in. Then she says, I hear the police think it might be Pete.

Tess stares at Nora's thighs, imprinted with checks from the canvas chair.

The police had come to her place asking. She told them Peter had relatives in town – and enemies.

Girls, says Stefan. Inside!

Tess looks at the dry earth almost reaching the foothills now. It has not rained, it has not rained. The bees have nearly all gone. Fifty hives in the bee yard stolid and empty. José's entire colony – stolen. Everything, waiting. The dirt on her father's shoes fine as talc and holding to nothing, not even the roots of trees, not even to itself. On the mountain, when they fell the ancient eucalypts, there's a second when the trees hover, suspended by a final splinter of trunk. Dust whirls up from the weekend tourists' four-wheel drives, from the semis that rattle through town in the morning. Tess arrived at school last week covered in it, eyes watering. Mr Parker offered tissues and asked did she need some privacy? She stood by the lockers and rubbed her eyelids, but only scratched the grit in deeper. She wanted to tell him that she'd gone up the mountain, that she'd seen the commune ruins and what had moved in after everyone was gone. She wanted to ask about the Rilke poem on the whiteboard.

> the fathers who lie at rest
> in our depths
> like ruined mountains
> and the dry riverbeds
> of earlier mothers
> the whole

> silent landscape under a clouded or
>
> clear destiny – girls, this came before you.

Because she thought she understood about the fathers at rest in our depths, thought maybe she'd figured it. But her silence was bricked up, it was a habit she could not break. She coughed instead, and dust flew out of her mouth.

As Nora steps off the porch a soaring, vertiginous feeling overtakes Tess.

Inside, the phone starts ringing.

Tess? Meg's saying, one hand on the door. You OK?

Better get that, Meg, says their father.

Tess, whey-faced and shaky, stays fixed to the chair as Meg dashes inside. Nora's hand is on Tess's arm, patting, patting. Put your head down, Tess, she's saying. On your knees if you can. Her voice, sounding submerged.

A faint, Nora's saying. Some water, Stefan!

Tess jerks her arm free of touch, she turns towards the creaking door, her father's back disappearing. The static air with its black lines of frantic bees.

You're breathing too quick, Nora's saying to Tess. Slow down, sweetheart.

Don't touch me, says Tess, and her voice, a dry forgotten croak, surprises even herself.

19

Tom Tucker wanders out. A dirty sky, flecked with altocumulus. He sniffs the air for particulates, tastes them on his tongue. Then turns to his native bees. He'd set their hives just below the fence so the neighbour couldn't see. Annette Turrell, a swatter of insects, a Baygon can permanently in her hand. A collector of dolls. Twenty glass-eyes follow Tom whenever he passes the side window. Girls in uniforms of the world. Tartan kilts, feathered headgear, grass skirts, Swiss-maid aprons.

When she was sharper his mother had joked about this collection. Afternoon tea at Mrs Turrell's, she'd say, like a UN meeting at the Playboy mansion. His mother had once been queen of the barbed story, the wicked quip, but illness had white-anted this part of herself. She'd lately grown dogged and literal; tunnelling deeper into some more temperate trait.

Now she'll stand on the threshold at Turrell's, date scones in her gloved hands, not seeing how overdressed she is for neighbours. It was after the commune she'd turned churchy, quickly shedding the cheesecloth and tie-dye, the tinkly anklets and nose-stud. And ever since has favoured skirt and jacket combos, high-necked blouses with bows and buttons her arthritic fingers can no longer master. Now – Sunday hats! Gloves supplied by the charity shop, impossible snub-toed, cube-heeled shoes. Her hair grew higher every day, scaffolded with pins, nets and sprays, haloed by its own toxic weather. Despite years of this, there remained something unpractised in her get-up – all that outdated tailoring and inexpert make-up – Tom often thought she looked like a person in drag.

He walks to the first bee hut. Something white, slotted in the entrance. The bees frantically zapping, trying to get in. Closer, he sees paper jammed inside. He pulls and twists, then opens the hinged lid and sticks one hand in the combs to get it out.

An envelope. On the front, instead of a stamp, one of those chemist reminder stickers for organising his mother's medication. *Monday*. Beneath this, an address and the half-familiar name of a man.

Mr Ian Tucker
Yellow Hill Holiday Park
155 Palms Road
Little Haven

Only the bees witness Tom's flamboyant rumba of surprise, one fist tugging the air, *YES!* From a distance you might think he'd been stung, the hand in the hive then fisted like that. Whoever posted it must surely know that native bees are stingless.

Tom scrawls a note for June, for his mother, then kicks the tyres on his old Ford, gladly noting their buoyancy.

Four hours' drive north of Bidgalong there he is, pottering about his caravan garden. Tom watches from his position outside the holiday park as the man fondles his green tomatoes, their skins cracked from lack of water, then weaves some starveling beans up a pole. Potatoes, wilting, aphid-infested broccoli. After a quick reconnaissance Tom had chosen this scrubby corner, half-screened by blazing wattle.

From here he can observe Ian Tucker weeding with one hand, taking his time about it, pausing frequently to smoke in such long, stertorous drags that his cigarette is in seconds more ash than Marlboro. He sits now in a rusting deckchair. Its canvas so low to the ground he might as well have put his arse right in the dirt. He reads the paper, folding it in quarters and holding it hard against his eyes. Racehorses. He puts some biro on the page and says aloud: Lucky Susan five to one. Through the caravan door, an oddly spotless kitchen, everything cleared, everything *shipshape*, a word that ambles into Tom's memory. *Everything shipshape, son, before your mother comes home*. Now and then a figure passing the caravan windows.

And there Ian sat, for pretty much the entire afternoon. Other residents coming and going, nodding, gesturing, saying little, but confirming that this was indeed Ian. Ian was top-notch, and feeling much better now, and look – he held out his arm, all healed up.

No more run-ins with plate glass then, Ian?

No, Stavros, not likely. Ian's laugh was short and wheezy.

There is, said this Stavros, such a thing as a door.

When you gotta go, though, eh? When a man's got debts he exits the fastest way he can.

Stavros laughed, and walked off, firing gun fingers at Ian Tucker's head.

Now a dry coughing comes from the caravan. Too deep, Tom thinks, for a woman.

Ian wears a baseball cap and his small grey, eczematic dog trots about, licking the skinny shin exposed when the man sits. Tom sees then how that body is a facsimile of his own – tall, slight, the hairless ghost-gum flanks. A face that matches the photo Tom found among his mother's things. A fair man standing beside a dark-haired boy, the kid's arm wrapped around the man's thigh. On the back, *Peter and Ian, Greendale*, 1980.

As Tom shuffles further behind the park perimeter, as he hops on one foot gone numb, the man removes his cap. On his bald head a long red scar. Beneath this, the sheared-off, geometric planes of his skull.

Tom stares and stares until he fears that Ian Tucker will detect the heat of his gaze through flowering Murraya on the last day of spring, through chain-link fence and heady, orange-scented air. *Those who are fatherless, think of me.*

Tom lines the two men up in his head. Hodgins v Tucker. And sees that Ian's no giant, no protector – this probable father – cruelled by illness, fate or accident, one withered arm uselessly dangling, his left eye swerving inward when he looks up suddenly now, as if the eye had come unhinged whenever the skull had.

The sound of coughing again, more intense this time, from inside the van.

You OK, son? Ian turns to the caravan door. Have a lemon water, buddy, put some manuka honey in, he says gently. And then he goes alert as an animal, then he stiffens and seems to hearken at a sound. It is his paler, younger boy; it's Thomas Adam Tucker, bolting away.

Tess will go out, on to the motorway. An act that was arrested, years back, before its completion. I dare you, Pip would say. All the sisters had by that stage of her illness were games, confined to the farm, to the house and finally, to the bedroom. And Meg and Tess had done their best to entertain her there; it was gold to make her laugh.

The third dare had been: walk along the Eastern Freeway without undies. Tess had gone through with it, waiting for passing semis to blow her dress right over her face. Every afternoon for one week.

Some days the traffic was jammed right along; the truckers call that a *parking lot*. Some days it was just *hood ornaments* – that's motorbikes, buzzing like hornets, paying her no attention. An eleven year old in a school uniform, blinking away her excited fright. But mostly you could rely on a big-rig to get the wind up, and whether they saw your bum in their rear visions wasn't really important. It was just the fact of having done it.

One afternoon, though, the headmistress drove by. When Pru Jackson saw a girl's bare arse and the school colours by the Edgeware turn-off, she veered her Renault right and braked. Tess, in the passenger seat with her knees pressed, put a Scout's hand up and vowed not to do it again. Her parents had enough troubles right now, with Pip so ill, Ms Jackson said, and Tess ought to know better.

I guess that's you, Meg said later in the bedroom, to Pip. You are *Troubles*, and they all flopped about, laughing. The girls called Pip this name for the next few weeks, hysterical whenever they said it because of how *Troubles* conjured Tess's pale, skinny bum on the highway, and Pip, up to so little in those bed-bound days, gloried in this amplified power.

In lesser dares Tess had mixed foul smoothies designed by Pip. Bananas, mustard, milk, salmon. Quinoa, peanuts, tomato sauce, tuna. Potion Afternoons. Tess would carry these cocktails into the bedroom and very gravely sip while Pip kept time to see how long before Tess retched or bolted to the bathroom.

Tess cut a hank of her hair, underneath, then shaved it right to the scalp. She ate a fly and went to school wearing her uniform inside out. She'd completed the Letterbox Challenges, with a final delivery of three live bees in a box to the Woolfs, the neighbours who'd complained, not long after moving from Brisbane, about the Müllers' irritating electric *farm noises*. If Pip would name it, Tess would do it. And the doing kept them all from thinking about what lay ahead: the autologous transplant, the sibling allo-graft and what these procedures meant for Pip, and for Meg, whose bone marrow was HLA-matched. The whole family rhesus negative, except Tess.

The next dare Pip made was: hitch-hike. Go as far as they'll take you.

They were in the bedroom, trying on some horrible hand-me-downs, scarlet flares with rhinestone-encrusted pockets. A babydoll smock striped with rick-rack, fit for a pregnant ten year old.

Meg looked from Tess to Pip, saying, Not hitch-hiking. *Nyet!*

Tess shrugged. Why not?

How could you even prove it? asked Meg.

I'll bring a souvenir from the chassis. Fluffy dice. A David Hasselhoff CD. A pack of NoDoz, Tess replied.

Some psycho might pick you up and dump you in the state forest, said Meg. You'll – she cast around – you'll have to eat at a truck stop from the bain-marie!

All three girls drew breath at that one.

Before the three-hour trips to and from St Catherine's, their mother had always packed sandwiches. And as they approached a Mobil or Shell, their father would enquire, Can I interest you in a little something, Lina, from the bain-marie? *Coq au vin? Boeuf bourguignon?* One day Pip had struck a deal. If *she* had to eat from the hospital trolley, it only seemed fair. So one evening, after saying goodbye to Pip, the family had stopped on the journey home to dine at Reg's Roadhouse, with its six-seater wipeable tables, and Dolly Parton sizzling through dented speakers. Under the fluoros with their cockroach silhouettes, the Müllers ate fried chicken wings, fried rice, greasy potatoes and what their father called murdered carrots. They toasted Pip with Raspberry Slurpees and ginger beer while Meg filmed it on their father's phone. They'd breathed easily that night, for the first time in months, as if they were a regular family out for a regular meal with the regulation amount of sadness.

When Pip came home again the girls would not go anywhere but school or medical appointments; their lives shrank to the bedroom. But Tess and Meg were rarely bored. It was Pip who hated stillness and required greater feats of entertainment, though later Tess wondered if Pip had really made these demands. Had Meg and Tess invented them just so they could feel useful?

Tess had always picked dare. But Meg went for truth.

One cranky day Pip said, You must sometimes wish I was gone already.

Don't be ridiculous, Tess replied.

But Pip, very intent, said, Meg chose truth.

No, said Meg, I thought we'd all live for ever.

When I go *you'll* be the youngest, Pip was pointing.

Big deal, said Tess, steering Meg away. You really think she cares about that?

Pip shuffled under the covers. The older girls stood in the burnished lamplight, blinking dully. Tess felt a weariness she did not think ought to belong to children. Outside a dank fog had swathed the house. They were drifting off then from everything dependably real.

She'll go out now and walk the highway. Should she leave a note? What had June said at The Hive? To make a person disappear was always popular. Such a trick helped people forget the lostness inside themselves. She recited this in the green tone of something freshly learned from a book. She'd been practising the Vanishing Woman for months, she said, with a sprung chair and some sculpted wire which looked, when rigged beneath a sheet, like a person was still sitting when really they'd gone by stealth through a lower trapdoor. As they rode home on the white mare, June shouted out the logistics of this and other magic. By Lunar Lake the horse slowed, and they watched the water building, the foamy crests on the jerky waves. It was then some half-stories had connected in Tess's head.

And now, as she plans her route down the highway, she thinks she's figured it out, *the whole silent landscape under a clouded or clear destiny – girls, this came before you.*

Who's her father? And why has everyone kept it from her, for all this time?

Three

... the individual must sacrifice himself for the race,
and substitute for visible things the things that cannot be seen.
Maurice Maeterlinck

Sylvie Bellamy strides through the market in maxi dress and silver sandals, bare-shouldered in the fierce morning heat. She hadn't expected such handsome women, she says, pointing to the queue at the Karma Massage tent and linking arms with Jim. The natural tans, and sun-gilded hair, the tautly compact yoga bodies. She'd imagined way more calico and dreads. Or muddied Blundstones and badly sawn hair. She thought everything would have the dull recycled patina of hippie DIY.

As she fills her basket from the biodynamic stall, Jim wanders off for coffee. But when he returns she's gone. He swings around, scanning the crowd in a minor panic. Then finally spots her. She's standing at the Honig Farm stall, face to face with Evangeline.

She'd turned up yesterday, unannounced. Well, Jim hadn't answered her texts or calls, how else could she forewarn him? She'd flown in from Sydney, then hailed an airport cabbie. Jim heard the whole saga as they sat on his porch in the evening. The goddamn journey, Sylvie said, the drunken yobbos delaying the plane, the turbulence and consequent spewing, the prognosticating cabbie on the drive to Bidgalong with his visions of frog rains or was it dogs or fish and his tarot garland obscuring the view. At the sugar cane burn-off – the exploding inner tube. And then, the electrical storm. Whether to sit in a cab while the driver changed the tyre in the rain? Or pass the jack, and hold the brolly? A modern woman's conundrum.

Finally at Fox's Lane, they'd pulled up short of the cabin. I wanted to surprise you, she told Jim, as if it wasn't enough to show up uninvited. But, as she stumbled in wedge sandals down the rutted road, she quickly regretted this tactic. Her wheeled case jammed in potholes and was soon talcumed in sticky dust; she'd nearly twisted an ankle in a burrow, which some confused creature had built *on the road*! Soon she'd passed that quaint farmhouse – the kind of double-fronted, sweeping-verandaed, fixer-upper her colleagues would mortgage themselves to for life, then saw the little huddled doll's houses in a field.

I thought it must be your place, she'd said to Jim. She'd felt ready to take up darning or the cold-fingered art of pastry. Then noticed the broad-shouldered blond tending cows in the twilight. Sort of sexy, she said, in his wide stance with his slow, curious wave. This, Jim realised, was Stefan. All that land, all those animals; Sylvie soon twigged it couldn't possibly be Jim's – let's face it, she said, you're just not that farmy.

When she reached his cabin, he was standing on the porch. It took an age, she said, for him to notice her, he was so intent on the farmhouse.

Hooroo! she'd called in mock country-fashion. Bet you can't guess who!

He visored his brow. Without his glasses, she was a butter-coloured blur. *Sylvie?*

He came slowly down the lane with his head tipped sideways and gave her an awkward hug. Then looked very stonily at her luggage.

Very brotherly, she said, with one hand on her hip.

Huh?

Your hug was very brotherly. Look, I know it's a surprise – but you never return my calls. And I don't have to stay here. Of course if you have a spare little cushion for me then – you probably only have your bed but...That's assuming you live alone, that you haven't moved on already, but if there *is* someone...

He watched and listened, waiting for her to exhale.

Inside they'd glanced around uneasily, as if both seeing the cabin anew.

Very cosy, she said.

He laughed, Meaning?

An adjective, she said. I think it means snug, or homely. Conducive.

To what? he asked as she flopped on the lumpen couch, then began scratching her thighs in their thin cotton skirt. She plucked at the hessiany fabric.

What is this, James? Horsehair?

From my neighbours' shed, he said.

The bee people?

She pointed out to the house and fields, all shimmering in the last scraps of daylight. It was so olde worldy! She'd completely forgotten farmers existed.

Yes, the Müller family, Jim said in his most schoolteacherly voice. He watched Sylvie's eyes dart, then stare. On the back of a door, the flowered robe.

I'm just assuming, she said, still eyeing the robe, that you haven't hooked up with anyone already.

Sylvie, he said. You turn up with no warning...

But she was examining her phone, frantically scanning the icons and apps, all promising to take her elsewhere, to do something with her unquiet mind.

The problem was that the body remained, didn't it – paining.

Now, as he sees Sylvie leaning over the Honig Farm stall, Jim attempts a saunter. He tries keeping a neutral face, swallowing the urge to shout and run.

Sylvie, eenie-meenie-miney-moeing the stacked honey jars, points a finger as Jim comes up beside her, and says, Bloodwood.

He's mouth-breathing, in a sweaty funk, his forearm scalded with spilt coffee.

Evangeline barely looks up as she wraps the honey, scrunching the yellow and black tissue. Impossible to read her serene face. Jim looks, instead, at Sylvie. Sooty under her eyes, because she hadn't slept well, she said, on his musty couch with the scratchy blanket. She'd had a fit of sneezing, and then of itching. And so, sometime before dawn, Jim had taken pity; he'd let her crawl on to his futon. Then went out on his bike so she could sleep in peace.

At breakfast that morning she'd promised, I'll find a hotel tomorrow. A premises with a day spa, wet-edge pool, thick white robes. Luxury products – Payot, Decléor. Someone to put their impersonal hands on her and pummel them up and down. They both knew she wasn't invented for the country.

Evangeline counts Sylvie's coins very deliberately into a tin. Jim decides she's trying not to look at him, her jaw pulsing at the angles. He downs his short black. He's been floating calmly since that dawn spliff by the lake. But hardly needs caffeine now to take the mellow off.

Sylvie, pointing into the stall, says, You ought to get a stool.

Evangeline rubs her belly. The taut skin beneath her shirt, so eerily translucent over the baby. Has he ever touched anything more erotic in his life?

In this heat. You must get tired? Sylvie sounds hopeful.

I'm pregnant, Evangeline says. Not disabled.

Jim, drawing breath, looks very concertedly away. Then braces himself.

It's just that – when *I* was pregnant, Sylvie says. Don't you remember, Jim? I felt sick all day. Just lay there eating buttered Saos till you came over. Now even the Arnott's logo makes me ill. The rainbow lorikeet, the wheat stalk. Ugh! And I can't eat butter any more, though it's back in vogue, have you noticed?

Evangeline's eyes go stony.

Jim feels it rippling through him – his confused loyalties, the dope and coffee. He has an urge to rend a hank of his own hair.

Sylvie smooths her fringe to one side. When he returned from cycling that morning, he'd found her in lacy underwear, straightening her hair in the kitchen. She looked shocked when he walked in, like a 1950s wife who must hide her ablutions from her husband.

Anyway, I miscarried, Sylvie's saying now.

I'm sorry, says Evangeline. But doesn't sound it.

Jim, thinking he must have misheard, turns around slowly.

By now, Sylvie says, it would have been … I mean *we* could have been …

…A family, says Evangeline, looking at Jim. But you still have plenty of time.

Jim, blasted with the chill of exposure, is soon frozen by another thought. *Miscarried* – is that really what Sylvie just said?

But Sylvie's wearing her silencing look, her lips gone thin and bloodless. He puts a hand on her neck, tries steering her away.

You wanted sourdough, remember, he says at top volume. The good stuff's usually gone by nine so we'd better …

But Sylvie is ignoring him. *You* must be due any day!

A few more weeks, says Evangeline.

And Jim sees that she is privately absorbed and completely unmoved by this glimpse of his history. The disappointment is so crushing, he can hardly bear it. He tosses the coffee cup, missing the bin. His eyes begin to throb. He has a sudden memory of running a playground to hide uncontrollable tears. And another, from school camp, of balling wet pyjamas and burying them in a backpack. In the spidery night, through dense scrub, the toilet block had been another continent.

But you look so much more … Sylvie's saying. How exciting!

Another pregnant woman passes in a beaded choli. Her exuberant health, her nut-brown belly, bared from navel to hip, seems a provocation to them all.

Looks like there's an epidemic, Sylvie says, of babies. And, well, *fucking* of course. In Sydney everyone I know seems to be on IVF.

Not much fucking in the city then? says Evangeline. Have they forgotten *how*? And she casts Jim a sly, cryptic look.

Both women laughing now. Jim thinks he might be sick. He feels as if someone has knifed him clear from groin to throat. Soon his guts will spill on to the market table.

Shouldn't joke about IVF, Sylvie says, it'll probably be my fate. And then she tips against his chest.

Are you all right? Evangeline raises an arm. You're super-pale.

Sylvie clutches the table with both hands. Then bends to rifle frantically through her basket.

Vertigo, she murmurs, then comes up with sunglasses and a bottle of pills.

Jim offers a small back pat, but he can't get over how she's just lied, or misspoken. Had she chosen the word miscarriage just to mask the more morally awkward truth?

He scans the market for some private space as his feelings swell. But he won't cry – not for their child, a mere idea, suppressed; not for his mother; not for Evangeline and her memorial tree with its tiny shoes; not for this new baby belonging entirely and only to her. He'll always be at the mercy, he realises, of some woman's decision about family. He is powerless to summon it alone.

Let's get you some water, he tells Sylvie, sit you somewhere shady.

But she's still so intent on Evangeline.

Thanks for the honey, she says weakly, dry-gulping a pill. Then leans over the market table.

Don't you think it's strange, she asks, with Jim allergic to bees, I mean – moving next door to something so potentially fatal?

Tommy, sit.

Evangeline gestures to a kitchen chair. She looks tired and dishevelled, the baby's growing fast and she is carrying low. Something has happened to her chin that he guesses will unhappen when the kid is born.

He looks at the framed paintings on the kitchen shelves, the flowers drooping in vases, the sunken candles on the mantel. When the Müller girls were younger, and he'd visited more often, when he'd been just like family as Evangeline said, they were always busy, mucking about with old shoeboxes, string and tape, and the results were plausible, noteworthy. The sisters' word for these: *creations*, and how their mother displayed them, on small tables with lamps trained on, turned the most incomprehensible or minimal sculpture aureate. All that care – he'd wanted to be part of it – the wonder and the noticing. But after Pip's death the Müllers had asked not to be disturbed.

After The Hive he'd had nothing from his childhood; everything had burned. Even his beloved storm glass had shattered in the heat.

Stefan round?

He's taken the hives to Rossdale, she says. It's boiling bees up there, apparently.

Not the canola? Isn't he worried about the neonics?

Tom stops himself droning on. The other day someone at the market called him a *doomsayer*, and last week Dr Paulson suggested that the preoccupations in his *Survival Report* could be adding to his depression. He'd had a copy at the ready and tapped page three with his Pfizer biro. Why does one need a simple wire snare loop? Why publish instructions on how to make a stone adze? Thomas, if the Apocalypse comes do you really think all our technological knowhow will just disappear?

And then, after his trip to find Ian Tucker, Tom binned his script. He's been cold turkey on the Venlafaxine for two weeks now. Restless legs, dizzy spells, night sweats, but worse, the sudden electric zaps in his brain. The terrible nightmares, full of scenes from The Hive. Jack Hodgins with a giant hand on Evangeline. Infants in the nursery, beneath a solid shelf of smoke. Some recurring fly-like figure in a motorbike helmet. I believe in nature, Tom told Dr Paulson. What else could a person cling to? And where else had he experienced such wonder as on a clifftop conducting a cloud spectre, marvelling at mackerel skies, or skimming the pebbled floor of Repentance River with the young Evangeline.

They'd once been so fearless. Now he's on the ginseng, the St John's wort, the Omega 3s. Each morning he anoints himself with spikenard, two drops on the solar plexus. He'd thought life would get easier, that on exiting the commune, like emerging from a coma, he'd enter a world shining with possibility. Instead, it was desiccating around him.

Subjects of Hope: that's what he overhears the teens saying as they wait at the crossing. That's what they want to study now.

He gulps his tea, scalding his throat. Fresh bread on the Müllers' kitchen bench. Actual wildflowers, in non-jar vases. His place, since he'd packed his mother's things, is even more stricken-looking than when she'd been inside calling everything the wrong names, compulsively zapping the air with fake lavender, hyacinth. She'd grown terrified of stinks and germs, flushing the toilet till the water turned an unearthly blue. But she didn't realise she was their primary source, refusing to get in the *water coffin* as she called the bath. Sometimes, mid-negotiation with this new child-mother, he had an urge to fall laughing to the floor, to weep and chuck heavy breakable things; sometimes her condition was a kind of contagion.

He pictures her, stretchered after the final bad fall, badgering the paramedics and calling out. Peter would never have abandoned her! she said. Tom had ignored her. He'd gently stroked her clammy hand against her will through the long ride to the hospital.

There were often serious, regressive dementia episodes after accident or illness, Dr Paulson said. But even if she levels out, it's time for the 24/7 care.

Gah. Evangeline puts a hand at her side and leans against the bench.

He leaps up. Are you? Having it?

No, it's weeks off, just … Braxton Hicks.

Do you remember my mother ever talking about someone called Peter? he asks.

She straightens, blinking fast, starts slicing carrots, celery. Back to him, knife in her hand. Thwack, thwack, chop. Some pieces flying.

I've pretty much forgotten the Peter I knew, she says.

She opens the fridge which casts a polar glow across her bare feet.

Was it you I saw at the teacher's house? Tom asks. Very early, foggy morning, the other week?

She turns slowly.

He's a neighbour, she says.

Just rumours then?

As she narrows her eyes Tom winces, ashamed. He is so hungry for everything she has – family, love, sex, children – all the riches of entanglement. Even the affair, if that's what it is, gives her life greater meaning, substance. His is cauterised. He can't leave his mother alone in the Home, move away, start over. Who'll look out for her? His life in town as futureless as in the commune.

Look, he says, I work on my reports, my website. I'm a lollipop man. Big fucking woop in my high-viz vest. Now I've got Sunday visits to the dementia ward. Apparently I have a father. Brain-damaged from a tumour. He wouldn't even recognise you, my mother says when I asked her. Coming from her that's funny – she's the one who calls me Peter. I could use some family. No one else will tell me about him. Not even Nora.

Finally, she sits beside him. Why ask Nora?

I heard they had a thing – her and Peter. He dossed down with her for a while, or so José says.

Evangeline goes pale.

He shakes out a Marlboro, matches it.

She stares. You smoke now? Look, I thought I knew your brother, she says, sweat on her temples. He was sweet, but wild. We had no future together. After the baby came I asked him to stop visiting The Hive. Then once I started seeing Stefan, he never forgave me.

But … how come I never saw him! Tom says. My mother never even said!

Evangeline shrugs. He didn't announce himself when he came up there. He and his friend were skulkers.

Then she stands, kneading her side, breathing hard, saying, Ow.

They were using. Dope – meth – something, she says. On the day of the fire they turned up, really high. Peter said he'd come to take what was his.

Tom draws hard on the cigarette, searches around, then ashes the tip in his palm. I don't understand, he says. What was that?

My baby, she says. Tess.

They shoved me in their van. They wanted to spook me.

Now she grows silent, very compact.

He swallows, did they do something to you?

I fought them off! she says brightly. Lost a tooth see, she taps the white incisor. No big deal.

And that's all she can say for now, she tells him. Because it takes a toll – all this remembering. She has to save her energy. Pretty soon, the new baby. In fact, even now, these contractions…

He stands, lopes down the hall and in the toilet vomits twice. He leans on the basin and stares at the mirror. His breath constricted, his heart swamped with speeding blood. Thinks about leaving the front way, unseen. How long has he been in here, sweating madly, struggling for air? The tap runs and runs but he does not heed the wasted water because the sound is soothing. This is how it is then, to actually feel. After months cotton-balled in Venlafaxine, he's newly raw and unprotected.

Tommy?

She calls quietly, puts her head against the bathroom door. Distraught men in bathrooms, alone. Such things happened to them in those novels of Scandi noir – they ran taps to disguise precarious business; they climbed out windows or located razors; they were seen many hours later in different territories with new clothes and hair. When Tom was a kid, he'd risked his life carrying her baby from danger then running back into that fire. He'd done almost anything she'd asked. She owes him the truth. But shouldn't Tess be told first, before it comes to her sideways, warped by embellished report? Who her father is, what exact variety of man?

Be a minute! Tom calls.

And squints at the red face in the mirror, pitted from teenage acne, his large, blue unseeing eyes. He really is just a fucking drone. That's what Hodgins had called him once. Until he'd run from the nursery with Tess and set the fire alarm. After that, some called him a hero. And he had not disabused them. Maybe he'd saved Tess, but he'd abandoned those other babies. Still, he'd let the story of his manly feats run its course; he'd taken praise and a little glory.

Now, it seems, he has a brother. Hold fast to that, he tells himself. But why would Peter want Evangeline's baby?

A sudden image. Evangeline, backlit by flames, and running.

On the basin, three flower soaps. Waxy gardenias in a bowl. The little touches, axing his heart. He rubs his hands on the Müllers' green towel, buries his face in it. The scent of young women with their whole lives ahead drowns out his stale yearning. He turns off the tap. Still dripping. Sticks his head under, then dismantles the whole contraption. An abraded washer probably.

3

Datsun, Subaru, Hyundai; Tess watches the colours fade now the highway lights are gone. Would Pip have become a girl like this, out in the dark on a sister's dare? No, Tess thinks. Pip wasn't dreamy, she'd have said this was stupid. Probably her dare had been a joke.

The centre line of reflective lozenges casts a pitiful glow along the road. Should have brought a torch, Tess thinks, or at least taken her mother's phone from where it's stored on a high shelf, the harmful rays well away from their tender brains. Should have worn something warmer than T-shirt and shorts.

Now the sun's heat has passed from the tar, and the path, at first lined with shady trees and verges, has dissolved into a mean, shoulder-less highway. Now she must walk on the road to avoid the razor grass and bramble. Her narrow hips in tattered denim, her thin arms batting flies and moths, her eyes searching the scant moonlight.

Where does she really belong? Is her whole self a lie? Where has she come from? Does she even want to know? Her mother had carried her away from that burning mountain when she'd been just a baby, June said, but it seemed impossible. As they rode the steep mountain trails on June's horse, Tess became mired more deeply in silence. She'd had to hold tight to June's hips to keep from tipping off that Appaloosa. That night at the cold supper, she'd examined her family, a bunch of strangers now you thought about it, with unmatched hair and eyes. She stared at her father the longest, chewing with his half-open mouth, the full glass beside his plate, the bottle also on the table. And felt a tiny fury. Her mother was idly studying her nails. Meg was kicking her shins beneath the chair. No one with a sec to tell her the actual truth.

Tess's father, catching her burning look, had said, What? Then tossed his knife and fork, muttering, *this family*, and left. Tess saw her sister's eyes fill; she watched Meg gnaw her lower lip. Her mother's face was very pinched, one hand on that belly. Another child for her touch, Tess thought, the baby already drawing her mother's attention. Sometimes she had a fantasy of popping that stomach with a hurled fork, of her mother zipping through the air and slowly deflating.

Their father came back in for the bottle, then strode outside again.

Here we go, their mother said.

Had they all known? Had Pip, taking the secret with her? If I was born on the commune, why lie about it? thought Tess, scanning Meg's body for signs and clues. Tess knew she looked nothing like her father but Pip was the dead spit, their mother said, of their father's mother, Gretchen, a distant German *Oma* they'd never got to meet.

Tess's silence is bound up with this, walking along the shadowy highway with her hand outstretched, and one thumb up, carrying nothing but a cross-body bag into which she'd shoved ten dollars twenty.

Cars pass and she wills them not to slow, though when it's over, the worry will be gone. Worse waiting to find out what type will pick her up and where they'll want to take her.

It's one thing to risk being lost, quite another to be found. Mr Parker had said this gently. Then asked her to try first person in her journal. And she'd wondered, who's that? before remembering how in *Robinson Crusoe* everything was seen through I.

I found, under my mother's pillow, some baby clothes that once belonged to my youngest sister. I found, in her drawer, the small envelopes of our baby hair and teeth. Everywhere mixed with my mother's things were the things of all her daughters.

The amplified sound of a dog barking in a house or garage. Tess's feet pound, and her pulse, and she concentrates on these rhythms to distract herself from what she's set out to do. Small points of brightness appear – distant houses, streetlights – reminding her of the deeper dark when only stars or tail-lights will mark her out on the unlit roads.

Soon she hears an engine slow. It can't be large from how it sounds, she thinks, it has a humming smoothness. Definitely not a truck. As it draws alongside she watches the passenger window go slowly down, electric.

You right there, girly? Where you headed?

A luminous plastic hand suctioned to the dashboard. Its up-yours finger pointing skyward. From the car radio, she hears a song about fire and rain and she is suddenly aware of what she's doing and what she's done.

4

Meg's fed up waiting for the right things to happen. At night she grinds her teeth. She's supposed to wear a plate. It makes her feel she'll choke. It makes her feel muzzled as a dog. Each morning a pain crackles from jaw to temples. I hope it's not hereditary, her father says, passing her frozen peas in a flannel, so Meg knows, *she* must be his. Or he wouldn't say *that*, would he?

She rides out now past the new development because she can't think where else to go. Tess had not returned and her mother had come home, then at nine pm gone back out searching.

If you know what's going on with Tess, tell me now, she'd asked before leaving.

Meg, sick of always saying what her sister would not, shrugged, sighed, raked fingernails through her tidy hair. But it was impossible to escape her mother's stare so she said, experimentally,

Nora phoned. Asking about the dead man. Says she no longer thinks it's a person called Peter and that you'd like to know.

Her mother stepped back. What's that got to do with your sister going off?

How'd I know?

When Meg had finished blinking her mother was gone. Outside on the porch – her umbrella – even though the sky was very low and bloated, and way off you could already see the fine needles of rain.

Just ask your mum if she's seen Pete lately, Nora had said.

Ask her yourself, Meg replied.

OK, put her on, Nora said.

She's not here.

We both knew him, said Nora. If he's dead she'd know. If he's alive that changes everything, especially for Tess.

Here she goes, the smallest in her family, fiercely pedalling along the fresh bitumen of Borrodale Road, hunched over handlebars, squinting into the dark. The rain falls in a gauzy curtain, then swells, hammering the ground. Meg, quickly drenched, cycles out to where the blond, identical houses are replicating, past golf-course gardens, the monster cars behind SilentGlyde garage doors. Meg strikes the bell on her bike and sees with glee lights flash on in three houses and curtains jerking and a figure at an open door, beaking into the street.

Nora will tell her everything. But when Meg pulls up at her house it's dark. Beside it, the vast lake pitted with rain. Nora's Corolla gone from the drive. Probably in the pub, getting hammered. Getting smashed. Getting liquored up, pissed, 86ed. Getting gourded or shickered. *Ich bin sinnlos betrunken*, said her father one stumbling winter afternoon.

Meg sits on the porch, then jimmies a window with a garden fork and climbs in, landing on a tower of boxes. As her eyes adjust she sees the room is packed to the ceiling with stuff. A smell of Nag Champa and mint. She feels along one wall, smacking her shins into piles and stacks until she finds the light-switch. Some kind of storage area? But every room in the house is crammed with furniture and objects, magazines, books. In the kitchen she makes an almond-butter sandwich, sniffing all the bottles on a shelf. Whisky, rum, gin, bourbon. Empties sentried along the bench. Not all chaos. Every pile is tidily stacked, there's no grime or dust. But why keep so many things?

Meg swigs the Grey Goose and then, in the lounge, pokes around Nora's desk. Boring papers. Bulldog clips. Staples. More mini bottles in a drawer. She pockets two, unopened. But hold on – photos. Mum and Nora, arm in arm. People at The Hive with spades, smoking. One of Dad! On the back, someone's written *Stef, 1990*. Who calls him that? And then, her mother standing with some other women, all pregnant. Meg peers at the background, the familiar rustic cabins, her mother's clear, untroubled expression. Pregnant with who? Meg takes another swig, though it tastes like something witches have invented.

Beside the desk, on the wall, a poem. She reads it twice.

Lord, the air smells good today, straight from the
  mysteries within the inner courts of God.
A grace like new clothes thrown across the garden, free
  medicine for everybody.
The trees in their prayer, the birds in praise, the first blue
  violets kneeling.
Whatever came from being is caught up in being,
  drunkenly forgetting the way back.

One man turns and sees his birth pulling separate from
  the others.
He fills with light, and colours change here.
He drinks it in, and everyone is wonderfully drunk,
  shining with beauty.

I can't really say that I feel the pain of others, when the whole world seems so sweet.

And then, as Meg saunters through the house, emboldened by vodka, Rumi follows: *Birth pulling separate from the others. Whatever came from being is caught up in being.* She wonders about the drunkenly forgetting, picturing Nora staggering down the main street. Her father pulling over to drive her home. *Don't tell your mother, Meg, she'll only get upset.* Nora had repeated *Ich bin sinnlos betrunken* and laughed. Her bare feet curled on the front seat making her seem even younger than the girls, her sudden weeping frightening them. The feeling, later, of holding the secret reminded Meg of the day the pressure cooker exploded and the boiling stew hit the roof; of how she and Tess had stifled their excitement in the face of their mother's dismay.

In Nora's bedroom a bed so immaculately made that Meg tiptoes around it.

She climbs back out the window with the bottle, and from the porch watches the moon rise behind the pines and go ballooning in the sky. She turns to the black water, the steely rain, then sits, crossing and uncrossing her small knees, waiting for lake music. But there's only an insect tick between downpours. No harp sounds or electric wires. No celestial sounds or human voices, which Nora's heard. Last April, hundreds of fish had leapt from the lake. With Tess she'd biked out to watch them dying onshore, their mouths full of sand and pointless air. Meg looks back to see the waves burnished with luminescence. She scans the purple-black bent-over trees, the bushes crouched around the house, the buttery roses and stephanotis. All throbbing with expectancy. She cranes around to the back of the property and sees an odd shape dangling from Nora's clothesline.

It can't be? She clambers up. A body, chopped at knees and neck? Then her heart slows. A wetsuit, hung out to dry. Still, it's weird – everyone knows Nora doesn't swim. A man's wetsuit, Meg thinks, looking at the proportions.

Cold air constricts her throat. She sees the escalating rain, how the lake is lapping already at Nora's yard. She frisks her wet self for the inhaler, then remembers it's back inside by the empties. She's drunkenly forgetting, her breath obstructed, her flesh glowing like burning wax, as the tide comes surging across Nora's front lawn.

5

Where you headed then, missy?

Tess shifts in the passenger seat. The belt welts her neck as she strains towards the window, away from the man's onion scent. Hard rain beats the car, blurring the road ahead.

I'm off to look at some stallions, he says. They breed them super-fast at the Golden Stables. Superior outfit, 'bout yay far past the Jericho Swamplands. Very fine racing horses.

His right hand rests lazily on the wheel, the other raking a bulgy thigh. Tess stays quiet, inventories the car. Itchy-looking backseat blanket, empty chip bag, carton of strawberry Moove with gnawed straw. Freckled sausage-fingers, petrol-station sunglasses taped on one side, a quarter head of gingery hair. A compulsive snorter, a sinusy voice. A whole story, right here, for Pip.

Name's Edwin P. Murphy, but she can call him Murph.

He fumbles for something, inverts a tube of mints, scraping one out with teeth. His top lip, peeled back like that, reminds Tess of horses. She doesn't know whether to laugh or cry. Murph! So she stays very fixed on the road as if she's the driver, not him swivelling his head, yawning, switching the high beam on and off to see the way better in the rain, adjusting his seat so he's leaning right back, with his arms straight out towards the wheel. The rain slows as they pass an occasional house, and an old, dented phone box with its receiver hanging like someone's just bolted, mid-conversation. They pass stables and barns and rusty hay-balers and now a long stretch of nothingland. She hasn't eaten since morning and feels hollow and unreal.

He twists his head, asking, What's that? as the car jumps the kerb and bumps back on to the road again.

On the rear window, see? he says. Fly, wasp? It's not a hornet, is it?

Tess cranes around but can only hear the innocent buzzing, the insect body butting something. From the sound, though, she can pretty much tell.

Wind your window, girly, so it can escape.

Rain spits in and her arm is soon wet and cold. Outside there's a clean, stony scent, as if from the stars. We're part of that, her father had said. We're part stardust, did you know?

Her father. Which isn't even a fact any more.

The flies they got round these parts bite, he says. Horseflies. Doesn't *sound* like a fly.

Edwin flips off the radio. Listen carefully, he says. We'll find the bastard.

Tess folds her hands, crosses her legs, subtracting herself. She might have vanished from her questionable family, but now the bug-eyed gaze of Murph. Harder than she'd thought to simply disappear.

Fields of electricity towers, like space beings stalking with arms up; their wires powering TVs, computers and electric tooth-brushes, iPhones, blenders, porch lights. All the houses, darkened, with their people and their machines turned off inside. Think about it, Mr Parker had said, how we live is nothing like our parents did. When you turn on a tap, a heater, the world's limits rush into your house. We're so much more aware than they were, of our limited resources.

Tess thinking of *limited resources* pictures Pip, running out of tomorrows, confused to the end, about the limits of today.

Where are your bags then? Where you staying? You got family waiting?

Murph swats wildly at the air.

Jesus, girl, it is a bee! You didn't even say!

Tess tries not to laugh as he bats at the insect, only making it angrier of course and more likely to sting. She goes very calm and wonders where the bee's from, maybe in the car the whole journey, perhaps even a city bee, happier and healthier, Tucker claims, because the cities are greener now than the country. Country life is what damages you: the unreported mine leaks, the rolled tractors, the pesticides. At Vinegar Hill, your mother says, the kids stay inside to avoid lead poisoning from the smelter. You cannot hang your washing, or let your babies crawl on the ground. You can't grow veggies because of lead in the soil, air and grains. You mean some other country? Meg asked. No, said your mother, a small town just a few miles away.

... I sold her when she was twenty, he says. But she was strong for ten more years. Then he turns to her slowly and asks, How old are you then?

Tess stares at the fogged horizon. She holds up two hands, then another.

He nods, squinting. Underage, he says. *Illegal.* A bit of spit goes flying.

Tess, sliding closer to the passenger door, feels the solemn thudding inside her chest.

Quite a few never wore out. The large one, Sukie, she was whip-smart, and the red roan ran like the wind. I called him Windy.

Krazy Town Alert! If Meg were here they'd be pissing themselves, but Tess pities him, something seems ajar in his head. She grows drowsy, listening. She pinches her arm to stay awake.

Tess drifts, picturing her mother's paintings, the horses huddled in a deep field, one blindfolded. The bits she'd repainted, with the past showing through. Then recalls that cloud, suspended by an artist in a stately room. Mr Parker had shown it to her. He'd called her in from the hall where he'd found her alone, eating an apple and watching the school clock wrenching its slow hands through the lunch hour. An artist who must also be a chemist, he'd said as they'd puzzled over it. And then he turned very suddenly to face her and said, Tess, I don't believe your silence actually belongs to you.

Her eyes had darted around frantically then. Inside her chest, a searing. Everyone seemed to know something of her inner life, though she'd tried so hard to brick it up.

…That one was a dun with a black mane. I never saw such an animal, very deep-chested, quite long of tail.

Tess's eyelids grow heavy; the vehicular air is close and depleted, smelling of peanuts, and now of roast chicken, of the thousand meals that have passed through Murph's car.

When she wakes, the car's empty and still. The world beyond, liquid dark. That prickly blanket tightly wrapped around her body. She yawns and sees, in the cold cabin, her own white breath suspended. Remembers that cloud artist and thinks, well, anyone can make such a work. You only have to exhale in the right kind of weather. It gives her a delightful second of hope.

She searches the dark beyond the car and, now fully awake, remembers to worry and fear. She turns to the black block of unlit house. The man has completely vanished. But has she?

6

Evangeline in the kitchen, under harsh pendant light, flicks through Tess's schoolbook, frantic now for clues or signs. She's soaked to the skin after dashing from the farm to Jim's to ask – had he seen Tess, had something happened at school? Jim would say nothing, or had nothing to say. And hadn't he suggested, some days back, that his loyalties were divided? Even more since that Sydney woman, using up all the air in his cabin.

How about her friends? Jim had asked.

And when Evangeline replied, She doesn't exactly *have* friends, the ex-girlfriend's lovely face was racked.

Young girls go off, Sylvie said, when finally recomposed. That's what they do. And if there's family trouble?

Evangeline sensed this was not rhetorical. But was suddenly struck by an image of Peter. How long since she'd last seen him sauntering out of a shop in town, then boarding a bus at the corner? More than two years surely. She'd marched over to Jim's work table then, with the woman's gaze searing her back, and searched till she found the journal she'd given Tess years ago. If you cannot say it, then write it. Some empty maxim from her own childhood: *better out than in*, as if emotions, contained, were a force for ruin.

It's after nine. Meg, out looking. Stefan, driving the bees. And Tess? Evangeline stands at the table now, head bent, wet hair glued to her neck, and turns the pages. She gnaws a fingernail, shifts from foot to foot, redistributing baby weight, easing the sacral muscle spasms. She's ticking, on the verge of a cry or scream, full of anticipatory restlessness. She reads it over again, lips moving, one finger travelling beneath each word, this account of a time she'd not been part of, this glimpse of Daughterland.

Undertow

Ever since she was small, Pip had confused her todays. Every morning she'd want to know, 'Is it tomorrow, Tessie, or yesterday?' You marked time by what she could see from her window. The day of Watery Sun and Cumulo Nimbus. The Blustery Day of Bowing Trees. The day of Three Wombats and a One-armed Joey.

This one night Pip woke and said yesterday was too far off and she wasn't tired AT ALL. 'You mean tomorrow,' said Meg, yawning. It was past midnight so tomorrow had come already and now it was today. There was no weather to describe to Pip that night. Only stars pricking the sky. 'How many?' Ten thousand, you told her. 'Lots more but we just can't see them.' 'What are their names?' You looked them up and read them out until she closed her eyes. Zaurak, Zavijah, Zibal.

Yesterday came and went, for everyone but Pip. She hovered, not awake or asleep for three more days. She took no food or water. You told her the story about the lost and injured man who crawled for days and nights down a mountain till he found the light of safety. He crossed a glacier, and in his thirst he heard running water. He crossed the hard snow on his belly until he could no longer tell when his days became tomorrows and he began to feel part of the mountain, the ten thousand stars, the rocks and the dirt. Zaniah, Zuben Elakrab, Zuben Elakribi, Zuben Egenubi, Zuben Elschemali. No today, no tomorrow, no yesterday. Just Pip's breath and the wheeling stars. In another room your father's crooked beeswax candles were burning slowly down.

At first, Evangeline scans for one word only, thirsty as that crawling man for her youngest's name, for any new fact on the child she's lost. But when she rereads it she hears a sound gone missing from their lives for so long. She hears Tess recording what was lost and what might still be saved.

7

Before Stefan takes the northern exit, he heads up the mountain to see what he's seeding, what he has sown. His farm bees are stacked on the truck. They'll do their work under the avocados, eight hours north where the sun beats in a flat plane. Fifty hives left on the farm. But first he wants to check the wild bees in the elevated air. Wild swarms are naturally driven to build comb. Trucked bees get stressed by their journeys. Which colony will fail? Which, if any, will thrive?

As he grinds the gears on the Upper Mountain Road he thinks of that wreck on its lower reaches. The coroner had deemed the death suspicious. Plastic-wrapped drugs and money had been found in the back of the van.

They were both called in – he and Lina – separate rooms. Nora had given the police a name, Peter Tucker, and said he was known to the Müllers also. In fact, she said, *related*.

Had he ever laid eyes on such a van? the detective asked. White Hyundai, plates DMG 765.

Stefan sat with the plainclothes man in the airless chamber, walled with the stench of sweat, air freshener and cigarettes. He said there were many such vans around the mountains, every second backpacker hired one.

How about the man that was in the van, and now dead?

The detective showed him an identikit. It looked yeti-like, in the way of such things, it looked barely human. Was it Peter? Or Gus? Stefan struggled to recall either face. He shook his head, shrugged. But swallowed.

Interesting fact, the detective said, the deceased did not seem to have been the driver. The driver had fled perhaps, or gone for help and disappeared, leaving his dead or injured associate. Yet the wreck was never reported. The drugs and money were left behind. And no one had witnessed the accident or filed a Missing Persons. The crash wasn't so far from Honig Farm. There must have been noises, comings and goings, after.

You heard and saw nothing? the detective asked.

Is a big property, said Stefan. I don't farm every corner. Actually I have never been before in that section.

The detective blew his nose theatrically.

I'm often away, Stefan said. The bees, you see, what I have to drive. I'll ask my wife if she heard anything...

The policeman tore open a pack of Fisherman's Friend.

Your wife had amnesia after the fire? A head injury? How was she wounded?

A long story, said Stefan. I'm sure she tells it better than me.

Then he asked for water. Showed the pills. The room had begun to flare and pulse. His right eye swam with dark, oily blots.

I have a script, Stefan said. Migraine. So, nothing unlegal here.

It's illegal, said the detective. The word is illegal, Mr Müller, not *unlegal*.

Stefan dry-swallowed the pill, coughed. He had nothing to hide but a minor infidelity. But the real story – of Peter and the fire – was his wife's to tell.

We did a sweep. In the back of the van, said the detective, we found a tooth.

Stefan pictured Pip's incisor, set in gold, which Evangeline wore around her neck.

And then he knew the whole scenario as he heard them say, *it is a match with your wife*, and he wondered again if it was Pete or Gus who'd died in that crash – neither had been seen around town for so long. And he tried not to hope – because the thought alone made him culpable – tried not to wish that it was the father of his child.

Stefan checks his phone as he changes gears on the incline – a message, two familiar numbers. Nora Roberts. Lina. Then the screen fades. No reception up here, or it's the battery. He sticks an arm into the mountain air. Even the bees in the ute have gone silent now, sensing the altitude perhaps, or saving energy for the feed ahead.

Twenty minutes later at The Hive, he stands by the rocky escarpment and looks down into the valley. The farm grids, partly shadowed under a shelf of cloud, the threads of river and tributaries, the eerie planes of Lunar Lake. He'd never liked swimming there. That lake mysteriously draining and filling. He does not like things without pattern or season, he needs to believe in these or how else will he farm? Rain driving in slanted lines on all the houses. Up here, though, it's very dry. A faint eucalypt scent slinging him back to when he'd first visited Evangeline at The Hive.

The memory comes in fragments: her waist-length hair around his fist; her long neck, arching back; her belly still soft from the pregnancy; the beat of a high, hot mountain sun. And the baby, who he'd soon call his, falling silent as she was put to the breast. All three, lying in sweet, dry grass. A new contentment, a revelation – this instant family. It had felt bestowed by some higher order, it had felt entirely natural. But Tess's father would arrive at The Hive, then hover, pissed off because Evangeline had changed her mind: she hadn't given up the baby, she'd given him away instead.

This new family had been the counterpoint and balm to the other strobing scenes in Stefan's head: his father with a hand at his mother's throat, or bending him out a fifth-floor window to make her beg. It had been his brother, Gerhard, who'd shown how he ought to feel. From Gerhard's horrified gaze, Stefan learned emotions he'd not been capable of mustering for himself.

Hasn't thought of Gerhard for some time. He'll look him up when he gets home. Maybe visit. Hamburg, is it? Bonn? It's time to tend his mother's grave, to skirt the borders of where his father's still living. Talk with Gerhard about anything but the past. *Gemütlichkeit*, the word comes back, and the unthinking way his mother had used it, even though nothing in the house had been cosy, or nice; everything had been utterly fucked.

Now, as he crosses the grass at The Hive, calm. Up here he'd found a woman educated in little but peace. In those early years he'd never heard her raise her voice. The limited facts she had about the world astonished him. But he did not disabuse her – he needed to believe in her purity, her quaint faith. How she took her clothes off, so natural! A man and a woman in the long grass, God-made, essential. He's fed off that memory for years but it can no longer replace reality. A woman who no longer wants to share her body, wants him to insult her while *using it*, as she says. Her new circuitous route to pleasure. He can't fool himself any more. After the fire and her forgetting, and then, after Pip – she'd become, like his mother, another woman bearing the unbearable. It was not the men, she said to him once, who'd damaged her most. Before losing Pip it had not been the men, but the fire.

He looks out beyond The Hive. An opalescent sky. Through a rent in the banking clouds he can just see into the stormy valley. He picks out the farmhouse, the tiny grove of hives, now the band of the creek, wider than usual, sees the cows in a place they oughtn't be. They must have trampled the electric fences; is the power out? It takes a while for his eyes to adjust and then, the realisation: he's looking at a maelstrom. Great cliffs of cloud massing in the north and east, and now a sudden, swift stream of vapour dropping the temperature. Up here he's at the eerily tranquil apex of a coming storm.

8

Before their mother returned from searching, Meg arrived at the empty farmhouse, drenched from the lake, with her teacher. It was nearing midnight. Mr Parker had doubled her on his bike all the way from Nora's – and the journey through dark streets, teetering on handlebars with the oiled whirr of his pedalling behind her, was surreal and wondrous. Had she ever felt that pure relief of rescue? She'd waded, wheezing, alone through black water while he came towards her, hands out. Nora's porch was ten centimetres under. Meg's inhaler nowhere to be found.

Once home they stood in the empty kitchen wondering where Evangeline had gone in her searching. Meg found her spare puffer and sucked the cold Ventolin down. She took her wet clothes off in the bedroom and when she returned found the teacher on the porch.

Mr Parker coughed hard when Meg offered some of her father's dry clothes, smiled awkwardly, then declined. He stayed there, shivering and wet, scanning the mountain and far fields, as if he could summon mother and daughter by purely focusing, by a quiet abiding. Soon he'd closed his eyes, chanting something in a low tone.

But when a vertical line appeared far off, he leapt up, his torso bent forward the whole way across the boggy paddock, his stride long and quick. From the porch Meg watched and wondered.

When Evangeline reached the house her face was grey and pinched. Her soaked hair clung in snaky ropes to her face and neck. The colour on her skirt had run and her feet had gone blue from the dye. She had the look of a person clawing back from some limit. She'd walked too far in the rain for someone so pregnant, Jim said. Rest, he'd keep searching.

Meg put her arms around that wet, cold body. Because of the baby, she could not join her hands at her mother's back and did not know how to arrange them. She glanced up. Her mother hadn't said anything yet about Meg's going off or getting stuck in that flood, or the smell coming off her, of the lake's miry stink and Nora's liquor, though surely Mr Parker must have told?

Evangeline stepped back, releasing Meg, and then began to shout.

What if the road, what if Tess had gone up that mountain alone. What if someone had taken her!

Mr Parker tried to quieten her.

Don't shush me, she said. I know what happens to girls on their own.

Then call the police, he said, stepping off the porch, and Meg heard his neighbourly voice turn back into a teacher's.

But try to be calm, he said, for the baby.

And he slogged across the marshy field, then wheeled his bike towards the lane while her mother called after him, Fucking hilarious telling me that!

Then she walked inside and tore all the curtains from their rods and switched off the lamps so she could see more clearly through each window, in every direction.

And Meg crossed the morass that was once the back paddock to ask the western neighbours, had they noticed Tess going by? But when she reached the creek dividing their land she saw how swollen it was already, that soon it would be impassable. She made her decision and leapt the flooded bank, and in the time it took to quiz the Stones – all five of the family filing in from different rooms and blinking sleepily at this new, ballsy Meg who'd braved the storm and now stood in mud-caked gumboots violently wheezing – the creek had become a bloated river seamed with fast-running currents.

Now her mother cannot be reached, not even by phone because the mountain lines are down say the Stones. And Meg notices the candles and torches, the muzzy light in the rooms of their house. The road is closed now and dangerous and there's no reception on any of the family's five mobiles, because the friggin hopeless wireless in this hollow, though they all humour Meg by poking their devices, very blatantly, very sober-faced, at the kitchen table. So Meg must sit with her warm Milo and raisin toast in the collegial glow of the Stones' concern and wait till it's possible to get back home.

9

Wait there. Tess remembers now what the man had said before she'd drifted off.

Won't be long, Murph said as he clambered out, tweaking his puckered trousers at the crotch and slamming the car door.

Groggy and starving, dry-mouthed from sleep, Tess peels off the blanket. A wet creaturely smell on her, her skin smarting. Horse blankets? Gross! She blinks at the car windows, her broad face reflected back, brows bent unhappily, an uncertain shape to her mouth. She hears the unfamiliar silence after rain, and breaks it with one word.

Outside, her eyes adjust quickly. All things aglow in the pallid moonlight. Puddle mirrors on a concrete path. A square brick house with statues out front. An angel, a ... frog? The lawn is clipped low, the bay windows black to the street. She leans against the car, watching the open moon and some stringy clouds, seeing the darkness changing, the swirling lilac and grey about the house and along the road. Where is she? It must be past midnight; tiredness tugs her limbs. But she isn't scared, she's just turned single-focused. Merely a maths problem, this disappearing. She must get from A to B. But where is B? B is simply *away* from where she no longer seems to belong.

Now, she remembers – Murph had gone down the side of the house. A parcel – some package he had to deliver, or collect? Off he went, loping, a thick heavy body, those poor horses! Tess hobbles along the path, dead-legged from the car. Peers in a side window with cupped hands, then hears singing, high and lilting, pure and hesitant. She moves past conspiring agaves, motionless potted jade. In the dripping, overgrown garden there's a young woman on a garden bench. A long fringe over wide-set eyes. Good evening, she says as Tess goes wooden with fear. The woman holds out a hand. On every finger, rings. Silver set with cloudy stones. Beside her, a wooden guitar.

Am Marta, from Ukraine, she says, entirely unsurprised at this vision, this pale teen-wraith with her shroud of dark hair, shivering in a T-shirt.

She offers a wide, gap-toothed smile. But have only three guitar strings! she says, exhaling smoke. Total bummer!

Marijuana. Tess recalls the scent from her mother's room. Pain relief, delivered before and after Pip, by Nora.

Marta starts singing again. A song about stars, mountains, the sea.

What's the time? Tess asks, the words creaking out. Where are we?

We are Fifteen Avenue Holmwood. Hold on, Marta grins, stamping out the rollie, I have Swatch … Is two twenty am!

There's an engine sound out front. Tess panics, turns to check.

Where's the man? Edward – Edwin?

He was toilet, says Marta. Hold it, she puts a palm in the air, then jogs towards the sound of acceleration as Tess stays in the yard, mouth-breathing. The house is blank and quiet. White moths on the black windows, avid for light. Gun-metal clouds wall up the sky. And now, terse and rapid rain.

Marta reappears, saying, Is gone!

Then she sits, ignoring the downpour, to roll a cigarette, the Tally Ho paper dancing on her lip as she pinches out tobacco. When she finally glances up she takes in the terrified eyes, the girl's hands compulsively wiping her shorts, the bare, rigid knees and struggling mouth.

Oh! Don't worry, little chick!

But, why did he leave?

Is spooked probably. Does it look good, I ask? Picking up some young girl at night. What if he's stopped by police? He already has a record. Lost his licence even. DUI or an Apprehended Violence Order, I can't remember which.

She takes Tess's hand.

Sticking with me, kid, OK? Am also having to get out of here.

Stefan. Is it you?

Evangeline looks nervously down the hall. No one there.

Outside, the weather's built itself in: long pillars of rain, a ledge of slate-coloured sky. Tess, and now Meg, and maybe Stefan also, out in that somewhere.

She puts a hand on her stomach, feels the muscles constrict. These are no Braxton Hicks but she's lied to herself for the past hour – more, her heart speeding at each new contraction. Birth, no avoiding it. She leans against a kitchen chair, then feels that slight subsidence and watches, disbelieving, as the flagstones slowly darken. How long, after her waters had broken, had it been with Pip? Two hours? Less? A frantic birth, but without injury. With Meg, though, delivered by instruments, she'd been certain she would die. The surgeon's face through the anaesthetic haze, the nurse's cryptic comment as they tried to staunch the bleeding, what are you going to do about that? *That* was her body, scissored apart. This baby in even more of a hurry. Three weeks early.

OK, she thinks, and turns strict, pragmatic, lucid. You've done it before – three times. Breathe. Better here than at St Catherine's, where everything would remind her of the body's frailty, better than The Hive birthing cabin under Hodgins's tobacco hands while Lana Beaufort paced nearby, waiting to get a look at the baby she'd been promised.

Evangeline walks gingerly to the bedroom, starts peeling away her wet things. But what's the point of drier clothes; they'll be coming off again soon enough. The girls – if she's in labour – who'll make sure they're safe, who'll find them? Stefan would be miles north by now. She turns to the weather, a sheer pane of rain partitioning her from the world. And then the two lamps blink out.

Back in the lounge she gropes in the darkness for the phone, always left somewhere obscure – in a pot plant or down a sofa crevasse – but is ambushed by more insistent pain and must sit, empty-eyed, then lie on her side on the couch. She remembers what the women had taught her at The Hive – a signature incantation for breathing out the contraction. Everyone has their own sacred tone, they'd said. Hers was a hum with a hectic timbre. But why believe them? Hadn't they been out to get her; in labour hadn't she'd just been the means to an end? Lana Beaufort, priestly and waiting in her white linen shift and silver bangles, which Evangeline, in the dissociated delirium of transition, was certain she could hear clinking. Someone had informed Lana of the labour, or she would not have travelled up the mountain from the town. That someone, it turned out, was Nora. She'd done Hodgins's bidding, when she ought to have sided with Evangeline. When Evangeline asked Hodgins, Why is Lana here? he'd said, because you promised. And then her mother had stepped in. For the two days and nights of that first birth Anita became newly gentle: attentive, wholly present. Time enough for negotiating when this is done, she'd said to Hodgins. An odd word – *done* – as if giving birth was like making a meal or a bed when it had ground on for more than thirty hours and was not progressing despite acupressure to ankle and foot. In the lunacy of that total, unyielding pain Evangeline became sure: her mother and Hodgins, and of all people Nora, were against her.

Now, when the high-voltage peak of the contraction dulls, she levers herself from the couch. Heads for torch and candles under the kitchen sink. If this rain keeps up, the creek will break its banks. There'll be no getting in or out of the farm. OK then, time the contractions, and maybe towels? The old ways, what did they do? Hot water, whisky?

She spies the phone, inserted in the bookshelf, plods over, stabs at the numbers, buggering it up because of her shaking. How about a bath, the shower? But, Stefan first. She pokes the buttons again, puts the phone to her ear with a quizzical look. Dead. So the power lines are down.

Her mother had stood back with her pinched lips, she'd let Hodgins step closer and put his hands where they shouldn't be. Throughout the labour Evangeline had told herself the baby was the first thing in that shared life of the commune that would belong entirely to her. But Hodgins was determined to see his property deal through. Everyone was starting to bail out of The Hive – even Jack. The Beauforts had ample, fertile land in the valley. Jack might have a use for some. And Anita had put her hand up too. Just a small section, she said, for my retirement. It was only later that Evangeline realised: her baby was the down payment. Jack was the first to touch her daughter. Crowning! he'd said. Push! And finally, out she jolted, bluish and crying like a cat. She was side-eyed with oil-black hair and seemed wholly possessed of herself already, just seconds old. As Hodgins reached over to take her, the cord still attached, the small red lips mouthing the air, Evangeline said, Tess. Then bit down hard on his forearm. It wasn't birth that had made her an animal, it was life, and she would hold fast to the one good thing she had conjured from herself.

All right, she says now, on her hands and knees in the lounge. Back then she'd wanted to labour alone – but now it was happening she wasn't sure she had it in her. The pain was tidal, ebbing and surging, with an undercurrent of wrecked and ruined things. Barely a minute now between contractions. From the roof, the unceasing buckshot of rain.

In the short lull between contractions she goes fugue-like; stares at the far wall where a small painting hangs. An awkward landscape in limpid, imported tones from Europe. She'd finished it years back, at The Hive. She starts thinking of those outlawed pigments, now obsolete, with their hazardous or rare ingredients. Uranium yellow, arsenical Paris Green, volcanic Giallorino, Mummy Brown – a story that had delighted the girls; a tint that had contained actual Egyptian mummies. The name hinted at some sorcery they imagined in her studio where the long gone was summoned, and transfigured. Orpiment. Cinnabar. Hartshorn. Smalt. As she stares at her amateur canvas, she feels hardly worthy of her daughters' wonder. The uncontrolled palette, her austere brushwork. She'd used the round sable and the goat-hair rigger – both had been gifts from Lana, they'd been *her* down payment. As the pain cranks up Evangeline thinks she has not been brave, that her art has risked nothing, that painting is an almost autistic with-holding. Her works barely even communicate to herself. And then she realises what's missing from all the aborted works in her studio: flame.

At the next contraction, more flotsam dragged up in the wave. She slogs through the pain, unaware of her creaturely sounds, her soaked hair, how still and compact she becomes, how husk-like and purely at her body's service, and then, how writhing. And she dimly recollects the spell for bearing pain – how the urge to escape amplifies the hurt. Try to stop running away.

After some indefinable time, her jaw slackens. Still kneeling she bows to the cooler floor. Then, a sudden fanaticism for her husband's stash of liquor and drugs. She crawls towards the dark kitchen, wondering which substances might tend the woman's pain without reaching the baby, though she knows the two are inseparable, that the baby's cells can cross the placenta and remain in the mother for life. When she'd learned this, after Pip, it had been a comfort. The cells – *chimeras*, the doctor called them – sought parts of the mother's body needing healing. It was solace to think of Pip, chimerical, still doing invisible good.

Evangeline gropes for the first-aid cupboard as the next contraction ratchets up. She runs a hand across a shelf of jars and packets, outdated prescription medicines. Somewhere in there, the locked box of hard drugs she'd kept after Pip's death, the serious pain relief she'd once administered to herself, and she feels a surge, inside and out, but is it the baby, or herself, emerging into being?

Once they're halfway down the Old Mill Road Tess sees right away: it's impassable. Marta had hailed the taxi to Bidgalong, offering to pay the fare. She's in the backseat now, still singing, her guitar flat across her lap. When she catches Tess craning her head towards the flooded Honig Farm, her melody trails off.

Is your place? Marta asks, then puts one slow hand over her mouth.

The house is a dark cube on a lake that was once a field. A torrent has torn up the tar of Fox's Lane, gathered fence posts, wiring, rubbish, branches, then flowed across the Müllers' land. Though the wind and rain have died, the house, marooned, unlit in the motionless water, looks flimsy and defenceless.

Tess's face is chalky, her eyes rimmed red. Her gut churns. Are her family inside or have they left for higher ground?

Where are you going? the driver calls as she slams the taxi door and strides towards the flooded road.

Marta's struggling with the door handle, she's hammering at the taxi window.

Tess! she calls out. You absolute cannot!

But they have no idea how strong she is, what a swimmer, how she's timed herself underwater at the town pool and in the bath. She tugs her feet through the grabbing mud and considers how long it'll take to cross the front field and which way the submerged currents are flowing.

Four

Your aim is clear to us, clearer far than our own; you desire to live,
as long as the world itself, in those that come after...
Maurice Maeterlinck

I

Jim takes her out in a borrowed car. Sylvie wants to see the hinterland, where the new, intentional communities have sprung up. They cross a timber bridge. Built, he says, entirely by hand. Blackbutt piles and cross heads, corbels and stringers of grey ironbark.

Way too much time, says Sylvie, wiping grime from her window.

Huh?

On their hands, such artisanal people, she says.

I helped them restore it, Jim laughs. It was really interesting, learning all those old skills.

Around a bend, a yellow horse grazing in a dewy paddock.

Oh just look, she says.

A mare in white veils of rising mist, fairy-tale perfect.

Jim had been very solemn all morning. He was tired, he'd said, lips tight at the corners. So much had happened in last week's storm; they'd had to shelter in a community hall, and he'd left Sylvie there with strangers while he cycled out to help the emergency teams find those who were trapped or stranded.

Because of the floods Sylvie had to extend her ticket home. One day left.

Nice car, Nora of the lake, Sylvie says, fingering the dreamcatcher dangling from a sun visor. On the back bumper *Magick Happens*.

Nora had dropped the car off that morning, then waded through mud to the Müllers'. Evangeline was still in hospital, three hours away, and Nora had food for the family's deep-freeze. This news had made Jim stand from the table and look at his hands as if he should have done more with them, delivered the child maybe or cut the cord.

Actually, Sylvie's saying, dreamcatchers are meant for Native American *infants*. Surely Aussie adults can cope with their own subconscious!

Funny, Jim says with a half-yawn, because you're the one trying not to look at something right in front of your face.

She groans. What are you now, my guru? My shrink?

What's going on with you? he asks.

Sylvie turns to watch the paddocks zipping by. Jim drives fast and reckless on the rain-spruced, carless roads.

After a while she asks quietly, But why move next door to bees, Jim?

The bees are all disappearing, he says. Some kind of mite, or virus.

Ha. Apiarists must be used to that. Isn't it just stock loss?

He looks at her. You know very much about farming?

Later, on the clifftop platform, they stare down the two-hundred-metre waterfall. Out beyond are bright hills and cabins clustered in the ferny hollows.

What do you even do in the evenings? she asks. You're not painting. Which, I'm shocked. Does the gallery even know? I thought you were going to have a show this year? What happened to *Twelve Rooms*? And you're not a gym person. You're not Footy Guy. And there's nowhere much to go out. So, I can't imagine. Meditate? Mark homework?

He gives her a cold stare. *Twelve Rooms*. How could she have remembered his proposed show, when he'd entirely forgotten?

Jesus, he says. You're pretty shack nasty. I guess you're not used to it.

Your cabin? she rolls her eyes. I'd be worried if I was!

Then she laughs, It's so totally you to choose a mother. But what will happen to her daughters, your students ... ?

OK, Sylvie ...

... if the school finds out?

He stands, hands on his head, ducks, trying to contain himself, and he sees that she looks frightened, as if worried about what he might do to her, or her to him, now they've reversed back to being strangers.

Don't you realise people already know? she says.

What people?

That survivalist from the market. We had this nice chat while you were off somewhere. Tom Tucker. He's quite taken with me.

Jim makes a throat noise. Tucker. The crossing guard?

Oh, who could possibly want me if you don't? says Sylvie. But, if you're after town history, he's your man.

Jim steps back, tugs his T-shirt.

Aren't we going to walk this track? she asks, and stretches a foot. Her yellow-striped Nikes look nuclear against the dowdy vegetation.

Go ahead, he says.

You're not seriously going to sit here sulking?

What the fuck do you want from me?

Just consider what they'll do to her – or you, Sylvie says, in Tiny Town.

But, he says, it's you who wants to punish me, right?

He starts pacing, in his dark blue shirt, and the leather belt she'd bought him, years back, from Melbourne.

Jim, she says, hooking one finger into the belt. I didn't have the abortion. But anyway, at about sixteen weeks, I lost the baby. It wasn't just blood, it felt like a proper labour ... and I was like some beast, alone, on the floor, at home. Later they told me I have this condition – incompetent cervix. It's stupidly short or something. Very hard for me to carry a child.

Jim looks at her, astonished. Miscarried. It was true then, what she'd said.

She ought to have told him sooner, she says. But hadn't known how to describe the weight and creaturely heat of what had slid out of her that afternoon. And how, not knowing where or what to do, she'd wrapped it in a towel and buried it later in the yard. What could she say except how she'd felt, during and after. A terrible, scraped-out despair.

You and I had a baby. But I don't even have an ultrasound photo. There's no trace of him at all.

He puts an arm around her. It takes him a moment to register. A boy?

But Sylvie has turned to the forest, her eyes behind her hands.

He has a second's doubt, that it's a kind of trap, then says, We never talked about if you wanted kids.

Do you?

Yes. But I don't think I'm ready, says Jim.

You've hooked up with a pregnant mother. You'd give up your profession, your reputation ... ?

...I don't have to explain myself, he says.

But you had a chance with me!

She dries her cheeks with the back of her hands. I haven't even asked, she says, if that beekeeper baby is yours.

Come on! Stefan appears, sock-footed, smelling of leaf sap, hewn timber, engine oil.

Get in the car, he tells the girls.

Time to visit Mum! Meg announces, an unbelieving light in her eyes.

She swings off her chair and scouts the kitchen, listing aloud what they ought to take. Healthy snacks because of hospital food, essential oils to hide hospital stinks, herbal teas, Bach flowers. Their mother used to keep them packed in a bag, for when they visited Pip.

Meg pauses, says, And Asher!

And Stefan leans across as he passes, tugs Meg's neatly braided hair. Of course, he says. You didn't think I'd forget your brother?

Tess, watching from the doorway, is very still and sombre, some element of herself suspended since her mother had been stretchered and carried off. She'd floated away with newborn Asher in a rescue dinghy while Tess stayed back with the emergency-services woman till the floodwaters subsided. Asher lay on her mother's chest, wrapped in a sheet that slowly discoloured. Tess couldn't figure out who all that blood belonged to, and during the long wait in the house she replayed that receding sight. She leans against the doorframe now, chewing her lower lip. She hasn't spoken since her mother departed and doesn't know any more how, or what, to feel.

They find her in lilac-coloured Ward B. She's sitting in the bend-able hospital bed, still pale after the transfusion, but her colour rises when she sees them all coming in. She reaches across to Meg and Tess, wincing, because her lower body has been stitched. She takes their heads in her cold hands and kisses them on the forehead. Someone, in a curtained bed beside them, burps. Someone else rattles a cup. Their father has carried wailing Asher out into the corridor, he's gone to ask the nurses when they can take their mother and brother home. The nurses' station. Tess used to wish she could stop with the nurses, back when they'd visited Pip. She would have liked to remain at the station with no destination, just a glossy mag and an open box of thank-you chocolates, running a finger down a clipboard.

Was it some kind of plan, you two going off? their mother is asking. She's looking everywhere but at their faces.

The girls glance at each other.

Hitch-hiking was Pip's dare, Meg pipes up, her fingers hovering over bedside levers.

Please don't pretend what you did has anything to do with Pip, Evangeline says.

The other women in the ward are all curtained, but through fabric gaps Tess glimpses wedges of flesh, huge breasts, dark nipples the size of saucers, tiny feet and fingers, folds of belly, bandages, blood. She tears her eyes from this tableau, the infants, just days ago alive inside those women, now out and eating,

261

sleeping, shitting, breathing. So needy, so noisy. They'd have been safer staying put.

Meg's murmuring something about those dares made years back. She glances at Tess to check if she's put the right spin on it for their mother.

But why would Pip ask you to do *that*? their mother says, her white fist holding the bed rail.

Her anger, missing from their lives for so long is a surprise and relief. Her anger confirms – she's fully present, feeling something.

Maybe because she couldn't go anywhere, Meg says, very quiet.

Evangeline bows, visoring her eyes with her hands.

Sometimes, she says, I worry I've damaged you more than grief.

Tess stands by the bed, very grave, saying nothing, even though she has recently shouted while hammering the front door in rain and flood. *Mum, are you there?* She might have been asking that question the whole of her teenage life.

She'd found her, in the kitchen, a small, damp boy in her hands, his cord uncut. Beneath them both, the blood and the peculiar veined sac that had cradled her brother, and looked wrong on the floor, and seemed somehow still alive.

A hospital trolley clangs past and a gust scented with mashed pumpkin and gravied meat makes all three Müllers briefly lock eyes, and grimace. *Yerk.*

When I was young – just seventeen, Evangeline says, looking hotly at Tess, I got pregnant.

Both sisters stare, their bodies tilt closer; a feeling, in that ward, of the antiseptic air giving on to an otherworld.

But she hadn't wanted to stay with that particular man, she tells them. So their grandmother, Anita, and Jack Hodgins arranged to give the baby to a woman in town. She was connected with an art school, a gallery up north. In exchange for the baby she'd promised some of her land.

And for me, their mother says, she promised art lessons, painting supplies, even an exhibition at a city gallery! I had all these small canvases. Little painted scenes from The Hive ...

... The ones in the lounge? asks Meg.

Yes, those, she laughs. I actually believed I was gifted. But, I couldn't give you up, she says, turning to Tess. As the months passed I made up my mind. I had you. I kept you ...

... But then ... says Meg. Who's Tess's father?

Their mother's gaze jumps from one to the other.

You're *all mine*, she says very quietly. Does it matter who your father is?

Should I be worried where this conversation is going? They had not noticed Stefan entering the ward. He pauses then bends over the boy in his arms and inhales the air all around his head.

Whether it matters, he says, well, that surely is up to the child? He turns very deliberately to Tess.

Tess wants to know, don't you? Meg asks, urgently pulling her sister's hand from where it's hanging limp and passive by her side.

When a baby's born the whole world's unfamiliar, says Evangeline. But its mother's voice is a bridge from the womb to the world.

Tess listens, aware of how her mother is, even now, changing the subject. She feels so flimsy, she could float away. Where did you say you are from? she'd asked Marta, in that strange garden, in the rain. And she'd replied in a deliberately mystical voice, nowhere, and everywhere. Now, a curtained baby hiccups. Tess hears the whimpers, the lusty wailing and primal sucking; she listens to the low harmonies of all the mothers, soothing the newly born.

Babies know *nothing*, Tess thinks, feeling hot and tight as if she's outgrown her own skin. All they have are feelings. Disgusting, to realise she is plagued by the same affliction.

I've never forgotten the sound of *your* voice, her mother is saying. Even in the eighteen months and seven days you've kept it from me.

Tess stares at her mother's desperate face. Somewhere inside, there's the relic of a will – to be heard, to be seen, even if her mother's sufferings outclass her own. And so, fighting everything walled up, a shaky, depleted feeling running through her, she asks,

Well then, who was he?

And all the Müllers turn as one, eyes very bright and only just noticing that glassy timbre, and how Tess speaks – atonally – like a person who has never spoken before.

Three weeks later, the small boy governs their home. His routine dictates how quiet or loud they may be, whether anyone can finish what they've begun before his cries reverberate down the hall and beyond to the yard where the girls have hung a baby monitor in a tree. Such volume! Their father seems especially proud, as if Asher's sturdy lungs guarantee him a brilliant future.

This morning, though, he's asleep in his hammock as Meg and Tess follow their mother over the bee field. They pass the hives, noiseless in the hesitant light, pass the sleepy Charolais, their steamy shit in the low grass. The roos are down, but wary; they hark as the three approach, then bound off, daubs of grey through the forest green.

Inside the studio, the pram in the corner, a faint smell of turpentine. Then they see the largest canvas, the fresh sheen on it, radiant in the gloom.

But when did you? Meg asks.

Her mother whistles a bit through teeth. At night, when I couldn't sleep. Before Asher, she says. I still have some way to go.

The girls stare at the painting with its raw backing frayed around the edges. The new details give the scene an eerie urgency.

Why horses all the time? Meg asks.

Evangeline sighs, looks nervy. She leans against a trestle table, scuffing the floor with a bare toe.

I started noticing, on my walks, how even animals turned from me. Only the Petersons' horses ever looked at me squarely, she says.

In the foreground, the hazy shape of a baby. In the distance, two twig figures, a van on a hill.

After a long silence Tess says, You're really good at doing horses. It's so hard to get the heads right and the legs. Not to mention hooves.

Evangeline turns, her grey eyes grown milky.

Tess, she says, you don't have to make me feel better about the things I've done.

But isn't that what families are for? Tess thinks. And if not, what else?

Not long after Pip died, I went into town, Evangeline says. A woman came up to me. She said, I heard you lost your youngest. I was so desperate then for any kindness. I told her yes. And then she said, an eye for an eye. And walked away.

Who was she? asks Meg, making fists, a small force, out for her mother's own good. What does that even mean?

Evangeline doesn't say how Lana Beaufort had paused in her leaving. How she'd turned back to say, Your art was utterly shit. And that whole story about the gallery and your talent – God, what a ruse and you bought it! A couple of sable brushes, a tube of Quinacridone Gold and you're Michael-fucking-angelo? Her laugh was forced, erratic. But Evangeline heard the grieving undertone and knew then how alike they'd become, hauling their losses around.

Did you ever see my dad, in town? asks Tess very brightly. You never said where he's at.

Had she passed him many times, in the street, at the market? Did he know her, or was she a stranger, with same-coloured hair and eyes? Had he spoken to her once or twice, by accident or deliberately? Had he sought her out? And what, come to think of it, even was his actual name?

Tess met the city girls one open-skied morning. Three green coaches turned down the main street and rolled in, slow, important. These girls from Sancta Sophia had crisp navy pleats in knee-length tunics, their hair sleekly pinned despite hours on the Bruce Highway. Blazers and straw boaters, shined black shoes that dulled as they leapt from the high metal coach steps into Bidgalong's red dust. Some had badges on their lapels. This one Prefect, this for Public Speaking, that for Good Citizenship. In the raw morning sun the pins zinged off gold arrows of light.

Tess stood, waiting to meet them, with the other seniors from the River School. A ragged bunch in mismatched cream and burgundy. Their socked legs, lined up, graphed varying degrees of care. Seeing these immaculate girls file out, Tess bent to pull her knee-highs, but their cheap elastic was failing. She finger-combed her rampant hair, then stood very straight as the city girls shrugged their backpacks on to the street.

They'd come two hundred kilometres to join the River School in planting five hundred saplings on Stan Baker's land. The trees had arrived the day before. Hardy pioneer species.

Forest oak, doughwood, rough-leaved elm. They stood in black hydroponic bags by the Bakers' drystone wall. The girls had come for the reforesting – not just for their future, but for the generations – and they'd felt so exulted, journeying out, do-gooders with very clean, manicured hands. But they quickly forgot all of that; they were city girls in a new scenario and they looked up and down the street, paused and locked eyes with the locals. Scowling boys with mussy hair and the surprising shoulders of men. So pleased to meet them, the girls extended their soft palms, hello!

After the planting, there was a cookout in Stan's field below the Ghost Mountains' tallest peak. The paddock, once kept trim by Black Angus, had been cut that afternoon by Tom Tucker demonstrating the art of a hand-tooled Austrian scythe. Chairs and mats were laid out, lanterns hung from the Moreton Bays and a line of tables was slowly filling with trays, platters, cutlery, bottles. Older locals brought Flo Bjelke Peterson's pumpkin scones and sponge cake, their adult kids decanted gluten-free – quinoa salads, chia breads, claggy pomegranate molasses. Guests from the intentional communities offered invasive species: salads of fat hen, wood sorrel, turkey rhubarb; a crock of wild blackberry and humanely trapped rabbit. The miners and their wives had all declined to come.

Tess sat by the entrance to Stan's. Beside her crouched Nikki, Sachiko, Kate and Aggie from Sancta Sophia's Year 8. They'd spent all afternoon together with trowels, compost, dung and Seasol, stamping fresh-dug earth around the new trees. As they worked they'd quizzed Tess on the boys who sauntered by, pretending not to look at this new variety of girl. Now they watched the locals coming along the lane with Eskies, Tupperware and rainbow-coloured sheetcake. Tess named each arrival, her hands folded, her cheeks flushed, newly indispensable with her local lore.

There's Nico and Lute, that's Nora with the coloured hair, said Tess.

And Tom, no longer in scything clothes, looking pretty scrubbed actually if you ignored the beard, arm in arm with Marta Boronski, her guitar slung across her back.

After the food there'll be a show, Tess told the girls. Marta's a singer.

Totes pretty! the girls said.

How she's done her hair, sighed Aggie.

I first heard her sing the night I went hitch-hiking, said Tess. I mean I kind of discovered her. Just playing guitar in some crazy guy's garden at midnight in the rain.

The girls stared, slack-mouthed. They said, Hitch-hiking? as Tess, nonchalant, clawed a fake itch on her forearm.

Marta had her head on Tom's shoulder now, her fishtail plait looped across his back. She'd stayed in the town six weeks since catching that taxi with Tess. At first at the Red Lodge, and later at Tom's after he'd advertised a room.

Tess did not tell the girls that Tom was related, that he was her actual uncle! A fact so fresh she was yet to believe it and could not even shape the word in her mouth.

Here comes Jackson G. Hodgins, and his twins, bounding in light-up sneakers. And June, on her white horse with a bag of easy tricks to teach the littlies, and later, a magic act she'd mastered after eight and a half months' practice. She tethered her horse by the gate and the girls followed Tess over to stroke its creamy, spotted flank.

Stefan was the boss of meat. He stood, far out in the field so no sparks from the fire could catch, carving dark ribbons off the spit lamb, his knife arm sawing in long motions up and down. He looked so lonely, bent over like that, the smoke uncoiling around him. Tess hesitated, what to call him?

Two days ago he'd driven her into the mountains. When they arrived at The Hive, Tess said, Follow me. He'd do whatever she asked, out of guilt maybe, or love, or just to prove he was there and had been from the start even if he hadn't fathered her. Together they climbed the long, steep track till they reached the clearing. Then Tess took her father's hand and pointed ahead.

There, she said. Go and look.

But what if she hadn't remembered right, and the bees had been an illusion? They might have swarmed and left, like they had a long time back, their mother said, when she lay in the burning grass and the bees flew above. Bees were programmed to react to fire – at the first scent of smoke they'd stuff themselves with honey and swarm.

Her father walked very slowly into The Hive. He put one foot directly in front of the other, his arms out like a high-wire walker, humouring her in some unfathomable way. Then he disappeared behind the nearest wall. She could hear them – but how many? Enough to make the air sing, and the scent of honey, real or imagined, to meander by.

It seemed ages till he reappeared, scratching his head, his eyes veined red.

You found it, he said, a hand on her shoulder. I should've known you'd be the one.

Tess felt his hand's tremor, how he was tensing the sinews to keep it steady.

June showed me, she said.

From the Red Lodge June?

She comes here because of the graves. Tess pointed to where June's mother was buried.

He'd come to her room when he'd returned from the orchards, after hearing how she'd hiked down that highway, how she'd swum a field that had become a lake, then broke the front door to find her mother and new brother on the kitchen floor. He'd sat on the edge of her bed and was quiet for a long and awkward time. And then said he was sorry he wasn't the father she may have wished for.

But she had no wishes then, about fathers. Only wishes about mothers, sisters and silence.

Biology – some say it's important. But I disagree, he'd said.

As they stood among the remains of The Hive he said he knew the girls didn't like him killing the queens. So he'd decided to set up some old-lady colonies, maybe there was some wisdom in leaving them be. After a time, to his surprise, they multiplied. Up here, with only blossoms, no pesticides, without his interfering. They've done very well, he said.

Old-lady bees, said Tess.

OK, so I really hate to say it, he said. But Hodgins was right after all.

I've taken no honey, not a drop, he said. But I am so curious. What do you think it will taste of?

And together they circled the remains of that commune hall and stared at the mass of wild combs, and her father carefully prised one open with a stick, barehanded, no bee suit or helmet, no smoker. Calm, Tess thought. And she loved this fearlessness in him and knew it was a thing she'd loved for all time. He ran a finger across that glistening honeycomb then held it out.

Come on, he said. Actually I know you have impeccable taste. Try to guess. Which flowers made the honey?

She'd walked towards him, and then, without hesitating, he'd put his finger in her mouth.

Now, watching the city girls as the smoke rose and the toasty scent of baked lamb and burning wood drifted by, Tess felt suddenly sleepy.

That's my father, she told them. From Germany.

She had no other word for him. She thought of that Ghost Mountains honey, those aromas you couldn't distinguish. In wild places, her father had said, the bees weren't discerning and their honey was so beguiling because you could not place its source, you could not absolutely say — that flower there is where the flavour came from. Somewhere else around these parts, her mother said, her real father existed.

Did you personally know that lamb he's got? said Aggie, pointing to Stefan and the spit. Poor little thing with the stick up there! she said. And the five girls collapsed on the bindi lawn laughing and cringing.

We have cows, said Tess when she could breathe again.

Cows, bees and chickens, she said. Not sheep.

I'm definitely going vegetarian, said Kate, who'd never seen meat in animal form, only red isosceles defrosting under Cling.

When Tess turned back she saw a stranger, or rather, his shape, backlit by the fire. Tall and angular and talking very lively to her father. Something about how Stefan was leaning with his hands at his hips made Tess wary. She turned. In the distance was Stan, coming from the farmhouse with a tray of potatoes.

Tess pointed, and told the girls about his divining.

Can he really find water with twigs? the girls marvelled. Like some kind of wizard?

The slightest thing enthralled them. When it was time to eat they filled their plates twice over and said, *yummo, de-lish*, so Tess wondered what kind of life had armed them with so much capacity for delight.

They'd bagsed a picnic mat some distance from their teachers so they could discuss pashing and head lice and a pop star who, when Googled, could be seen doing pranks like farting in supermarket dairy aisles then filming the exodus of disgusted shoppers. They talked about sex, which Sachiko had had, and which she said was, like, forgettable. Though she remembered the feeling after, the secret pride and disappointment.

Tess told them about the mountain commune, that she and her mother were saved.

Are you religious? asked Aggie.

No, Tess laughed.

Why so funny? asked Kate, fingering the gold cross around her neck.

Tess held her breath, desperate not to break the spell. Just… oh…, she said, then pointed to Tom.

He was the one who carried me out when the commune caught fire. Up there, she pointed to the west side of the mountain.

The girls turned as one and blinked at Tess. You were seriously, like, in a bushfire? asked Kate.

I was only a baby. I was safe. It was my mother who got burned, Tess said.

You were rescued, that's epic! said Aggie.

She did not tell the rumour about who'd started that fire. She did not say, as June had, the word arson.

Then Nora appeared. She'd shaved her head on one side and dyed the spiked regrowth purple. She leaned down towards the girls, her breath very piney, and took Tess's hands.

Don't forget the show, she said. June's finally mastered the Vanishing Woman.

When, when? The girls leapt up.

Nine thirty, said Nora.

Your hair's so cool, said Sachiko. Wish I was allowed.

Who's vanishing? asked Tess.

Yours truly, Nora laughed, then sauntered off, her pockets clinking faintly.

D-runk, laughed Aggie, did you smell?

Nora passed through a rain of ash from the fire. Tess watched her talking to Stefan as she leaned against that stranger. Then tugged the man's arm, very urgent. Red embers jittered above them like gnats in the night air. The three seemed to be arguing, or maybe celebrating – it was hard to tell through the ash and smoke. Their shadows strung out along the bladed field.

Evangeline was sitting far away so Asher would not breathe in smoke. When Tess took her over a plate of food she could hardly see her new brother, curled tightly in his sling. But could hear his constant sucking.

Why's he so thirsty all the time? Meg, irritable from early waking, had asked in the early weeks. He'd been put to the breast nearly every hour back then.

Takes after me, Stefan had said, unsmiling.

Milk's for lots of things, said Evangeline, eyeing Stefan. Not just food – it's also comfort.

Grown-ups drink because of their childhoods, said Meg, staring hard at her father.

Who told you that? Stefan asked. No – let me guess – Nora?

He put the bottle down then and picked up his son. He rocked him in his arms and sang a song they'd last heard him sing beside Pip's empty bed.

> *Schlaf, Kindlein, schlaf,*
> *Der Vater hüt' die Schaf,*

Die Mutter schüttelt's Bäumelein,
Da fällt herab ein Träumelein ...

Their father had chosen their brother's name. Asher Azha Müller. Asher for *happiness*. Azha, a star in the Celestial Meadow. Asher had dark frowzy hair and lapis-blue, wide-set eyes. Who does he look like? everyone asked, then held their breath as if scared the answer would be Pip. Tess wondered if parts of herself would float up in Asher, some traits that also belonged to her mother.

For a time Evangeline had gone peculiar from lack of sleep, dropping things in the kitchen and staring out the window. She'd mix cakes and forget to add the agave syrup, she'd wash clothes without powder and wear her T-shirts inside out. Tess slept in her parents' bed, because her mother could not lift the baby after the surgery and their father was still on the couch. Farm life meant early rising, and no one could do that after tending to Asher all night.

Tess would wake when he started crying and though she was groggy she loved that moment when the boy was in her arms, and the rest of the Müllers sleeping deep. She'd walk him down the hall to stand in the glow from the glass transoms above the front door. His face in that green or sea-blue light full of unseeing wonder, the colours unknown to him yet, only her voice tethering him to the world. She'd pretend the boy belonged just to her, that she'd made him – some wizardry without sex or a father – and he'd rely on her for everything, he'd love her, having nobody else. But then she'd think of the sister he'd never meet, and who belonged, just as much, to him as to them all and she'd have a second's guilt for selfish wishes and would say as much, aloud, to Pip, to the numinous dark beyond the front door, to the fields and cows, to the bees who were struggling each day to do what they were fated to, flying with their burdens of pollen. She pictured them swarming from the doomed hives to that higher place, where they'd made their purer community. Then, when hunger brought Asher's cries again, she'd pass him to her mother, who fed him lying down, or tucked under one arm in the football hold. These nights, in her parents' bed, watching this boy, so dear, so dependent, made Tess very homesick. Once she'd been connected like that, and now, nearly fifteen, she was drifting in another direction.

One night she woke to see her mother standing at the window. The weather had closed in for a week. At first, hail and its blue, mystical scent. The girls had gone out in it, pressing handfuls against their cheeks. They'd filled a bowl, labelled it for Pip, then placed it in the freezer. The next morning, an iron-coloured sky. The ground a tide of mud. They'd forged through it to school while their mother stayed behind with Asher, waving his fist at the door.

Tess watched as her mother rubbed a line on the window and said, *Like a heavy mane across our eyes, rain.*

What's that? Tess asked, yawning and stretching.

It's from a poem, her mother said. By a woman who lost nearly everything. Her name was Marina. She lived far from here, long ago, in a place with much more heartbreak.

I've learned it, she said. It's a comfort.

Evangeline was still staring towards that empty cabin on Fox's Lane. But just as suddenly she jerked the heavy curtain, blocking it out. They hadn't forgotten who used to live there. After Asher was born Mr Parker had left town. He was the only other person Tess knew who read poems. Was it he who'd taught her mother the poems of Marina?

After the food and speeches, after Stan accepted the Mayor's Award for his philanthropy, for bequeathing his land for regeneration, after the endless thank yous, it's time.

June stands in a tuxedo. On stage, a wooden chair draped in navy velvet on a square of flokati. Some pop music comes on. Tess recognises it and the city girls leap up, whipping their hips and putting their hands in the air – a dance from TV and YouTube. After a minute June snaps her fingers. Silence descends, louder than any music.

I call this, says June in a grave monotone, the Vanishment.

There are coughs, giggles, a cork being popped. Seventy-three people from town and city, ranged on picnic rugs and quad-fold camp chairs, their breath starting to show as the damp rises from mountain and field.

Our willing participant, says June primly, then gestures stage right.

Nora trips up the stairs and on to the platform. She sits with bare knees pressed. Tess can see that her hands, even jammed between her thighs, are trembling.

Your honour, I beg mercy. I've done nothing wrong! says Nora.

Oh really? comes a voice from the audience.

Funny, Nora says. Can't you see our magician's concentrating?

June, scowling, pinches Nora's arm.

OK, no ad-libbing! I forgot, Nora says as she straightens.

In just minutes, says June, I shall make this fine lady disappear!

Fine lady! Hilarious! Hurry up then, says the same voice. Get rid of her!

Who *is* that? Nora visors her brow and scans the crowd. Pete?

Tess hears whispering, feels the ripple of unease in the crowd. Nora looks fidgety and worried. Tess turns to search the dark for her mother, the name Pete a faint, disturbing echo. But maybe this is just part of the act, thinks Tess, part of the whole suspension. *Obvi!* as the city girls say. Adults are expert, after all, at all kinds of pretending.

June stands in front of Nora so all Tess can see are her bare feet. They look so vulnerable sticking out like that.

Behind the crowd, two policemen. Tess recognises one, from the time they'd come out to the farm. Their squad-car lights are trained on the Bakers' field. The car, all lit up, looks ready for something. Had they been invited?

Nora is scanning the crowd. Who called the cops? she says.

But June interrupts with her *Abracadabra!* and then Nora's gone. Just the shape of her body beneath the velvet cloth.

Tess whispers to the city girls; it's bent wire beneath the fabric that gives the illusion of head and shoulders. June had told her all about it, as they rode the horse from mountain to valley. A magician needed also to be a sculptor, June had said, to do an expert vanish. It was not easy to do a false transfer or to banish the awkwardness in a limb that might give a trick away. Such tension was mostly caused by the magician's guilt. And so she'd taught herself the difference between deceiving and convincing.

Peter – is that what Nora said? Tess glances desperately around but the smoke has cast a thick haze in the dark; it's turned the whole community illusory. She hears an engine, then sees the taillights of the squad car, heading for the access road.

A little later, Tess runs into the dark fields with Kate and Aggie. All the freshly planted saplings are backlit by the bonfire, their roots safely tucked underground. Meg has gone back out; she's tamping dirt and hosing the last of them, taking special care with the spindliest trees.

Seeing her sister, so young, so serious, her fair hair gathered over one shoulder, her face smeared with ashes from the fire, Tess remembers how it was to be twelve. How everything comes running in, how breathless you feel all the time. Worse for Meg, she thinks, who's developed early, whose breasts are already larger, whose blood came when their mother was in hospital with Asher.

Tess squeezes Meg's shoulder, smells bonfire smoke in her hair. Kind of odd, she thinks, that they're burning wood while planting trees that will provide some future fire with kindling. Meg has tied a tag on one sapling. There's a drawing on it of a frail, narrow plant. Its limbs held up like a person surrendering, or praising: *Hallelujah*.

And then she sees the miniature handwriting – Meg's Krazy Town writing. They used to compete to do the smallest – and Pip was always champion, her letters so tiny, like an ant had written them with its feet.

Beneath Meg's sketch, two minuscule words. *For Pip*.

Tess straightens and looks at that mountain where her mother had taken her and Meg, after Asher came home. She'd showed them a tree, its huge roots protruding from the forest floor, its trunk covered in mementoes of Pip, a quandong with buttress roots, old and solid by the Repentance River, and Tess wondered, was this where she'd disappeared, going there to maybe think of Pip, the one they'd all loved without complication or error, the one Tess had rallied to distract and comfort till her final hour? Her mother had not cried but touched the tree and said it was like a poem with all its meaning privately unfolding.

She's over by Stan's house now, jigging Asher in his pram. Tess can no longer see her father. After three attempts to rouse her, Nora had finally clambered out from behind the stage and began to berate June, then run about wildly searching. The crowd stood and then dispersed, gathering children and refilling glasses and forming clusters of threes and fours, heads bent, discussing. The police car has gone. They've taken him in for questioning, Tom had said to Marta. They say it is my brother. It was then Tess realised: the stranger was her father, as if conjured in a reverse vanish by June. Maybe it's a relief, Marta said, for a person who's been hiding for so long. The city girls gather closer to Tess as ash falls on her damp cheeks, and drifts across the fields.

4

Sometimes, in the middle of some austerity, Jim will begin to hallucinate. A sea of honey, cascading down a mountain. When the honey tide's just metres off, he runs. He's wearing his mother's gown and army boots. The boots feel leaden and the flimsy robe snags on twigs and thorny branches. As he runs, he knows he's ruining it and he begins to cry for the things he's damaged by trying to save himself, in his struggle to escape. He's destroying it all, this relic of his mother that retains in its folds a vestige of her scent.

This scene will float up on a Forest Day at Hammer Wood where, on weekends, he helps clear the paths of invasive plants. It will amass in his mind during meditation vigil and he'll bid it gone so he might continue to reach for emptiness. In the shadowy forest the bhikkhus pass him with muted steps. They're forbidden to clear the weeds but will come to gather the chopped branches of sweet chestnut to burn for heat in the monastery. He walks behind, their skulls so naked beneath their stubbled scalps, their feet hidden under long robes so they appear to glide across the forest. In the shadowy copses, en masse, they seem very vulnerable, and he feels oddly protective towards them. Later, in the crisp light of the hall, scratching their itches, barking at a wayward acolyte, dog-earing a Marks and Spencer Christmas catalogue, they fall to earth, newly human.

On weekdays he crosses Clapham Common to Brigham Private through heavy, crusted snow. For his class of twenty-one boys he broadens his ocker inflections, embellishes stories of towns where native animals mix freely with the locals. The boys tell him of their own fauna, of badger culling and the moles that have excavated ancient ruins – unwitting archaeologists, ploughing up the British earth.

In London winter the world is slate-coloured and hard and glimmering with hoar frost. It is statuary and occasional cobbled roads on which some old Roman once ambled by, cursed and shat and spat, Jim thinks. When he compares it, Sydney seems so illusory. Its faux-gothic cathedrals, colonnaded verandas, the slate roofs, lancet windows, gables and buttresses. His memories centre on that broad swathe of land from the Art Gallery to the Quay. His particular Sydney, alien to Sylvie whose suburban childhood steered her imagery in other directions: bushy tracts of development land, air-con shopping malls, main streets with fluoro signage. He thinks of the Moreton Bay figs under which he spent so many hours. He tells the boys how these can sprout in a host tree, their adventitious roots trailing towards the earth. From *advenire*, he says, *to come or be superadded*.

A queer feeling to be here then, at the heart of a mental Britishness construed from convict histories and Captain Cookery, from his mother's sun-bleached photos of pastoral East Sussex. It all comes back: her tales of school dinner ladies presiding over liver and kidney, of the fountain pens the children refilled at large metal sinks so her young fingers were always blue-tipped, of carolling in the snow and being bitten by a neighbour's dog whose chair she'd dared sit on, *a dog called Rex* she'd say, laughing and showing the scar, and boy was he fucking royal on his Regency chair! All of those stories, imported, diluted, make fresh sense now he's at the source of Veronica's lore.

On weekends he takes the train from Euston station to Berkhamsted, then a taxi past Hoo Wood and Hill Wood and St Margaret's Copse to the Amaravati gates. As he passes grids of farmland he remembers Veronica's final reveries. In the hospice she'd described a school public-safety film. Six children killed, one by one, in gruesome farm accidents: drowned in slurry, crushed by a tractor and a gate, poisoned by weedkiller. It was called *Apaches*. This last death had especially disturbed, because the girl seemed so unscathed after swigging the poison. But later, she said, you saw the light go on in a room of a house in a village just like mine, and then the child's agonising scream. In the hospice Veronica would not talk about her own death; she talked again and again about *Apaches* and its spiteful, B-grade editing. Jim had not recognised the story as a parable of her own terror, only that in dying there was no quietening. The world will go on, she said, in a moment of lucidity, of trying to comfort. It will go on without me.

Back in Australia, before leaving Bidgalong, he'd driven up to St Catherine's Hospital. Three hours on a monotony highway, window down, elbow out, yelling in the Mack truck tailwind, *I'm gone again, I'm out of here*. He decided, then later resigned from the River Primary.

At the hospital, three flights up, Maternity. He crossed mopped linoleum, gleaming and stippled as a lake. There she was by the window, feeding. And there was the boy, dark-haired, a grizzled old-man face when he was shifted from right breast to left. Evangeline wore an expression he had no name for. A glazy look that reminded him of Veronica, so he thought such contentment must surely belong to the Endone, some other analgesic. But no, Evangeline glanced up, her eyes swimming with new intensity. She was off the pain relief and healing well.

That's good, he said. I'm glad.

He was stripped to such banality in the face of her new radiance, at the sight of the baby, blindly groping the air at her breast. He was and wasn't happy for her. He had a childish fancy for her suffering to return because she'd needed him once in the thick of it, but now it seemed she did not.

Here he is, our nameless new boy, she said.

And he was struck with a terrible injuring emotion in the second he took her *our* to mean *his*. Rain rapped the window, and the scene outside, so eternal, dragged at him. This lush, drizzly region; its people with their own unfathomable weather. He'd thought of Tess's journal and had an urge to ask for it back because it had given him hope to see what had thrived from the Müllers' losses; a girl, unspeaking, but writing, it seemed to him, for her life.

In England he's seriously considering signing up for the year's Buddhist training. But first must become an *anagarika*, a homeless one. He must shave his head and devote a year to the Eight Precepts. He's given up dope, alcohol. His mind cobwebbed for six weeks and then, walking by the filthy Thames, he glimpsed a clearing, an intermittent spaciousness recalled from some dim untrammelled corner of boyhood. This clarity helps him face his delusions about what such training will bring. The delusion of peace, for example, which he knows can elude till your last breath. Still, the idea of it drives him out of the city and past the lambing fields to join the ranks of sober, cross-legged devotees.

Now he seals the envelope and crosses Clapham Common in grimy snow to post it. The fading day. As he returns, the lights come on in all the houses and the snow turns pristine, as if lit from within. His footsteps are still visible. He fits his feet inside them like he'd done years back, trying out his mother's shoes.

At home, five new canvases, a study in simultaneous time. Each painted object enfolding past, present, future, illusion. One night reading, Jim had leapt up, then rummaged madly for a paintbrush, suddenly knowing the style and tone, the composition. The next day, he bought the fresh canvas.

He tried to capture how folded paper had done away with time, the attenuated moments on his mother's bed before her death, the feeling of being borne away, a chancy, adrenalin river. He saw very starkly, as he painted, how fateful that meeting, in a clearing, by the water and that he knows barely a thing about Evangeline. She'd just steered him back towards who he'd lost.

He has mailed it, his proper goodbye – Rilke's first elegy – to Evangeline.

> Perhaps there remains
> some tree on a slope, that we can see
> again each day: there remains to us yesterday's
> street,
> and the thinned-out loyalty of a habit
> that liked us, and so stayed, and never departed.
> Oh, and the night, the night, when the wind full
> of space

wears out our faces – whom would she not stay for,
the longed-for, gentle, disappointing one, whom the
    solitary heart
with difficulty stands before.

5

The Year She Went Missing

I said, 'I'll write it. Maybe telling will help you remember.' We were sitting under the laurel magnolia. It was the summer I turned seventeen. The tree was full of creamy flowers and at night those glowing petals looked like sheaves of paper blown in a squall. 'All right,' my mother said, 'I'll tell it and you will write it.'

Inside the house our bags were packed. The next day, we were leaving.

'I'll begin with Peter Tucker,' she said. And I knew he was the source of my mother's forgetting and also the source of myself. I looked at her translucent scar from back then. It ran from her temple and crossed her right eyebrow, causing the hair to grow more finely there. It did not detract from her loveliness, though, which wasn't the regular kind of handsome but something enlivened by asymmetry. She crossed her legs and folded her arms as if gathering herself, shivering even though the breeze through those magnolias was breath-warm.

'You were just three months old when we moved here, you were happy, an easy child. You did not even crawl, you went from dragging yourself to upright in a day,' she said. 'This house was new to us all so it didn't matter that I still couldn't remember other places from before; the Repentance River, say, or the Goat Walk from The Hive to the cliff. Or even further back, when I lived in town with your Grandma Anita and I'd be sent to visit my grandfather twice a year and help in the stables. All this came back to me later when I retraced my steps, the names and places lighting up, except for where those boys took me on the day of the fire.'

'Boys,' I said. 'You mean Peter and his friend? You mean my father.'

'He came to The Hive saying I had something of his. It was time, he said, to give it back.'

'What was it?' I asked.

'It was you,' she said.

Peter and Angus drove her to the falls. They put her on the edge of the viewing platform so she could hear the treacherous water and she tried to guess what they had planned for her in that place, on the edge of a cliff. The two-hundred-metre drop; the cairn below full of jagged rocks and fern. She wondered if it was some kids' game, and worried that she'd missed the rules for such a game, which other children *growing up normal*, she said, might have known, but she, raised in the commune, did not. When they reached the place with horses she was not as scared as she might have been if she'd been left completely alone. If the men were with *her* she knew I was safe at The Hive. 'Back then,' she said, 'I did not know what women had to fear when taken by vengeful men. I was never told about the Lincoln boys and the Jepherson incident. Hodgins didn't let us read the paper, hear the radio or TV; he didn't like the world coming into the commune to despoil.'

My mother thought maybe those boys were under orders from elsewhere. Maybe from the Beauforts, who'd been so angry when she'd refused to give me up. Or Jack Hodgins who'd lost his parcel of valley land when the adoption fell through. Still, she said that Peter cared.

Cared was a funny word, I thought, for someone who'd kidnapped her in a van and blindfolded her. But was it a true kidnapping if a person you knew had taken you? If it was someone you'd had a child with, maybe then it was a kind of game. 'I did not know, even then, what kidnapping *was*,' she said, as if guessing my thoughts. 'I thought they were playing around, they never seemed the type for menace.'

'They drove me into some forest. We were quite near the commune, but I could not see and was disorientated. When they let me out I tried fighting back. But they pushed me. I hit my head, lost a tooth. After that I had only one weapon left to use.'

I asked her what it was.

Small enough to hide in a pocket, she said. It was a lighter.

I remembered those articles she'd sliced from the paper and tucked within her crossword folder, each a story of things that men had done to girls so that after I'd read them all one thundery afternoon I had to fill the bath and lie still till I thawed out. I floated under the lip of water. I held my breath and counted my way back into my body. It had been news to me how much and in what unthinkable ways some women suffered and that it was usually the men who claimed to love them that unleashed all the violence.

At first she'd reported her incident. But then changed her mind. He was my father. What if, in revenge, he made some claim for me? And there were troubling gaps in her story. By then she was in hospital because of the burns and the head injury and the doctors needled her pain away and soon she recalled very little, and for a long time, she remembered nothing of that incident at all.

'In the new house, in the new town, it was easy except when I had to believe, for your father's sake, that he was decent. My mother visited, just once, before she moved away. She ran to Stefan in the bee field and hugged him. In the kitchen she patted his hair and said, "Good man." That's what she'd called him. She wasn't afraid to leave town now he was in my life. I saw her relief, I saw that she was palming me off. But she trusted him. Stefan came over then and put his hand on my cheek. And I thought, OK, he is gentle.

'Later, he told me what he could about The Hive and how he'd fallen in love with me there. He told me what I used to be like, which is really a myth, I mean how he says it, as if I was some virgin birthed in a forest, when he knows I was damaged. He didn't speak of Peter and so I had to piece him together myself. Walking helped – it seemed to unlock my memories. And whenever I saw horses some shadowy parts of my mind would clear.

'Through all of this there was little you! You kept me in each moment so my past didn't seem important. I knew you were mine, no question. That was simple and bone true. You were asleep or awake, your world was unfolding. Cup, Mum, book and chair. Your first words. Horse and crow. Moon, cow, tree! I started painting again. It was like dreaming. A simple colour could just ... realign my thinking. Sometimes

I couldn't even get the brush to the canvas. I just liked to mix on the palette. Phthalo Blue, Aureolin. You'd watch from a mat on the floor. Red, you'd say. Green.'

She paused then as my father and Asher came out of the house, both in bee suits. Through Asher's veil I could see his toy rabbit, Kaninchen, coming along for the walk to the hives. He was learning already how to handle the bees, how to identify the *mama bien*, and the *papa bien*, as he called them. We waved and watched them cross the fields together, my father shortening his stride to stay aligned, Asher gesturing to the sky, to trees, and cows. And then remembering me, she turned.

'When you slept in the pram I took the furthest roads on the edge of town. I didn't realise I was searching. I thought I was just walking,' she said. 'But when I saw those horses in Peterson's field, their breath of broken hay, the lonely sound of their tails, I realised this was where the boys had taken me. It began to rain and I remembered then all the names they'd called me. Names about my ruin, about my so-called reputation in and outside The Hive. All because I had not chosen Peter, but I had chosen you.'

'But you said he cared!' I told her. And she looked up, saying, 'He wanted you in his life.' His childhood was difficult. He had a true longing for love. 'Tess, you can make a life from the few good things you have. Besides, some of us don't get choices,' she said, her voice smoother now. And I knew that *some of us* included Pip.

She said she'd been lost twice. But it wasn't the boys who damaged her most, she said. After Pip, she wasn't sure she'd ever return to herself. I said she sounded very wise, and her laugh was unsmiling. 'You should know,' she said, 'I'm unschooled and still learning. Full of fault and unruly impulse, something like that,' she said as if quoting some other person even now, with me. 'And you're still the kid on the mat, watching me paint and naming everything you could see. Red, red!' and there was a sharp snag in her throat.

When she finished her largest canvas, I was surprised to see its new backdrop. But I soon realised that fire had always been part of the picture. In the narrow river at the bottom of the canvas, she'd painted reflected flames. They'd been there all along, but none of us had ever noticed.

I looked at the house. Inside, our bags, packed with sketchbooks and charcoal, our masks, suits and towels. It would be our first trip together. She wanted to see the world further north, before it disappeared, she said, or turned completely white as it had already in many parts. She wanted to look down on the glowing gardens, the rippled turbin-arias, the staghorns that make up the reef's construction force, the destructive Crown of Thorns. We'd all thought she'd choose overseas – anywhere you like, my father had said, Meg and I will hold the fort, and Asher spun the globe then slapped one small hand on Zimbabwe. But she chose the Barrier Reef, with its drifting seahorses. 'Where, where?' Asher asked and Meg pointed north, which was skyward. 'Up there. You can swim right through it,' Meg said, her arms winnowing through the kitchen where bread was cool-ing on the table. 'It's an underworld,' Meg told him, 'a whole other world beneath us.' Twelve loaves, one for every day we'll be away, my mother had said, and I recognised her labouring with that dough as love.

I look at her now, the wide band of grey in her chopped hair, the way she sits very straight with her face tilted away, and

I try to imagine how she must have been, years ago, hair to her waist, her gaze fixed on some other scene while I was forming my words. Turn around, I will her, as she looks beyond the magnolia, past the bee field with its abandoned huts, the insects stricken with collapse disorder, with rapture, with disappearing disease or spring dwindle, past the knot of cows and the dark stand of pines that walls our property off from wilderness, and further, towards the Ghost Mountains. 'So much has gone,' she says.

One day I might meet my father, on a street in the town. But probably I'll be far off; by the time he's free, I'll be in some other city of the world. If I met him I might hear another story of my life. Or one about his own troubles, about why he'd left a friend after the accident in that van. It was hard to confess to a fatal mistake, my mother said, after you'd already run from it. She herself had put harm in others' way and for this she was ashamed. As for Peter, he's doing his time.

'So much has gone,' my mother says again. And I know what she's thinking about, as her eyes search the scarred ridges and crests, the mists or dusts furling around the remaining forest trees — I know who. 'Yes. Pip is gone,' I say, willing her to turn towards me. 'But we are here. Look, here we are.'

ACKNOWLEDGEMENTS

A generous community fostered the research, development and creation of this novel. A special thanks to Michelle Moo for her attuned reading through several drafts. Huge thanks to my family – Blake Ayshford, Evie, Emile, Madeleine, Roger and Guy Juchau and Yvette Vignando. My gratitude to Helen Garnons-Williams for her thoughtful editing, to Sarah-Jane Forder, Elizabeth Woabank and Oliver Holden-Rea. Thanks to Kate Cubitt for her calm guidance, to the dynamic Brendan Fredericks, to Lucy Barrett and to everyone at Bloomsbury for their enthusiasm and belief in my work. Thank you for wise counsel Jenny Darling, and for friendship and support Gail Jones, Michelle de Kretser, Karen O'Connell and Saskia Beudel. Thank you Deborah Levy, Pam Newtown, Jim Crowther, Rebecca South and Rebecca Leacock.

This book could not have been written without generous support from The Australia Council for the Arts and two artist residencies at the Bundanon Trust.

CREDITS